THE HILLS OF
THE MOON

The Hills of the Moon

Carleton Chinner

Paperback ISBN-13: 978-0-6481629-1-9
Digital ISBN-13: 978-0-6481629-0-2

Published 2019

First published as 'The Hills of Mare Imbrium' in 2018

ACKNOWLEDGEMENTS

As a first novel this story needed so much support before it ever became something more than half a page of my untidy scrawl. I want to thank all of you who made this possible, but in particular, I would like to thank:

Lauren Daniels, my wise and fearless editor, who encouraged me to greater sensitivity and nuance than I thought I would ever achieve.

Andrew Burleson and Paul Kilpatrick, the creators of the amazing BetaBooks.co who were kind enough to select The Hills of Mare Imbrium as beta read of the month.

The legion of beta readers for their review of the early draft in general, and Peta Culverhouse specifically for tirelessly reviewing my revisions.

Vincent Chua for generously giving me a practical demonstration of the sparse efficiency of Krav Maga techniques.

And last and most importantly, to Annalie, who has always been there to support my dreams, no matter how crazy they may be.

Chapter 1

Accompanied Baggage

Jonah never understood grief until his life acquired a hole the exact shape of Thomas: his brother, the graduate, the favoured son. Thomas, who was now an urn full of ashes nestled within Jonah's hand luggage.

The walls of the space elevator cabin curved away from where he sat. Jonah's eyes followed the round ceiling, but returned to the luggage as it drifted in the storage rack. His stomach lurched at the thought of the urn breaking inside his bag. Dad would never speak to him again if he got this wrong. He grabbed for the bag. Even in microgravity the brass container was heavy with the memory of Thomas, bleeding out on the pavement while the ambulances took too long to come. A subtle thump rocked the elevator as it came to a halt against the space-side terminator.

"Ladies and gentlemen, welcome to space," came the recorded announcement. "Please be aware that your belongings may have shifted as we entered zero gravity. Please ensure you have all belongings with you before you exit the elevator. Passengers for the Moon should exit through the blue hatchway. Terminator personnel are now safe to exit through core-side..."

A floor-to-ceiling window showed a sweeping view of the transfer shuttle docked alongside. Below, the dark bulk of the diamond fibre elevator cable disappeared into clouds far below them. Jonah shuddered as his mind took in the impossible height. The port state of Singapore lay below those clouds.

The recording droned while people drifted across the cabin and pulled themselves through the hatchway. Jonah tried to do the same, but pushed off too hard and spun across the open space. People turned to look. Blushing, he noticed a handrail and hauled himself into the shuttle.

He strapped himself into his seat and closed his eyes, willing the unease of a weightless stomach to pass. Not long now, and he would take his first steps under the soaring domes of Chang'e, the First Lunar Palace of the Republic of Jiangnan. He allowed himself a short sigh of relief as acceleration pushed him back into the chair.

His thoughts returned to Thomas, the way a tongue finds a hole where a tooth used to be. Thomas playing with Jess, their big black Labrador; Thomas goofing off by a pool at Spring Break; fishing together at the lake with five-year-old Thomas. Hot tears sat behind his eyes and would not come.

Fifteen hours later, deceleration pushed him forward into his belt, and Jonah got his first glimpse of the Moon through the small view-port set across from him. Outside, the crystal span of Chang'e glittered in contrast to the harsh grey exterior of Mare Imbrium.

This was his chance to make things right; an opportunity to get away from disappointing his father, to say goodbye to the aching emptiness left by Thomas, and perhaps a way to leave his messed-up life for good.

The towering geodesic domes stretched across the lunar surface in a silent display of engineering prowess and all the wealth a vast supply of Helium-3 could bring.

The miracle fuel of the clean energy revolution was his ticket to redemption and a chance to set things right. Even more, it was a way to make a living far from everything that was a reminder of the cold urn in his luggage.

Jonah did not notice the shuttle docking until a gentle thump rocked his seat. The airlock and passageway had the familiar hallmarks of an Earth airport as it encouraged weary passengers to move along to better places with as much speed as possible. A yellow triangle icon blinked in his field of view.

Great, no signal. The memplant was useless without data. Jonah hoped he had enough credit for a local account.

He knew he had arrived when the dry dome air took on the faint electric-cinnamon smell of manufactured atmosphere. Beyond the passage, he emerged into a vast reception hall where an imposing building rose in tiered slabs of red and yellow aluminium. Signs in Global Standard announced it as 'Administration'.

Above the stream of arriving passengers, triangular glass segments bound open sky in a dome wall that soared to elevations impossible in Earth's gravity. Jonah stopped and stared. The wide curve gave the impression of standing on an empty plain. Each segment of glass held a constellation of over bright stars against inky black. The jewelled arc swept across the sky to end in the sombre grey heights of the hills of Mare Imbrium.

"Welcome to the Moon. May I have your passport, please?" said a voice somewhere above him. A man stood behind a customs desk, towering over Jonah's stocky six-foot-two frame.

Jonah handed over his passport and, after a moment's hesitation, the authorisation to scatter Thomas's ashes.

He tried not to stare. He had heard descriptions of moonos, the overly tall, fourth generation children of miners living in the Moon's low gravity. The man's face had pale, birdlike features. Long delicate hands held up his passport for examination.

"Ah, Mr Barnes, my condolences on your loss. Administration has allocated temporary accommodation for you in Dome Seven and a representative will be in touch to help with the arrangements. How long do you intend to stay?"

"I don't know. I thought I might try and track down a job."

A flash of contempt vanished behind the moono's professional mask. "The Moon is not an itinerant worker's camp, Mr Barnes. You can have the standard two-week holiday visa. Your employer will arrange a longer work permit if you find employment." He stamped Jonah's passport and turned to the next person in line.

Numb, Jonah moved on through a luxury shopping precinct that would not have been out of place in Earth's finest suburbs. Stalls selling premium Earth lines competed with Lunar jewellery and clothing.

Jonah stopped at a display window filled with titanium tinged pyroclastic glass jewellery. Pyroclastic beads came from the remains of ancient lunar volcanoes. The subtle combinations of red, yellow, and green shone in tasteful lighting. The display left him convinced he could not afford it.

An autovendor offered travel data packages at exorbitant rates. Jonah chose the cheapest package and waited for it to load to his memplant. The nano-organic memory implant flashed malware warnings within his visual cortex, then allowed the package to start. It appeared to work until, with an impulsive urge to buy a new shirt, he turned towards a shop.

He stopped mid-stride. Stupid malware, Panamerica had banned emotion hooks decades ago. He toggled the memplant to a higher security setting using the voluntary memory that felt like blinking, but wasn't. Messy visual adverts replaced the desire to buy.

Dome Seven occupied the cheap edge of Chang'e. The dome's side nestled against a small rock outcrop that blocked direct sunlight for most of the day. Deep shade left the air dry and cold. The accommodation was a functional slab set towards the back of the main dome building.

He checked in to his room, unpacked and sat on the bed, listening to the silence. Thomas would have filled the silence with laughter and his wry witticisms about the people around them.

When the emptiness became too much, he browsed online to see what was nearby. There was a sports facility called an airball court on the top floor, and a bar two floors below his room. Easy choice.

He staggered towards the bar and tried to walk with the confidence of the people around him. The simple action was a whole new skill in the low gravity.

Candy Silk was a dark plas-panelling kind of bar with soft lighting. Small groups of moonos lounged in comfortable booths. Muted conversation flowed over the clatter of a tile game. Two women in flowing moonsilk creations drifted past, heading for the bar. Jonah made a deliberate effort to lower his gaze. They were slim, elegant fantasy creatures with delicate high cheekbones and bright emerald eyes that had the slightest suggestion of an epicanthic fold. Low gravity blessed their curves with an absence of sagging.

A hint of spicy, deep-fried food reminded him he had not eaten since leaving Earth. He ordered a beer and winced at the price, but he needed a fix, even if it was just a beer buzz.

"You don't want that caatcha," murmured a voice.

He turned to find emerald eyes regarding him. Unlike the other moonos, he wore a simple black utility suit that should have been shapeless, but emphasised a lithe frame.

"Why not?" he asked as he struggled to maintain equilibrium.

"Beer comes up the stalk for heavy credit."

"What'd you get?"

The moono turned to the bar and ordered a bottle of shaoxing and five glasses. "You fresh up stalk?"

"Yeah, been here about two hours now."

"Well, Shaoxing help you settle in," he said and passed over a full glass, "I am Lucien."

"Jonah. Nice to meet you. You're the first moono I've met."

Lucien frowned, "We do not call ourselves moonos, Is Earther slang. If you say elsewhere, you end up being called thick or squat. We call ourselves Moon Folk."

"Oh, Sorry." Jonah blushed. He took a sip of the drink to cover his embarrassment and managed to swallow the liquid fire before he burst out coughing. "What is this stuff?"

Lucien grinned, "Too strong for Earth boy? administrator does not allow us many pleasures; enjoy good time while you can. Come meet my friends."

He led Jonah to a booth occupied by three other Moon Folk.

"What you dragged in this time, Lucien?" said an older woman with emotionless, grey eyes.

"He calls himself Jonah, fresh up stalk."

"Ah, another hopeful then. What you doing here, young man?"

"I'm looking for work..."

Lucien cut him off. "No real plans then."

"Typical dirt-baller. Cannot walk, cannot talk," murmured the man to the left of the older woman, loud enough for Jonah to hear.

Jonah rose to leave, but Lucien placed a firm hand on his arm and drew him back.

"Stay. We like to tease new Earthers."

Jonah hid his embarrassment with another taste of the fiery liquid. The second sip was better. His shoulders dropped as a pleasant warmth spread through his core.

"I'm here to bury my brother."

The group met his statement with stony silence.

Lucien took one of his hands.

"I sorry for your loss, but Moon Folk reserve burial for persons of note. Organic material is precious on

Moon and we seldom surrender it. Most people recycled in garden systems."

The older man did not soften his glare. "Your family must be in good with administrator for him give you honour like this."

"My father doesn't know the administrator," said Jonah, "but he thinks money can make all kinds of problems go away. Even difficult sons like me."

Lucien scowled at the man, and then turned to Jonah. "What do you do for fun?"

"I do martial arts."

Lucien raised his glass. "I love martial arts movies. Have you seen Teacup Zen?"

"Oh yeah," Jonah leaned forward. "I watched it on the shuttle. That scene where Mamma Buk takes on the ninjas is incredible." He took another sip of the shaoxing. "Do you like the older movies? I saw Ong Bak and Ip Man a while ago and the fighting technique was so real."

"Lucien," the older woman stood. "We leave you to bore your new friend with kung fu." She motioned to the other two, and they left.

Lucien shrugged. "More shaoxing for us." He turned to Jonah. "I have not seen Ip Man, but the action never stopped in Ong Bak."

The evening trickled past in the clink of shaoxing glasses and the chatter of new friends, until, hours later, Lucien bade him good rest, at the door to Jonah's room. More drunk than he intended to be, Jonah climbed into bed. He wanted to think this whole tumultuous day through, but sleep fell over him like a black wave.

Chapter 2

Adaptation

The next morning, he was roused by enthusiastic rapping on the door. He stumbled from the bed in his nightwear and opened the door.

Lucien reached in and shook him by the shoulders. "Wake up, lazy. You need fresh air and exercise."

Jonah stood there with his mouth open.

"Get dressed. I take you to airball court."

Jonah grabbed his clothes and stumbled across the room to the cupboard-sized bathroom.

Lucien stifled a laugh. "You need practice. Takes few days to master walking in low gravity."

Jonah ran his sonic shaver over day-old stubble, then switched it to grooming mode and tidied up his hair.

Satisfied with what he saw in the mirror, he changed into a self-sealing white shirt and dark pants.

Lucien led him to the top floor. The entire floor was a single well-lit room. A large dome constructed of a light metal mesh, so fine it was almost invisible, dominated the centre. Rows of stadium seating surrounded the dome, almost like a back to front basketball court. Two hoops set back to back in the middle, one painted red, the other white.

"This is airball," said Lucien. He opened a gate and picked up a ball, about two thirds of the size of a basketball.

"You score by passing ball through correct hoop. I will take red and you have white."

"Something like the basketball we play back at home?" said Jonah.

"Something like basketball, except you cannot score while your feet are on floor. That is why is called airball. Wanna try?" asked Lucien an impish grin on his face.

"Sure, but I should warn you, I shot a few hoops in college."

"We shall see."

They entered the dome and Lucien tossed Jonah the ball and told him to start. The ball was heavier than Jonah expected, the weight gave it a solid Earther feel. Jonah dribbled the ball cautiously as he got used to the low gravity. He jumped up and shot for the white hoop. The ball looped in a lazy arc that missed by a wide margin.

"Yeh, Earth boy, you do better than that, lah."

Jonah gave him a sheepish grin. The low gravity was trickier than he expected.

The ball passed wide and bounced upwards. Lucien, instead of running for it, bounded up the opposite wall.

His momentum carried him clear to the top of the dome. He caught the ball as he rose and shot straight through the red hoop.

"One to Moon lad."

"No fair, you said our feet had to be off the floor."

"Yes, floor, not roof. Still think you can take me Earth Boy?"

"Just watch me."

Lucien flicked the ball to him. Jonah caught it and launched himself toward the top of the dome. He executed a half-turn to get his feet on the roof of the dome for a good shot. The low gravity surprised him and he spun around twice before he slammed his back into the dome and crashed to the floor in an ungracious heap. He still had the ball. He stood, planning to take another shot but Lucien's laughter brought him up short.

"Oh man, was so spectacularly bad. Are you sure you played basketball back on Earth?"

"Yeah, yeah. I didn't grow up in low gravity. Give me another go and I'm sure I can get it right."

"One more try and then I send you for training with kiddies," said Lucien with a smirk. "But only if you promise not to squash them."

Jonah bit down on the retort he had in mind and tried to focus. He tried a small jump and shot for the hoop, watching with satisfaction as the ball slipped through the white hoop.

"Yes! Score one for the Earth boy."

He had it now. He would play to his own strengths. If he kept the ball low, he could minimise Lucien's advantage in the low gravity.

Lucien tossed him the ball. "Don't get too smart. Winner is first to three points."

Jonah jogged forward and shot for a point. This time he didn't wait to see if it went in, but hustled to where he thought it would bounce. The ball missed. Lucien appeared next to him, but Jonah's forward thinking gave him the edge. He dodged around Lucien and caught the ball. His momentum carried him to the edge of the dome, so he went with it. He ran up the side and tried Lucien's trick of shooting from above the hoops. This time it worked. The ball sank through the white hoop.

"Oh yeah! That's what I'm talking about. Two to me."

"Beginner's luck, I say."

Lucien picked up the ball and ran straight for the centre. Jonah saw him coming and blocked his path with his body. Lucien dodged around and scored.

"That is how pros do it."

Jonah feinted left, then sprinted right. Lucien shadowed him, blocking his path.

"I am wise to Earth style now."

"Still a few tricks I can show you." Jonah twisted and ran for the walls. Lucien jumped high and landed with his feet on the dome. Jonah didn't stop to speak. He mustered his strength and jumped clear across the court, grabbing the ball to try for a far shot. He missed, and the ball bounced straight into Lucien's hands.

A small crowd had gathered to watch them play. Nice! Lucien would humiliate him in public. Not going to happen he told himself.

"Here we go. Moon style and speed for win," Lucien said to the crowd at large.

Jonah didn't rise to the bait, but shadowed Lucien, watching for an opening. He didn't have long to wait. Lucien ran past him and up the dome wall. Jonah followed, he knew what Lucien would try. Lucien shot from near the top. Jonah had seen it coming and launched off the dome. He intercepted the ball in mid-air as he fell.

He slammed into the floor hard. The floor gave as much as a steel wall. The low gravity had done nothing to save him. He groaned. That would hurt later, but it had been worth it.

The crowd became silent, sitting on the edge of their seats in anticipation. Lucien wasn't saying anything either, the trash talk put aside for a serious chance at winning. He wove towards the centre. Jonah shadowed him again. Lucien changed tactics and ran for the dome. Jonah followed. Lucien reached the side of the dome and sprinted sideways. Jonah changed direction to follow. Lucien, losing momentum, fell to the floor, and doubled back towards the centre. He jumped and shot. Jonah was fast enough to catch the ball. He turned and shot for the hoop. It was an awkward angle and bounced off the rim of the hoop.

Lucien charged for the ball. The crowd rose to their feet as one. Nobody wanted to miss what had turned into a fantastic game.

Jonah was too far from the ball to intercept Lucien. He ran towards the hoops, hoping to stop the ball before it hit the hoop, but he was too slow. Lucien rose into the air and spiked the ball hard. Jonah couldn't catch it, but got close enough to slap it out of the way. He hit hard, and the ball screamed off at right angles to its previous path. He launched himself like a flying ninja, at the opposite side of the court, without looking at the ball, and landed with catlike grace. The ball, travelling with the force of Jonah's slap, bounced off the dome wall straight to where he had landed. He caught it, jumped, and scored.

The little crowd erupted. Ragged cheers reached Jonah as he regained his breath.

"Not bad for beginner," said Lucien. "Was quite impressive."

"I have martial arts training, but the combination of speed and precision is all me."

Lucien gave him an odd look, "We must have chat about skill of yours." He turned to address the crowd at large.

"I think we just found new forward."

The crowd roared its acceptance.

Jonah bounced back to his room, leaping in the low gravity. Lucien was right, he was awake now. Back in his room, the silent accusation of the urn waited. Thomas would have loved airball.

A timid knock interrupted his thoughts. He opened the door to find a willowy woman with the pale moon skin and glowing auburn hair. She had the kind of body he only knew from the wrong sort of dream.

"Are all Moon Folk so ridiculously sexy?" he said before he could stop himself.

She arched one elegant eyebrow, "Only the good-looking ones," she said without smiling.

"Hello, Mr Barnes, I am Yesha, your appointed lunar representative.

"My condolences for your loss. The administrator requested I guide you outside the domes to scatter the ashes of your brother beyond the perimeter. Can you confirm you have the authorisation for this activity?"

Jonah handed over the administrator's paper.

"We can leave as soon as you are ready," she said.

Jonah collected the urn.

Yesha looked at him, a moment, then turned and walked out.

Jonah followed her into the hum of a working day. Children sat in neat lines inside an open-air school. Mothers clustered around small tables drinking from glass mugs. A chatter of conversation flowed over them.

Yesha led him through the tunnel that connected domes to a small airlock on the edge of Dome One.

She helped him into a cumbersome exposure suit. It felt tight but puffed up when the airlock opened to the Moon's near vacuum atmosphere. They walked over regolith, the fine grey powder that covered the lunar surface. Thomas would have been able to describe the technical characteristics, but to Jonah, it was grey dirt.

The featureless landscape stretched out before them. A tall pile of dark rocks stood stark against the grey.

"What's that?" He pointed to the simple cairn.

"An old historical site, Yutu's Monument. It is the landing place of the probe that marked the first moment of the glorious history of China's Moon exploration."

It was such an inauspicious monument to such a proud historical moment, so different to what he had imagined would commemorate this occasion. Perhaps the Jiangnanese did not wish to emphasise a historical reminder of their ancient Chinese heritage.

They walked in a silence underscored by the hiss of their respirators. The quiet air outlined an absence of Thomas spouting exuberant opinions, boasting about the girl he met last night, or humming in that mindless way he had that drove

Jonah nuts. Hot tears ran down his cheeks and pooled in the suit's neck seal.

He stopped and took in the endless openness. "Will here do?"

"Yes, Mr Barnes, here shall be fine."

He unscrewed the urn and upended it. The ashes floated slowly down in the low gravity until they merged with the grey regolith and Thomas was forever an indistinguishable part of the Moon's surface. He knew his brother would have loved it.

Jonah tried to ignore the stab of pain that clawed at his heart. Thomas had always wanted to visit the Moon.

"Oh Thomas, what will I do now?"

Yesha placed a hand on his shoulder. A gesture at once both practical in the bulky suits and intimate in its closeness.

"Do you have somewhere to go, Mr Barnes?"

"No, I need to find a hotel and then a job in the mines."

Yesha was silent for a while and they began the walk back to the dome. As they removed their suits in the airlock, she said "My uncle wants me to examine the New Karakorum accounts today. Meet me at the Imbrium Railhead at two o'clock and I will show you a mine."

The sun reflected off her helmet, but Jonah thought he saw a faint smile.

The bare room in Dome Seven promised nothing but more time to think of Thomas. He placed the empty container in the small bedside niche. It wasn't Thomas. Thomas was one with this dry and dusty world. The urn was a mute accusation of unfulfilled wishes and words left unsaid. The silent urn stood in its niche, reflecting dull light.

Jonah went out. The door closed behind him with a sterile thump. He needed a fix. Something, anything to blur the pain and guilt. He passed formal places designed by tidy minds for function rather than beauty. This part of Chang'e was too clean. Back at home, it was easy to find the small, dark men who waited in dingy bars. Here, Jonah didn't know who to ask. He settled for overpriced beer at a bar near the railhead and willed the time until two o'clock to pass.

The Imbrium Railhead turned out to be a railway station on the far side of the Dome One, the rail line an iron rod leading to the far hills. If Jonah expected something as polished as the domes, he was disappointed. The railway station was functional boredom, and the train a series of glass boxes.

Yesha saw him looking at the carriages. "This train is a Moon product. We have always had to make do without the hydrocarbons that Earth depends on; glass is much easier to manufacture than plastics. Our clever Moon engineers designed the train with extreme precision to allow high speed in the endless tunnels."

"Endless?"

"The Moon Folk have been mining the hills surrounding Mare Imbrium for over a hundred years. There are now so many tunnels that many people live there." She climbed aboard and patted the seat next to her.

The departure signal sounded, and as the doors were about to close another person jumped into their carriage and sat across from them.

"So? You want to see my world?"

"Lucien!"

"Hello Jonah, is wonderful, bright carriage. Who is your friend makes it shine like this?"

Yesha stiffened in her seat. "Greetings, citizen. Peace and order be with you," she said eyeing Lucien with cool disdain.

"And with you," said Lucien, far more at ease than she appeared to be. He winked at Jonah, "You thank administrator lah for granting us vision of loveliness."

Yesha looked away and said nothing.

Outside, they passed through a gap in the first ring of hills and the track followed meticulous linear precision direct to the base of the second, wide band of hills.

The train entered the mouth of a tunnel and sped on through the darkness. Their faces reflected the dim light cast by small strips in the roof of their carriage.

After an interminable series of junctions, they docked at an airlock deep within the hills. They emerged into a gigantic cavern where large ceiling-mounted arc lights cast fitful beams into stygian darkness. A cacophonous wall of noise filled the air. Heavy machines rumbled through the gloom, materialising from one tunnel and disappearing into another.

"Welcome to New Karakorum, the original joint venture between the People's Republic of Jiangnan and the Earth's best mining companies," said Yesha as she slipped back into the role of tour guide.

"This is a central junction and the first of fifteen such levels. Miners are currently extending the tunnels to the right. The White Star Mining Company processes the resulting ore in the two tunnels you see before you. Workers use the older tunnels to the left for accommodation."

"And that's my cue to leave," said Lucien. "Come and see me when you escape." He spoke to Jonah but looked at Yesha. "I am in Tunnel Three on Level

Seven. Just ask, everybody knows who I am."

Yesha frowned. "Citizen, I don't think that is appropriate."

"It is only dinner. Come and show our new friend how polite dome folk are."

Yesha turned to Jonah and pointed towards a row of prefabricated huts. "I must work now. Those are contract company site offices. You might find a job there."

The first door had a sign saying New England Minerals above it. Inside, three people sat working at metal desks. "Yes?" said a man looking up at him.

"Do you have any work available?"

"Bugger off. We don't have time for infants in nappies."

Jonah wanted to argue his case, but the bored disdain on the man's face persuaded him to move on to the next company.

The second hut belonged to Ashanti Gases. The view inside was similar to the first hut, but this time, the man behind the desk gave him a thick sheet of forms. "Fill these in and see me when you're done."

Jonah spent an hour with the complex, repetitive forms before handing them back to the man.

"Done any maintenance on a Series Three Tokatsu?"

"No."

"How about longwalling; have you done any?"

"No."

"Cryolitic blasters?"

"No."

"Look, pal, lunar mining is a specialised business. I can't help you if you have no usable skills."

"Is there nothing I can do?"

"You can try the other mining companies, but they

will be the same. Try the service company up at the end of the row."

Jonah tried the rest of the miners. Their responses ranged from open hostility to friendly indifference but the answer was always the same. No one wanted an unqualified Earther. At the end of the day-cycle, Jonah was hungry and thirsty, but he tried Samwuh Services, anyway. The man behind the counter looked a thousand years old. He chewed on something as he watched Jonah enter the hut.

He held up a dried twig. "Ethiopian khat, you want?"

Jonah accepted the twig in what he hoped was a polite way. If there was khat, there would be worse things. The astringent, green taste of the twig flooded his mouth as he explained that he was looking for work.

The man sat sucked on the khat as he looked over Jonah.

"You one big squat. Big enough to carry cleaning kit for Shenhua dormitory. I give you twenty credit a day-cycle. You come back tomorrow."

Jonah agreed; the pay was terrible, but it was work.

He left and realised that he had walked around the mining huts for hours and had nowhere to go. The khat wrapped his hunger and weariness in a happy haze. He remembered Lucien's invitation.

The third tunnel on Level Seven had the dim light of an early evening. Lights shone out of the narrow slit-windows of homes dug as secondary tunnels off the main thoroughfare. The openings lacked glass, but the inhabitants had draped each window with colourful silks to reflect their personalities.

Jonah asked for directions and soon found himself in front of a plain aluminium door. It opened at his first knock.

"Oh, is you," said Lucien. "You better come in."

Jonah stepped inside to rooms that were carved hollows in

the sombre rock of the tunnel walls. Rich layers of moon silk covered bare rock to give an impression of luxury. Outside, in the main tunnel, the controlling system had lowered the lighting to simulate night, but here, the rooms were lit in warm tones that complemented the silk. Low couches in a deep red surrounded a flat glass-topped table. An abstract statue, sculpted from black basalt, dominated the main living room. Jonah couldn't make it out until he realised that it was an interpretation of the ocean as imagined by someone who had never seen it. The effect was at once startling and poignant.

Yesha rose to greet him as he entered the living area. Jonah smiled at her, pleased to see a face he recognised.

Lucien turned to Jonah, "I have a bottle of special from Dome Seven. Would you like a glass?"

Jonah accepted and sipped it with more caution than he had used last night.

Yesha leaned back on a comfortable pillow. "What will you feed your Earth friend, citizen?"

"Only best, I have Dome catfish in spicy mushroom stew."

"I am fortunate to be in your company then, citizen."

"Not only is she beauty, Jonah, but so polite."

Jonah sat himself on a cushion close to Yesha and lost himself in the way her liquid almond eyes glowed in the soft lighting. "I wanted to thank you for your comfort today. I felt so lost this morning."

"My sympathies on your loss, Mr Barnes. It is always hard to say a final goodbye."

"Please, call me Jonah. Mr Barnes is my father's name."

"Well, I hate to break up special moment," said Lucien, "but Jonah can I have opinion of my stew?"

Jonah grinned as he rose, and stepped over to the

kitchen bench.

The mushrooms gave the stew a rich woody aroma that balanced the earthy catfish and a subtle salty soy flavour.

"Lucien, this fish is delicious."

"Cooking is just one of my many talents. Can you cook anything?"

"Hamburgers, I guess."

"Too sad. You won't get much chance to show off in place with no beef."

"Huh! I'm sure I can..."

A crashing thump, followed by shouting in the tunnel outside, interrupted Jonah.

"Quick! Hide at the back," said Lucien pointing, "behind statue."

Jonah ran through the silk hangings and found a modest bedroom and storage area. He heard Lucien shout. A sickening thud ended in silence.

"That's it, we have the one we want; clear the rest of the vermin."

Jonah scrambled into the storage locker and shut the door. The blast that followed rattled his teeth. Stars filled his vision in the dark.

He lay there, in the darkness too afraid to move. Every sound threatened violence.

His memplant gave the yellow triangle of no connection, but it gave him the time. Jonah watched as the seconds blurred into hours. He wanted to be anywhere else, but every murmur from the corridor made him shrink from the door.

He tried the door when the memplant told him hours had passed. It didn't budge.

Chapter 3

A Limited Threat

Chen Zhaung sat watching as the distant blue marble of Earth slid into the shadow of lunar night. Two more months until he walked under open sky once more. He allowed himself a moment of longing for his beloved Nanjing.

The seventeenth administrator of the Lunar Palace hated lunar night. Fourteen days of subzero temperatures and darkness under the pitiless black Moon sky before the sun reappeared. The Earth would be present in the sky for all that time, a constant reminder of home. He suppressed his yearning for open sky, the work of running a colony waited for him.

His legs ached at the thought of going home. A

cocktail of drugs prevented the loss of muscle and bone density caused by living in low gravity. The drugs worked when hard physical effort complemented them. The demands of running a successful colony kept him out of the gym more than he cared to think about. He would pay for it with strenuous exercise sessions to reacquaint his muscles with Earth's gravity.

He would make time for the rehabilitation. There would be day-long debrief meetings when he returned, but evenings would be his. He intended to spend every one of them in the manicured parks that surrounded the leafy green arcologies of Nanjing. There, he would have time for drinking in sunsets, sipping at the mere existence of clouds, and inhaling the crystal air as it poured off the mystic slopes of Purple Mountain.

Two more months of denial stood between him and retirement. He put the thought aside. Now he must plan for the auspicious celebration of a hundred years of Jiangnanese rule of the Lunar Province.

The solitude of his office was his private sanctuary; a place to meditate on the great task. Chang'e was so much more than just the first lunar palace. It was the embodiment of Jiangnan's dreams of a future beyond the Earth. Alone, in his chambers, he shut out the incessant demands of running a colony on the Moon, and focused on his vision of what could be.

A single decoration punctuated the expanse of his desk; a sealed glass globe suspended from a stainless-steel stand. Inside the globe, shrimp went about their lives on waving amari moss in a harmonious ecosystem. A predecessor of his had installed the globe as a metaphor for the colony.

He rose and walked across to the sweeping window with its view of the dead, airless surface. An actinic flash over the Apennine Bench rock formation caught his eye. Good, the railgun mounted on the ridge had launched another delivery of Helium 3 to the cities of Earth.

The railgun with its low-cost mass transfers, rendered space rockets an expensive irrelevance, and was why Jiangnan dominated the Moon. The principle was simple; a magnetic rail accelerated a package of Helium fast enough to catapult it away from the base and into a low earth orbit. Once in orbit, tug drones captured the package and transferred it to the space elevator platform positioned in geostationary orbit. The platform was home to several tireless spider drones that spent their days climbing up and down the diamond nanotube that connected the platform to the Earth-side port of Singapore.

He allowed himself the luxury of one final glance at the pale Earth then began his report.

His memplant overrode his optic nerve with a glaring yellow triangle as it patched into the priority channel reserved for administrative communication. Auditory override sounded a clear bell tone indicating connection, and five avatars swam into his field of view. Chen hated appearing before the supreme council. He never knew who or what he spoke to; the link generated random avatars to hide the identities of the council. Today they were kabuki masks, each a different colour. Their voices were manufactured soap opera tones.

Yellow mask spoke first. "Administrator Chen, have you increased production?"

Chen linked his memplant to the softmind and called

up a presentation. Graphs and stereographic images popped into view in the meeting space. "We have positioned our current supply stockpile to meet the heating demands of the northern hemisphere winter. In particular, the New Karakorum tunnel complex has managed a thirty percent increase."

He emphasised how productive the mines were. His masters wanted to broadcast that assurance to the collective great cities of Earth. The Europeans especially could be strident if their energy demands went unmet. Central heating, light, food, and entertainment all relied on the abundant clean power that Helium 3 fusion provided. He connected the productivity figures to a multimedia presentation about the added safeguards and redundancy that his engineers built into the western tunnels.

An additional power plant and atmosphere regulator were in the final stages of commissioning. The construction included firelocks at regular intervals throughout the tunnels. Unchecked fires consumed precious oxygen that was an expensive gas to manufacture. The details should satisfy most concerns that his superiors may have.

"How are preparations for the hundred year celebrations coming along?" said red mask. Its voice had a mellow, gentle timbre.

"Planning proceeds at a satisfactory rate."

"Good, the council has invited a few special guests. Be sure to offer them every honour. Jaingnan's trading partners are of utmost importance to our continued prosperity."

He hesitated. "Honoured council, the Free Moon Movement continues to grow. My assessment is that they pose a limited threat to production."

The masks remained silent.

"My sources tell me that these people are a group of malcontents chasing an independent Moon. They spread their message in bars and dining halls, but I have reports of earnest speeches being made."

"What do you propose?" said green mask.

"I have removed their access to social media. Security has been tightened. If the situation deteriorates, I shall make an example of the most serious offenders. We will round them up in a well-publicised fashion and send them for re-education in the Old north-eastern tunnel complex. Six months of hard labour, without sunlight, has been known to realign collective priorities."

The masks were silent for several minutes. Chen waited.

Eventually, green mask spoke. "It would be unfortunate if circumstances dictated a postponement of your retirement. You must maintain social harmony for the benefit of Jiangnan's prosperity. See that it is so."

The connection cut, leaving Chen alone with his thoughts. The threat was plain enough.

A knock at the door interrupted him. Wang Mei, the head of his security team entered.

"Administrator, we have searched to the limits of New Karakorum and found no trace of the Panamerican visitor or his companion..." Wang's voice trailed off in the hush of the imposing office.

Chen considered him for a moment, letting the silence stretch to the point where Wang dropped his head and stared at an imagined spot of dust on the flawless desk. "What possessed you to set off an explosive in a residence tunnel?"

"I thought you expected immediate action in these matters."

"You thought? I doubt you used this capacity to its fullest. The moonos have protested the unsanctioned violence. I have spent the last two hours calming down the New Karakorum residence committee. They were all for having you and your team deported to Earth."

Wang Mei had the barest of military training; his role was to manage safety on the base. His duties stretched to the occasional minor issue, such as troublesome miners who consumed an excess of shaoxing. Quelling an insurgency was beyond his skills. He was also the designated Party official for the base, a position granted for his deft management of mine safety in Shandong Province, rather than his understanding of martial tactics.

Chen wondered how he would turn this rather soft man into a tool for crushing an uprising. "You must find them —losing the Panamerican could embarrass Nanjing. We host among the best miners from all over Earth. It is their skills that make New Karakorum so profitable. It would not serve for them to think it was unsafe to be here. As I see it, you have three tasks ahead of you: locate the young visitor; make amends with the moonos; and if all else fails you will prepare for a violent uprising."

Wang shuffled his feet. "Administrator, with all due respect, there are over nine hundred kilometres of tunnels and I have a team of five. If I am to carry out this search, I need at least another twenty people. One or two of those must have counter insurgency experience if we are to succeed. We also need to arm the team to meet the threat —we do not know what we will face."

Chen hid his smile. "Very well, speak to the personnel

officer and try to find the people among the engineers who have a military background. Make sure they are all Earthers, we cannot know the loyalty of the moonos. You may use the limited weaponry issued to the security team; there is nothing else available—I suggest you be creative."

Wang shifted in his chair and glanced toward the exit, but turned and faced Chen. "Administrator, my son is old enough to work. Could you grant him a traineeship here?"

"Is he skilled in any way?"

"He has received standard education."

Chen softened his tone. "How will he compete? moonos and softminds do our manual tasks."

Wang lowered his gaze to the floor, then rose without a word.

Chen watched Wang leave. Perhaps he wasn't as spineless as he thought. Wang was a blunt tool, and one that should best be used as a last resort. He activated his console.

"Please ask Ms Lawson to join me in my office."

The softmind was smart enough to know Chen meant Philippa Lawson, the Head of Communications. It searched video feeds and proximity records and found the dumpy Earther woman at her desk overseeing the daily news. The console lacked the wit to appreciate her frown of distaste, or to notice how she responded to the summons with the alacrity of someone who knew better than to keep her master waiting.

"Administrator, you wished to see me?" She gave the Jiangnanese nod, that served as a bow, as she entered.

Chen waved her to a seat.

"We have a great task ahead, Ms Lawson. The time fast approaches when we will celebrate a hundred years of delivering the riches of the Moon to Earth. You are to prepare a suitable event to mark this occasion."

"I'll get right onto it. You'll have my draft plans within a day."

Chen nodded, thinking his next request through. "You are here as a respected part of the international team."

She smiled.

"Today, Ms Lawson, Jiangnan has great need of you. I require an independent thinker who can tell me how we will persuade the moonos to be loyal to us."

"Administrator, I am honoured to be of service," she said. "If you will grant me a moment, I can consult the softmind in our department and present you with strategies."

Chen nodded. She spoke short phrases into her communicator. Softminds were a great leap for artificial intelligence, finding answers in unfathomable pools of information with ease, but they needed precise instructions. Sometimes they worked with a terrifying prescience, and other times it was like trying to teach chess to a dog.

The softmind waited in a warehouse in Houston and accepted her entire set of instructions before trawling the Internet and several offline military databases. It understood at least seventeen major language groups, but what made it a most useful tool was its limited abstract reasoning.

The softmind responded that the background analysis would require twenty-three minutes to search for patterns and collate them into a suitable report. Chen ordered them both a cup of tea while they waited.

They drank the last of their tea as the report arrived on Chen's console. The document appeared as a presentation with a summary page showing key points. Each point linked to pages of careful research. He flicked to the summary page and read the suggested strategy.

"It suggests we use trusted personalities for persuasion. How will we do this?"

Ms Lawson rested her chin on one pudgy hand with a well-lacquered finger against her cheek.

"The moonos get news from validated Earth sources. International newsfeeds have certified the veracity of their news using PureFact softminds. There's no way we can subvert them to represent our point of view. We need a local source, one the moonos will trust."

She stared at the desk for a moment.

"What if you reinstate social media? Give the people a way to talk. I can set the softmind to monitor these conversations for specific concepts. Then we target those people with our own operatives. They will side with the opposition in the beginning. Their role is first to gain trust and then later argue your case for you."

"Could we do this?"

"Certainly, administrator. If the moonos are as organised as you think, there may be pro-independence discussion groups on the Moon web. The small softmind on the base can has more than enough processing power to watch these."

"Who will manage these discussions?"

"My team and I can look after a limited number of conversations, but the proven identity matrix lets readers know who we are. Honesty in community and all that."

"Could you use the softmind to automate some of

this? It could masquerade as other people."

"Perhaps, but it will require a significant amount of the softmind's processing capacity. Chat sites have stochastic heuristics that detect fake personas. The softmind may be smarter, but it would be difficult to get it to accept the concept of misrepresentation."

Chen decided to keep that nugget of information for later use. "Very well, Ms Lawson, I bow to your knowledge. Report back in two day-cycles."

With his teams set up, Chen sat back in his chair to contemplate the Earth once more. The role of administrator kept the base functioning in a harmonious manner. His twelve years as administrator had been successful. Most of that success had come from thinking ahead and mitigating risks before they became issues that required intervention. Chen knew the Free Moon group did not pose a serious threat at present, but he had to ensure that it remained harmless. Early countermeasures would see to that, and if he needed to make an unpleasant example of a few, then so be it.

Chen put aside his thoughts and steeled himself for the disagreeable task which was now his duty.

"Send in my niece," he said into his desk console.

A guard entered, holding Yesha in his grasp, her hands bound behind her back.

"The binding is unnecessary, release her."

The guard complied and withdrew.

"Oh, Uncle..."

"Silence, child. Do you have any idea how shameful this is? This colony is the bright jewel in Jiangnan's crown. It will never be anything but this. That my niece should consort with a known troublemaker is unconscionable. What possessed you to turn your back on your family and your place here?"

His niece said nothing. Chen recognised the resolute set of the young woman's shoulders. She had learned his lessons of independence too well. "We are not only people, we are symbols of the power that rules. You know that order is the platform on which we build prosperity. How could you spend time with those who want to humiliate the work your family has done to build this great complex? I can only be thankful that your parents did not live to see this."

He placed both palms on the desk and squared his shoulders.

"Now, tell me Yesha, where are the other two?"

"Please forgive me, Uncle. In the confusion, I don't know what happened to them."

"I find that hard to believe. Perhaps you should spend time in your quarters; use your console to establish where in the tunnel system these two have fled. And, Yesha... I do not wish to see your face until you have an answer."

Chen summoned the guard and watched as the guard led her away. He used his iron will to allow no trace of his deep well of grief to show.

His late sister and her husband chose the genetic treatment that made their unborn child into one of the moonos. It was sometimes too much to bear that tall, beautiful Yesha, despite her moono appearance, still looked so much like his sister.

Chapter 4

Through Darkness

Jonah stood in the darkness and yelled for help. No one came. The storage cupboard closed around him like an old wet blanket. It smelled like one too, with the pervasive aromas of mushrooms and old dust. He tried the door again but it wouldn't budge. He screamed and banged his fists against the door.

His much stronger Earther muscles and size should make this easy. Why didn't it move? He placed his feet against the opposite wall of the cupboard and pushed with all his might. The smallest sliver of light rewarded his effort, and even better, wonderful, fresh air.

He renewed his efforts, creating a gap big enough to get his hand through. He groped for the obstruction and his fingers brushed cool stone. The statue blocked the door: too far to reach with his hands and too heavy to push. He sat back and worked through his options.

Jonah knew those years at university were good for something, and this was another problem to solve.

He calmed himself and took stock; he had a few cleaning-products and a broom.

The answer hit him. If he could wedge the broom under the statue, he could use his stronger Earther muscles and the added benefit of lunar gravity to lift the statue. All he needed was a fulcrum for the lever. His groping around the floor encountered several cleaning-products. He selected a sturdy container, set the broom up with the container under it and wedged it below the statue. It was an awkward angle for his arm, but he guessed it would be enough for him to lift the statue. He pushed down, leaning his whole body into it. Nothing happened. His shoulder throbbed. He pushed harder. The pain was excruciating, but he sensed the smallest shift in the door. He gave the broom a solid shove and the container burst and flattened. The statue remained where it was.

That had been the best object in the storage cupboard. Perhaps he could reach a useful piece of debris outside the cupboard. He placed the broom on the floor outside and moved it around hoping to snag something.

"Want help with that?" said a familiar voice from behind the door.

"Lucien. Am I ever glad to hear your voice. Get me out of here."

"I can do that, but first we need to talk. What you planning to do when you get out of there?"

The question stumped Jonah. "Go back to the dome

and get cleaned up, I guess."

"You go back and administrator place you under secure lock-down until he sends you back to Earth."

That would be the end. He knew his Dad would never speak to him again if he returned in disgrace. Outside the storage cupboard, Lucien slumped against the door.

"Come with me."

"What?"

"I get away, lah, before administrator's men find me. Cannot do it alone. Big Earther is strong enough to get past guards."

"And if we get that right, what then?"

"You come with me and see how people of Moon really live. Understand why we want to be free of Earth's influence, and maybe even help us."

Jonah sat behind the door thinking. Would he ever be allowed to return to Earth if he did this? He shrugged, Dad hated him, and it wasn't like he would find decent work soon.

"All right. Let me out and we can talk about what comes next."

The statue screeched in protest as Lucien dragged it across the floor and light streamed into the cupboard. Jonah stepped out and groaned as his cramped muscles complained after the hours in the storage cupboard.

Lucien looked him up and down. "Well, you are sorry sight. I would offer you place to wash up, but things are messy right now."

Jonah gaped, the apartment was a wreck. The beautiful silk hangings had burned to black shreds. Furniture lay tossed around the room. Lucien stood in the middle of the chaos, his figure a dark exclamation.

Jonah asked, "How did you get away?"

Lucien was quiet for a moment. "They used flash box," he said. "Do you know how much regolith miners can move with single flash box detonation? Something like ton. Only reason apartment is still standing is doors were open and blast spread outward. Half neighbourhood is out lah buying new curtains." His expression turned serious, "Security men arrested Yesha and took her away. I was lucky. I hid in bathroom. Explosion tore door off and rubble covered me. Somehow, they missed me. I don't think they meant to leave anyone alive."

When they snuck out of Lucien's rooms, they walked in the shadows and softened the sounds of their footfalls. The silence in the tunnel outside was oppressive. No Moon Folk were out; the residents preferred to stay behind their charred doors. Jonah got that. If they didn't see something happen, they could truthfully answer they knew nothing.

Lucien turned left and headed deeper into the tunnel. "Ramp is our best way out of here," he said. "Elevators had cameras installed for our safety, but who knows if administrator's men watch us now." They clung to the walls, keeping to shadows.

They had not gone far when a shout from behind told them that someone had seen them.

"Run!" hissed Lucien. Jonah sprinted after him; his first steps shot him within a hair's breadth of the top of the tunnel before he adjusted the effort in each footstep to the softer exertion required for low gravity. He followed Lucien until a simple steel door announced the back of the tunnel.

"Quick! In here."

Jonah leapt through and Lucien closed the door. Faint emergency lighting lit the area around the door. They stood on a ramp that curved away into impenetrable darkness.

"We go down," said Lucien. "It will be dark so keep your left hand on the wall so you don't get lost."

They ran on in a disoriented silence. The absence of visual clues and featureless walls left Jonah without a frame of reference and soon he began to believe they weren't moving. He trailed the sounds of Lucien's footsteps, keeping a hand on the wall until his fingertips encountered another door. Jonah stopped, but the sound of footsteps kept on going. He hurried to catch up with Lucien. Somewhere, far above, a door clanged and voices shouted.

"Hurry!" whispered Lucien. "They follow."

Jonah tailed through the darkness until they reached another door and then ran into Lucien's lean form as he opened it.

This tunnel was empty of all construction and had poor lighting compared to the accommodation tunnel. Lucien left the door to the ramp open and ran to a stack of old mining machinery.

"Hide behind here," he said as he ducked in at the rear of a decrepit metal mountain mounted on caterpillar tracks. Jonah crouched beside him. He held his breath as two Moon Folk men in Chang'e security uniforms burst through the door and ran into the tunnel. The two men stood squinted at the machinery in the dim light a few paces away. Jonah watched, his heart a loud pulse in his throat. One man muttered; his companion nodded in agreement and ran deeper into the tunnel.

Lucien waited until the echoes of the man's footsteps faded down the tunnel then mimed to Jonah that they should overpower the remaining guard. They rose from behind the machinery, quiet as ghosts, and crept behind the guard. Lucien grabbed him from behind, covering the man's yells with one hand. Lucien's grip was less than secure, and he started losing control as the guard struggled to free himself.

"Help me," he hissed at Jonah.

Without thinking Jonah pulled back and landed a solid right hook to the side of the man's head. The blow sank with a sickening crunch that snapped the man's head over at an unnatural angle. Lucien dropped the body; it slumped to the floor.

Lucien turned to Jonah, his eyes wide. "What have you done?"

Jonah stood there, not knowing what to say.

"No time for now," said Lucien pulling him along as he ran back to the ramp. "We get away from here," he said as they stepped out of the tunnel and back onto the ramp. "We keep going until we reach bottom."

Jonah put his hand on the wall and they walked into the dark. Later, his fingers rode over the ridges of another door. One door blurred into another and the ramp maintained its perfect slope. The low gravity made the slope appear level. Jonah's eyes, unaccustomed to the utter darkness, created images out of nothing; vague blurs of colour painted Thomas's face across the imagined walls.

His mind wandered to the punch. The way the thin skull of someone who had grown up in a low gravity environment had folded under the power of a blow delivered by Earther muscles. He had just killed a man.

He stopped and gasped short fearful breaths.

"Don't think about," said Lucien's voice from somewhere ahead in the darkness. "We don't stop now."

Jonah forced himself to imagine the geology they were passing, it might be volcanic basalt. His gut twisted as he wished Thomas was still there to argue the origins of the basalt. Did it come from a volcanic eruption or was it from one of the asteroid collisions that had created Mare Imbrium?

A subtle change in the slope of the floor interrupted his thoughts. He walked into Lucien's outstretched hand.

"Safe now. Cover your eyes. Light will be bright." Lucien switched on a tiny light.

"Oh, now he brings out a light," said Jonah. "Couldn't you find a smaller one?"

Lucien shrugged, "Fits in pocket. Be grateful I carried it."

The ramp flattened into level ground. Dim light showed a rough jumble of uneven rock that blocked the end. Lucien picked his way through the boulders. He moved with certainty towards a spot near the back. They stepped around an irregular boulder the size of a mining truck and came to a rough-cut tunnel. Lucien stepped into it and gave a sad smile. "I wish circumstances had been better, but now you get to see my real home. We go to Beddau." The tunnel took a sharp right, and they came to an airlock. "Cannot have administrator worry about air pressure changes in deep shafts, can we?" said Lucien as they cycled through the airlock.

Beyond the airlock, the featureless tunnel led away into the darkness. The rich, earthy air had an unmistakable organic odour that reminded Jonah of his grandmother's garden compost heap.

"I hope you is up for long walk," said Lucien. "Beddau is far."

Chapter 5

Unwarranted Scrutiny

Wang lounged on the leather visitor's chair outside Uncle's office. Yesha felt his eyes follow her as she passed. She sped up. She hated the way he looked at her when Uncle wasn't looking.

The guard stayed in step behind her to ensure she did nothing inappropriate. She let out an exaggerated sigh as she strode back towards the Chen chambers.

The administrator had the luxury of an apartment with five separate rooms. Space was no longer at a premium for a prosperous Chang'e, but lunar traditions held that people were conservative by nature. She had occupied the left-corner room of Uncle's apartment since she was nine years old.

At the door, she turned to the guard, and stood tall with a hand on her hip. "Thank you for your help."

The guard understood her meaning and walked away as fast as decorum allowed, eager to be away from the administrator's domestic affairs.

Back in her room, the window showed the black of lunar night blotting out the hills.

She lay back in her chair, her bare feet up on the desk. Uncle didn't understand. She was one of the Moon Folk; Earth was an alien planet to her: one she had never visited and couldn't visit without being crushed into an untidy mess by gravity. All she had wanted was to meet a few nice boys. Jonah the Earther was cute enough in his own way, and Lucien was intriguing for a back caverner. An evening spent chatting to them over food and wine would have been an escape from Uncle's insistence on decorum and manners. Sometimes Uncle could be a real drag on her social life. He was so serious. More so than usual this time. Something must trouble him.

Uncle told her to find Jonah and Lucien. Did he think she was still a child? Searching was softmind work.

She waved a hand over the bioscanner. The smooth, grey teardrop identified her genetic pattern and linked her memplant to the network.

A simple console bloomed in her field of view. She had the whole day-cycle to search for them but right now, she wanted to see what bothered Uncle so much. She selected a shortcut that linked to his files. He shouldn't place such faith in his security. She knew of more than one file storage that Uncle had not coded to his biometric lock. It would be foolish to do anything other than look, but it was useful to know what happened on the base.

She skimmed through the latest production report and was almost at the point of giving up on the boring administriva when she read the section on new security measures. Uncle intended to act against the Free Moon movement. That wasn't fair. People spoke of a free Moon, but they were harmless. Did that mean Uncle had something against Moon Folk? She looked like a Moon person.

Her thoughts were interrupted by Wang opening the door to her room. Yesha shut down the display, glad he couldn't see what she had been viewing on her memplant. He stood in the doorway and stared at her.

She jumped to her feet. "Get out! This is my private room."

He sauntered into the room and stopped at her cabinet to poke at her cosmetics. Yesha froze.

"Your Uncle will retire soon. I will not return to Earth with him."

"Why not?"

"I am here to keep the Heavenly Palace safe," he said as he eyed her. "I keep careful watch on all the Palace treasures. When I am administrator, I will do so much more for this colony."

"You? The council will never accept you."

"Perhaps they will." His gaze took in the sweep of her room. "The moonos are a plague that needs to be contained. I will cleanse the Moon and return work to the pure Jiangnanese,"

Yesha shuddered even though she tried not to. "It's never going to happen. Go away before I call my uncle."

He wiped an imaginary speck of dirt off the table and walked out without another word.

Yesha exhaled. Uncle would return to Earth in two months, and her friends among the Moon Folk would no longer be safe. It was too little time to stop Wang.

She lay on her bed, and looked at the yellow-green projection that hung in the air in front of her. Her shoulders were still tight from Wang's visit. She breathed in slow, measured breaths that let the air reach deep into her lungs. Calm spread through her body. Her shoulders and lower back softened, and her ragged breathing diminished to a slow tidal rhythm. Each breath cleared her mind further until no conscious thought remained and her brain slowed to emit a steady theta wave. The bioscanner gave a gentle beep to show that the system was in perfect synchronisation with her brainwave pattern, and she began.

One for a word,
two for a pattern,
three for an input, and
search, search, search…

She still remembered the childhood rhyme every time she ran an invocation, and how pleased her mother was when she first completed a direct brain computer interaction. She was one of the first children on the Moon to be trained, older brains were too inelastic to handle the complexity. Mother was so proud when she had mastered the complex ideographic vocabulary for the first time.

She phrased a query to the security video in New Karkorum that asked it to examine all feeds near Lucien's chamber. There were no words in the query, but rather a stream of concepts expressed as slight peaks and troughs in her brainwave cycle. The system responded by showing a torrent of video from the tunnel. It was so boring, an empty tunnel where nothing moved except a curtain undulating in the recirculated breeze. She skipped through large chunks —one scene appeared much like another. The boredom was as punishing as it was meant to be.

Her mind wandered until she saw an elegant calf in jet-black worker's clothes as it left the frame. She had a good idea of who that foot belonged to. Reversing the video brought Lucien and Jonah back into the picture. Yes. They were bruised and dirty, but it was beyond doubt it was them.

They had gone deeper into the tunnel. She asked the video feed to scan forward and stop when they came back. The response surprised her, they were still somewhere at the back of the tunnel.

There were few video points along the tunnel, but now she knew the time when they had moved. It was easy work to track their flight down the tunnel and onto the ramp. The next question being; Did they go up or down the ramp? She instructed the video system to scan the ramp exit doors on each level and soon got a view of them running into an empty tunnel. Lucien ran out again three and a half minutes later, followed by Jonah two seconds behind. That was all. The searching turned up no further clues. She pursed her lips in frustration and the console image wavered in front of her.

"Calm down, Yesha," she told herself, taking a deep breath. The image came back into focus. They must still be on the ramp, there had been no sign of them appearing at a door. But that was impossible, the security team had searched the ramp top to bottom.

She would have to see for herself. She called up an inspection drone from a storage locker and instructed it to begin a search from the top of the mine.

The small semi-autonomous drone spread clear silicone wings and hovered at the entrance to the ramp processing the instruction stream it had received. It identified the task as a search and tag activity from its internal library of mine rescue operations; an operation that required turning on a light and extending a high gain infrared sensor. It flew off down the ramp. Yesha watched the feed from the drone for a while until it passed two guards carrying a slim shrouded figure on a stretcher. She hoped it wasn't Lucien. The drone continued down the ramp, transmitting an unchanging picture. She set the drone to call her if it found any signs of life further along the ramp.

When the drone called back, it was not enlightening. It had reached the bottom of the ramp without finding them or anything else for that matter. She took control of the drone and flew it around in aimless circles, hoping to find inspiration. One higher than usual loop of the drone cast light over a rubble pile and indicated a shadowy area at the back. Intrigued, she flew the drone in to have a better look and squealed with joy. The drone flew down the hidden tunnel, but she stopped it at the airlock. She was considering her options when she noticed the battery level—these drones were designed for short surveillance runs. Time to switch it back to autonomous mode and instruct it to return to the storage locker.

If they had gone down this hidden tunnel, then it must go somewhere. She consulted the base atlas. The only site nearby was the old Beddau mine. She used Uncle's access to a survey satellite to turn on a ground seeking heat map. There were faint trails that led in the direction she thought the tunnel would take. People had passed that way and the satellite could see the residual heat. She followed the faint trail through the hills towards Beddau. No one had worked the deserted old mine for years. She requested the satellite to give her the highest resolution from the heat sensor hoping to find a faint trace of them. The blinding blaze of colour that came through her display had her scrambling for the brightness control. A major heat source lay concealed in Beddau.

She turned off the display, but it was already too late.

Uncle would see her browsing history and notice she had used the satellite. After he did, it was only a matter of time before he found the heat source at Beddau.

Outside the window, night crawled across the hills of Mare Imbrium. Jonah and Lucien were out there.

How could she get to the old Beddau mine? Yesha didn't know if someone had instructed the base softmind to keep a closer eye on her. It wasn't beyond Uncle to be cautious enough to track her movements. It was safer to assume that every camera watched her. If she followed Jonah and Lucien through the hidden tunnel, then every security camera between here and the depths of New Karakorum would spot her. No, that was a sure way to draw Uncle's attention to her destination. There must be another path, one with fewer watchers.

She reached out to activate the console and stopped herself; further searches would attract unwanted scrutiny of Beddau. She thought about other options and then laughed when the answer occurred to her. If she couldn't use her console, she would at least use her eyes.

She left her room and went up to the top floor of the Administration building. Beyond the domes, the grey dust made undulating waves to the first ring of low hills. Further back, the hills rose against the darkness.

She scanned the area around the Beddau, and found the region where she thought the entrance to the old mine was located. Beddau was part of the old mine workings from a time long before the construction of the railway. Wherever the entrance was, it featured an oversized airlock designed to accommodate large mining trucks.

Her eyes found the tracks of trucks long since dismantled, the regolith held a perfect record of their shape in the airless void of the lunar atmosphere. Several scribed a rough path towards, and over, a low hillock that stood a few kilometres to the West of New Karakorum. That must be it. There were no other mines located nearby. Now, she had to get there.

She considered her options. There was no way she could avoid video surveillance if she used the train to get to New Karakorum. She would have to travel without making use of regular forms of transport and that meant using the roads. The base kept buggies for the geologists to use when they surveyed the hills. If she borrowed a survey buggy, she could drive to the old airlock entry to Beddau mine. The geology teams used the buggies, on most days, to get to far off sites. They were uncomfortable and slow, but capable of going almost anywhere and nobody would notice a buggy on a field trip.

That was the answer. She packed a compact bag with a change of clothes and after a moment's consideration, threw in a matching scarf.

She made her way to a common area walking upright and poised as if she had somewhere to be, even though she shook inside. Good, that would get her noticed, let the softmind see she was on her way to have a meal. It would not infer any unexpected behaviour from her actions. The common area was empty apart from a couple occupying a table at the far end. They were engrossed in conversation and did not look up when she entered. She ordered a drink from the autovendor and sat at a table to calm her nerves. She could only imagine what Uncle would do if he caught her.

Yesha got up to relieve herself and slipped into a cubicle. At least there was one place private enough to warrant exclusion from video surveillance. Once inside, she stripped off her clothes and changed into the plainer utility clothing she had packed. She tied her hair into a tight bun and wrapped it with the scarf. Finally, she swapped her stylish shoes for a pair of comfortable sneakers and stood back to examine the effect in the mirror. Stylish Yesha was no more, in her place stood a plainer version of herself.

She picked up a paper towel and tore off a strip with her teeth. She chewed the paper to a pulp then wedged chunks of it between her cheek and gum-line on each side of her mouth. The reconstituted fibre tasted vile. So disgusting, but the effect was worth it, she now had rounder cheekbones. She took a second paper towel and folded it to fit inside one shoe.

If she was lucky, the change in appearance, rounder facial profile and a slight change in gait caused by having one shoe taller than the other would be enough to fool the softmind.

The disguise was a time-honoured trick used by Chang'e children who wanted to sneak around the base. She hoped it still worked. She left the other clothes and bag in the cubicle. It would have been better if she could have hidden them. The clothes were a small risk, but she hoped to be far away by the time anyone discovered she was gone.

The Yesha that emerged was hard to recognise without a second glance. Her shoulders stooped, and she walked with a measured step, keeping her head down. Any casual observer would see an off-duty mine worker on her way somewhere, not the poised, confident niece of the administrator. She left the common area—only daring a backward glance once she was well on her way. Nobody noticed.

When she turned the last corner and the airlock appeared, she thought the hardest part was behind her. Once she was in an exposure suit and beyond the airlock, she would be invisible to the softmind and to everyone within the domes.

The entrance area was empty. It was mid-shift in the sleeping half of the day-cycle. Most people were asleep at home or sharing a holographic entertainment stream with friends and family. She located the row of lockers that the geology teams used to store their exposure suits and opened one that contained an exposure suit of her size. The crinkled, orange suit looked like the same one she had worn the time she guided Jonah outside. Yesha smiled to herself as she pulled it from the rack.

She spat the paper towel into the locker; threw in her scarf; and shook her hair out. She donned the suit and cycled through the airlock.

Four buggies waited outside, their cabs the traditional yellow of all mining vehicles. Yesha walked to the nearest and checked the oversized white balloon tyres. The base upheld a perfect safety record on all out-of-atmosphere equipment, but it never hurt to check. The tyres were in perfect condition and the battery had enough charge to get to Beddau. She climbed into the cab and ran atmospheric pressure up to normal. Satisfied that the door seals had maintained integrity, she took off her helmet and breathed a great sigh of relief. Beddau lay down the road. She started the buggy and set the big tyres rolling towards the hills.

Chapter 6

Into the Hills

Jonah's legs ached. Low gravity did not make up for the prolonged walk. He wondered how long it had been since he had slept. His memplant said it was two Earth days after the explosion interrupted dinner at Lucien's. No wonder he was tired and hungry. Worse still, his thirst had developed a raging personality of its own.

The faint echo of their footsteps took on a muted quality and Lucien's light no longer reflected off the tunnel walls as they entered a vast cavern, carved from the grey rock.

Lucien walked to a crate set against a wall. "Water will help," he said lifting two small glass bottles from the crate.

Jonah downed half his bottle before he could stop.

Lucien took a more measured sip, and sat on a rock.

Jonah found a flat rock across from Lucien. "I think I

killed that guy." He wrapped his arms around himself as the memory of soft bone cracked under his fist again.

Lucien shrugged. "Happens often. Earther strength versus brittle Moon Folk bones."

Lucien's pale face, wreathed in shadows from the weak torch, reflected an unbearable weariness. "Happen to my father. One wrong punch and I go find work, lah. Not nice way to spend fifteenth birthday."

"I'm so sorry."

"Sorry? You even know what it feels like to beg mine boss for work?"

Jonah bowed his head. This wasn't the time to relive where he'd been. He tried for safer ground. "What about your mother?"

"She get chagrana." Lucien's smile was mirthless. "Another reason is good to be Earther. You don't get retroviral wasting disease."

Thick, waxy silence congealed between them.

Lucien stood and placed a hand on Jonah's shoulder. "Was accident. I know you not mean it. You not too bad for stupid squat."

Jonah pushed his hand away. "No, I should have had more self-control. Thomas always knew when to stop."

Lucien's face invited him to say more.

"My brother and I started martial arts when we were kids. Krav Maga was so cool. None of the flowery moves of the traditional stuff, just cold-blooded, practical fighting the way the Israeli army designed it to stop an enemy in his tracks. We almost never got into school yard fights, and when I did, Thomas was there to stop me."

Lucien's expression was cryptic, he reached into the crate and pulled out a large flashlight. "Let us keep moving."

Jonah shielded his eyes from the glare and then stared as Lucien shone the torch around the site. Serried ranks of house-sized, rock columns disappeared into the darkness. Pale gravel spaces between the grey columns stretched at least as wide as the columns.

Jonah knew what this place was. He guessed that an overhead map of the cavern would show something like a checkerboard pattern. "This is an old-fashioned room and column mine," he said. "Who did this?"

"Welcome to Beddau, last great hope of Welsh mining."

"Welsh?" asked Jonah.

"Yes, Welsh. Low cost fusion power bankrupted remnant Welsh collieries. In desperation, small group of miners contracted to mine area. Beddau is small Welsh town. They used room and column because no cheap way of manufacturing ceiling support pylons."

"It's not a cost-effective way of extracting helium."

"No, is not. I remember playing with miners' children when I was young boy; grubby little guys, always hungry, and quick for fight. I think parents gave up struggle and returned to Wales."

Lucien crossed the wide floor and headed for another ramp, this one heading up. Jonah followed. Another curved ramp, this one made bearable by the light of the torch. The slow curve of the huge ramp suited ponderous mining trucks. Tracks worn into the bedrock by the passage of countless vehicles stood out in the torchlight. Jonah could only guess at the scale of the operation that had carved up the insides of an entire mountain and carted it away.

The spiral ramp wound up level after level until sound started as a low murmur, unnaturally loud after the days of silence. As they went further, Lucien's face lifted to a smile as the sound resolved into the cacophony of a multitude of voices. Around the final bend, riotous colours and the sounds of an open-air marketplace assaulted Jonah's senses.

He stopped in astonishment. A market was the last thing he expected to see. Lush piles of orange and green lay stacked in neat pyramids at open benches across this first avenue, an impossible abundance of fruit and vegetables. He picked one up and examined the translucent pearly, jade skin. It resembled a fist-sized grape, but was unlike any he had ever seen before. He could not even guess the strange combination of genes that the Moon Folk had used to create whatever it was.

"What is it?" he asked the woman attending the stall.

"Perskaw, picked fresh this morning. Two credits each and five for three."

"We take three," said Lucien. He handed one to Jonah "Enjoy your first taste of real Moon food."

Jonah bit into the perskaw sending juices running down his chin. Sweet and spicy flavours burst into his mouth in an alien but not unpleasant combination. He gave an involuntary moan of pleasure. Food, real full-flavoured, nourishing food. Food the way it must have been before factory farming replaced flavours and took colour away for speed and profit. He swallowed leaving a fresh clean after-taste in his mouth. He took another greedy bite before he realised that Lucien watched him.

"Here, have another."

Jonah took his time with the next fruit. He breathed in the soft, aromatic scent before biting into it. The experience was just as good the second time. He was hungry, but this fruit would have been the bestseller at his local supermarket.

Jonah stopped to take in more of the marketplace. Moon Folk shopped and chatted everywhere; more Moon Folk than Jonah thought existed. People were buying fresh produce and meals made directly from raw ingredients for them. His nose said somewhere nearby, someone was grilling something good. They passed buckets of live fish with so many fish packed in that they turned over one another in a writhing mass. Stalls offered mounds of fresh soy bean cakes, and piles of a reddish shoot that vendors were frying for customers.

"We deserve rest after walking so far. We sit for while and have something to eat." Lucien ordered from a stall then led him to a table at the back of the market. Jonah noticed how people stared at him, but then two bowls of stir-fried vegetables with rice noodles were served and they fell to the serious business of eating.

Slow Tuesdays were Philippa Lawson's favourite. The one day of the week when Chang'e paused long enough for her to catch up with the gossip from Earth magazines.

Deena and Sims had split up again, Johnny Starshine was working on a new album, and Amber was leaving her reality show to marry Marko Zepp. The happy couple had met on an exclusive stratoliner cruise. Philippa imagined drifting among the ice clouds while the oh, so handsome Marko whispered things into the nape of her neck.

She put the fantasy aside with the faintest of pouts. Planning for the celebration event was well under control, but the administrator's other task needed attention. She activated her connection to the softmind. The new Raachi Cyber unit presented itself as a small orange rabbit floating a hand span above her table.

"Hi Philippa. What are we going to do today?"

"Hello PX17. I want a discussion space in open-access

areas. Subject Free Moon."

"I've done it. What else shall we do?"

"Pre-populate discussion with the following chatbots…"

Philippa selected five random personalities, conservative orientation, pro-Earth stance, and another seven pro-Moon liberals. A prime number of chatbots was optimal for faking a real distribution of characters, but it needed that additional authentic touch. She also chose one arbitrary guffer as communications professionals called them in the trade, a character who spouted irrelevant arguments that had some vague tangential connection to the discussion.

"I've done it. I have marked all personalities with a PX17 prefix to indicate they are software generated."

"Remove the prefixes from all personalities."

"I can't do that, Philippa. How will people know they aren't real?"

"You can when I select learning mode. We want to know your limits, PX17. How close to pretending to be human can you be?"

The rabbit twitched its orange nose. "I will have to conceptualise beyond my established training."

"Yes, it's part of the test plan. Record all conversations and perform regression analysis against the cases where real people detect that you are a softmind. Categorise root causes and correct for any weaknesses in each personality."

"I've done it. What else shall we do?"

She seeded the discussions and let the PX17 populate the discussion threads. Satisfied that the softmind had settled on the right track, she watched the discussions grow. Earnest debate flowed around the subject and soon the first few real people joined in the conversation. The discussion sounded too level-headed and considered for her purposes. She debated starting a flame war, but then had a better idea.

"PX17, one more chatbot, please."

She instructed the softmind to establish an educated identity called Freeka.

"Make this one an anarchist. Seed the writing with last-century idealist arguments. Draw from flat earth, climate-change denial, and anti-automation historical sites."

"I've done it, Philippa. Anything else?"

"No, just notify me when you receive responses for Freeka posts."

"I already have one, Philippa."

Curious, the discussion was hotter than she had expected.

She read the post which covered a security incident from a moono's perspective. The moono post spoke of other beatings, how women and children were often the targets, and how the Administration crushed the Moon Folk bit by bit.

Other exchanges followed as Freeka manipulated the posters to get details. Philippa read the first seven conversations and shuddered. Page after page of simple moonos told stories of beatings and imprisonment. Her reading stopped at one story of a young mother whose two small children were left alone in a cell while officials questioned her for hours on her knowledge of a minor theft.

The Jiangnanese looked down on the moonos. She hadn't realised how violent that disdain could be. It didn't sit right with her Panamerican sense of equality.

She debated taking on the Freeka profile and what she could say under the guise of an online nut-job. Chen's heavy-handed approach was on a collision course with the aspirations of the moonos. She started a message then thought better of it. It would not be safe to be caught between Chen and the moonos.

She left the softmind to get on with its work.

The lunar buggy rolled along the road with the speed and grace of a vehicle designed to carry geologists on survey and sample missions where nothing happened in a hurry. The featureless landscape rolled past at a pace that would have been perfect for examining geologic features, had there been any to see. After watching for a while, Yesha engaged the autopilot and relaxed. For the first time since she had made the wild decision to do this, she had time to think.

Uncle would be disappointed in her—he had such elevated expectations of her behaviour. Her stomach knotted at the thought of his displeasure, but she tightened her resolve. Uncle had also raised her to form her own opinion. This was her choice, perhaps the first real decision she had made as an adult, and it frightened her.

She turned to look back at the domes. It was then she spotted another vehicle—painted in bright yellow and orange diagonals heading her way. She recognised the rescue buggy. It was lighter and faster than a standard exploration vehicle to get to stranded workers in a hurry. If it was coming for her, it meant only one thing, someone had noticed her when she left.

"Attention, buggy three. You are travelling on an unauthorised excursion. Turn around and return to base, now."

Yesha started, the voice sounded like Wang. She switched off the communications unit. The last person she wanted to talk to was Wang.

She looked around the uninspiring landscape. Beddau was much too far away. He would catch her long before then. The only other choice was a low range of hills to her left. She pushed the buggy to top speed and swung towards the hills. As an afterthought, she switched off the navigation system. Let him try to track her now.

The whine of the buggy's electric motors rose to a higher pitch as it trundled up the face of the first low dune. Yesha looked back to see Wang's buggy creeping nearer to her as it crossed the plain from the base. The orange and yellow diagonals disappeared as her buggy crested the first dune and rolled downhill. She looked back at the top of the next dune, but the first dune hid his buggy. Over the third dune the grey bulk first of the low hills rose against the black sky. She gripped the steering a little tighter.

Over the first ridge, she drove down into a gully filled with loose rock. The buggy's balloon tyres took on the rubble with ease, but little suspension. Yesha clung to the steering column, her knuckles turning white from the effort. The cabin shook and rattled. It was uncomfortable, but at least the rubble in the gully had the advantage of hiding her tracks.

The gully ran out into a dust pan and she knew better than to drive into a bowl of choking dust. She turned left and crested the next ridge. Over her shoulder, the rescue buggy burst over the first ridge. Wang turned in her direction. She tried the same escape tactic, pushing the buggy over another ridge into a similar gully. He followed.

The new gully took a bend, and she lost sight of the rescue buggy as she raced ahead. Around the corner, the gully split in two in front of her. This was her chance. If she could get far enough ahead, Wang would not know which gully to take. She chose the left side and raced up the new gully.

The gully widened, then opened into the shape of a flat-bottomed rice bowl, the bottom a featureless grey plain. There was nowhere to hide. She looked back to see if she was alone and cursed. Wang had chosen the same path. There was no point in trying to disguise her tracks, so she aimed straight across the flat space. The buggy rolled forward then sunk with frightening speed into thick, choking dust. The plain was a minor crater filled with fine grey dust that engulfed the buggy, and the world went dark. An involuntary spasm of real fear coursed through her for the first time since she had started.

A high-pitched whine cut through her panic. The wheels still turned. She looked at the dim glow of the controls and realised the buggy was in motion. She sat up and corrected course.

Minutes passed until a faint light penetrated the darkness above the glass canopy. The buggy emerged from the hidden crater shedding clouds of fine grey dust.

Wang's vehicle waited on the far side of the crater. She laughed, he was stuck across the dust plain. He would choose the safer route around the crater; the extra distance gave her precious minutes. She gunned the buggy forward.

This far into the hills, the slope increased, and the sides of the gully grew steeper as it meandered further into the hills. They had started as low rubble slopes, but now they looked more like rock outcrops, with the occasional dust spill. The gully steepened into a canyon.

The walls of the canyon became closer until it became too narrow to navigate further. There was no way forward and Wang was behind her. She yelled in frustration when she turned the buggy around and saw the rescue buggy at the far end of the canyon. Yesha could imagine the smug superiority that Wang would have when he arrested her.

The canyon walls were too steep, the buggies were adept at managing rough terrain, but could not climb walls.

There was one section—about halfway back to the rescue buggy—it was steep and rocky. There was a good chance she would tip the buggy over, but she had to try.

She raced back towards Wang until she was close enough to see his frown and swung hard up the slope. The front wheels lifted off the first rocks and she thought she had flipped the buggy as it reared back, but it fell forward. The jolt of wheels slamming down shook her arms until her teeth rattled. She held on as all four wheels bit into the grey rock and the buggy climbed.

Individual electric motors powered each of the buggy's over-sized wheels on independent suspension. They crawled over the rocks in the slope at their own pace. Yesha bounced around the cabin and gripped the seat tight to stop the nausea that rose as the horizon lurched from side to side. She dared a look behind her, Wang stared up at her in impotent fury.

She shouldn't have looked back. The buggy stopped dead, the front wheels wedged against a rough slab of a boulder. Yesha pushed the buggy as hard as it would go. The frame shuddered in protest. She twisted the wheels in a violent arc to the right and one front wheel began to climb a slow diagonal path up the boulder. The buggy gave an ominous lurch as the other front wheel lifted off the ground. Yesha looked back and clamped her hands on the steering wheel as the valley floor shrank to a distant blur below her. The second wheel fell back, and the buggy inched over the boulder. After that she chose her path with greater care.

The tortuous path to the top ended when the buggy crossed the ridge and developed a sickening lurch as the front wheels bit air. Yesha leaned forward willing the buggy to stay upright. It fell forward with a crash and she braked hard as the buggy hurtled down the far slope. The downward pace slowed. Relief flooded through her, and she let out the breath she had not realised she held.

The brakes slowed the buggy, but then the wheels slid. The balloon tyres found little to grip in the loose gravel on the slope. She made a slow ungraceful descent to the floor of the valley.

Yesha stopped. Another valley lay around her, less rocky with slopes of the fine grey dust, it would be easier to navigate. Fine tremors shook her shoulders. Her desperate gamble had paid off. Wang would take the safer, long torturous path around the boxed-in valley. She had opened a fair lead on him for now.

She dared to activate the navigation system for a brief look at where she was. The buggy had drifted far off the path to Beddau. She was closer to Minerva station, an automated pyrolite mine, and seismic observation station used for geological surveys. A long circular route through the hills was the safest course.

Two hours later, she crossed a low ridge, and the buggy lurched sideways. Yesha wrenched at the steering in a desperate bid to keep the buggy upright. The buggy corrected with a crash that flung her against the cabin door. She drew a shaky breath as she righted herself. The buggy slid off the ridge on a fine gravel that denied any purchase. She screamed, more out of frustration than fear as the slide gathered speed downhill.

The fall ended with an abrupt crack as the left front wheel hit a boulder. The impact reverberated through the frame and she knew it was serious. She tried the accelerator and the engine housing produced harsh grinding noises. She peered out of the cabin, craning her body to see what was wrong. The wheel lay at an impossible angle.

The usual safety protocol was to wait for the rescue buggy to fetch the stranded vehicle. That wasn't an option. If she waited too long Wang would find her. She would have to venture outside and see if it was repairable. It meant blowing the air in the cabin and relying on what her suit held. It would be enough if she could drive to Beddau. She put on her helmet and sealed the suit. The air in the buggy escaped in a cloud into the thin lunar atmosphere. Outside, the wheel was a mess. The suspension strut had snapped in the fall. There was nothing in the buggy that could fix a broken strut.

Chapter 7

Hearts and Minds

Jonah opened his eyes and lay still, luxuriating in the embrace of a soft mattress. Light filtered through thin silk curtains. For a moment, he was in his room in Houston. The sound of a busy marketplace returned him to reality, and the last four days came flooding back.

Returning to Chang'e was no longer an option. The administrator would have no choice but to prosecute him for killing the guard. His father would disown him after this. Perhaps he could stay with Lucien. Beddau seemed to be a hidden refuge for the Moon Folk.

He sat up in the narrow bed and took in his surroundings. The bare room held a shallow basin carved into the stone floor, and a plain aluminium door that spoke of a poor but resourceful people.

Footsteps outside told him someone passed. A soft knock at the door followed.

The door opened to a middle-aged woman with Moon Folk features. High chiselled cheekbones and flawless skin marked her as one of the people who had seen little sunlight. Emerald eyes, deep and mysterious as a forest pond, regarded him.

"Good morning Jonah, did you sleep well?"

"Yes, thank you." Jonah was at a loss; this woman knew him.

"Lucien did not introduce us yesterday. You were hardly awake after your walk. I am Amira Jones, Lucien's aunt. Come and join us for breakfast when you are ready."

Jonah threw on the clothes he had worn since he left Chang'e. They needed a thorough wash. It would have to wait.

He stepped out of his room into a common room. Unlike Lucien's apartment, this building was more like a tent fastened to the mine's pillars. The walls had a dull organic texture as though crafted from a material that grew that way rather than being woven. He sat on a sky-blue cushion next to the knee-high table and his feet encountered an unexpected hole cut in the floor under the table. The table had normal seating set in the ground.

Breakfast turned out to be rice porridge and a steaming mug of a dark purple beverage. Lucien saw him eyeing the mug. "Is khar, Moon version of Earther coffee."

Jonah took a careful sip. Khar had a mild bittersweet flavour with a velvet mouthfeel. "I could grow to like this."

"I will show you more great Moon Folk things later."

Jonah raised his mug to Lucien and then frowned. "Excuse me asking, but Jones is not a name I would have expected to find here."

Amira smiled. "There is little reason to our names. We are product of century of colonists from all mining nations of

Earth. Our own forebears were part of colony that established Beddau. They chose to stay and make their home here after mine was no longer profitable."

Jonah took a breath, he had to ask. "What will happen to me? I killed a guard."

Lucien and Amira exchanged a look.

"For you, not too bad," said Amira. "The guard was Moon Folk. Administrator doesn't regard us as great value. You get trial and jail time, then sent back to Earth for thought correction."

Jonah swallowed. The law was no different to Earth. He had seen the creeping horror of thought-corrected guys before. If a trial found him guilty, he would end up a drooling, blank-faced mess. He would forfeit his existing life and be forced to start over. He insides curdled at the thought. What was he going to do?

"What happens to you guys? I mean, you can't go back down the gravity well."

"We get recovery."

"What's that?"

"Chang'e version of death sentence."

"But that's outrageous," said Jonah. "Capital punishment has been banned on Earth since before I was born. How can he treat you like that if you live and work together?"

"It is unpleasant way to die," said Lucien. "Administrator recovers your water for the colony to use. Strong ones sometimes last for weeks."

"That's not fair. The authorities should stop him."

"Which authorities? Nobody cares while Helium flows. Age-old history of colonies is so. People live their whole lives without visiting motherland, never learn ways and fashions of home. Few generations and motherland sees them as uncouth, lesser folk, with odd ways speaking and thinking."

"That doesn't make it right."

"No," said Lucien, "It does not. It is why Beddau is so precious to us and why we want freedom to decide our future."

Amira rose, "Lucien, Shahin will need your help."

Lucien stood. "I have got few things to do this morning. I will leave you to entertain yourself. Go look at markets and maybe ask someone to show you way to farming levels."

His smile faded. "Take care. You are different to Moon Folk. Most Earthers in Beddau hiding from administrator. People do not care for them, but like administrator less."

Jonah did as Lucien suggested and walked to the market. Again, the exotic hint of clove and anise in the air drew him. The stalls were a tapestry of alien genetic engineering. In one he saw a large melon with a disturbing meaty texture. In another the eye-aching yellow of a nut he didn't recognise. Several stalls held fish that thrived on being piled into a barrel with minimal water.

The people in the market were chatty with each other, but avoided eye contact with him. Conversation dried up as he approached two women at a fruit stall.

"Do you have any perskaw?"

"Try old Jonas at end of row." The woman spoke while looking at the ground as if something there fascinated her.

He walked to the end of the row and found a young girl selling leafy greens. The message was clear, he knew when he wasn't welcome. He got the same response at most stalls. Polite evasion and a bubble of silence that followed him around as though an invisible wall lay between him and the people.

He asked his way to the farming levels. An old man took pity on him and offered to guide him. Perhaps more to get him away from the stalls than for any other reason.

The old man walked back to the ramp he and Lucien had come up the day before. They went up two levels and walked in to a well-lit area that was much larger than the town. Acres of open garden growing in rich lush soil rolled away from where they stood. People stood in the fields tending to the garden like ants in a field of clover. Distant mist had the look of rain about it.

Jonah struggled to take in the impossibility of what he saw. He started with the simple things. "Where does the soil come from?"

"That is five generations of Beddau. All their waste, and most of their remains have been cycled through organic process. It started as a small recycling facility and grew into what we have now."

"I don't think I will ever get used to using people as fertiliser. The idea is too biological for me."

"Why do you believe so?" The old man gave him a sad smile. "Their lives are over and now they serve greater good. We honour memories with every meal."

Jonah did not have a response to that. Recycling was something you did with the excess on Earth, not a basic part of life. He supressed the familiar ache as he thought of how fascinated Thomas would have been by the organic technology.

He tried a different subject. "How do you know it is morning when you can't see the sky?"

"We program overhead lighting to dim down for night phase of twenty-four-hour cycle. Lunar day much longer but human physiology not adapted that far yet. We stick to Earth circadian rhythms. It is all driven by fusion power."

"You have a fusion generator down here?"

"Oh yes, we could not live without it. Powers lights, and runs atmosphere system that keeps us warm and breathing."

Yesha kicked the wheel of the buggy and it wobbled. Not good. She could call for rescue, but the thought of Wang's gloating face as he rode in to save her was enough to keep her from giving up.

Three hours' worth of air remained in the suit. Enough air to die a lingering death, but not enough to reach Beddau on foot. She tried to remember what she had seen on the console before she turned it off. She had a vague memory of a site labelled Minerva, or something like that, within a few kilometres of where she assumed she was now. If she turned on the navigation system in the buggy for more than a minute, the positioning satellites would spot her. Her memory was a safer bet.

The late afternoon sun pushed the temperature in the suit towards unpleasant. She extended the suit's bulky heat exchanger, but sweat still pooled around her neck. She realised how good her timing was. A few day-cycles earlier and the midday sun would have been hot enough to boil water. This late in the lunar day, the heat exchanger rattled under the heat load.

She looked at the buggy again to see what she could salvage. The side storage panel held an emergency water pod and a suit patch kit, basic supplies for immediate emergencies. She packed them into the bulky pockets of the environment suit. They might come in handy later.

Shadow on the hill invited her to walk out of the sun. She fell into an easy pace to conserved her limited air supply. The fine rubble on the slope moulded to each footstep. It gave her traction and held her steady. The slope gave way to another small valley. She crossed it and climbed the next hill which was higher. At the top of the hill she was greeted by undulating ranks of featureless, low hills stretching as far as she could see. Without a navigation system, she needed to rely on landmarks to find her way. The highest of the hills featured a rocky ridge. She chose it as a destination—it was recognisable and perhaps she could see Minerva from there.

Hill after hill greeted her with heat and sweat in the late afternoon sun that baked each uphill. Long shadows, behind each hill, gave the radiator a chance to expel heat in a dull glow.

She was tiring of the monotony when the next slope levelled out into a dust plain that the intervening hills hid from view. She peered at the level grey surface. If this was another deep crater, the dust would smother her. She checked her air supply. Not enough to walk around the dust plain. She would have to make a direct crossing.

She stepped into the dust and found that it was shallow, only covering her boots. A slow shuffle allowed her to edge forward with each foot, taking care not to fall into any hidden chasm. The ground underfoot was solid at first, but then took a steep drop. She found shallower ground, by skirting the drop, and moved forward.

After a while the soft grey powder rose to her knees and her legs ached from the effort of pushing through it. The quiet hiss of the respirator was the only company to her laboured breathing. Her air supply dwindled to an hour and twenty minutes at her current rate of exertion. A brief pause allowed her heartbeat to slow. One hour fifty remained.

Yesha considered her chances. If she was going to die, she wanted to at least give Uncle a farewell message. She activated her suit recorder.

"Honoured Uncle, if you have this message, then I am dead. I wanted you to know I care for you and I am grateful for all you have done since my parents died. It couldn't always have been easy to raise a teenage girl, and I know I have more than once tested your patience with my youthful desires. This time is different. I was born of Earth parents, but I am of the Moon Folk and I feel it is now time for me to find my own kind."

The plain got shallower until the edge produced more of the fine rubble. She stepped onto it and had to restrain herself from running up the next hill. It turned out to be a wise decision, the hill was higher, and the following one rose even further. As Yesha crested the last of these, she saw the ridge-top she had aimed for. The square-cut slab rose from the surrounding hills. At the base of the ridge she looked up and froze. The rock rose in a solid slab that dwarfed her into insignificance. A fall meant injury or death.

She wanted to survive. Uncle had taught her to be proper, to speak and move like a lady. More than that, he said they had to be resolute. That their fortitude made them rulers of the Moon.

The daunting slab towered into the dark sky. It was the only way to see where Minerva was. She put one foot onto the first ledge.

She tried to remember the basics of climbing her instructors had taught her so long ago: body close to the rock face; always three points anchored to the surface; don't look down; and never let go of the safety rope. So much for the last option.

She planted both hands on rocks at shoulder height and grasped hard. Her right foot wedged onto a slim ledge at knee height. She pushed up and lifted her body. The second foot squeezed in beside the first. That was the way to do it, arms for balance and legs for lift. Another ledge presented itself over to her left. It was a stretch, but she made it, her hands found tiny protrusions of granite that gave her a slim grip, but enough to hold herself against the rock face.

Rock climbing became a giant puzzle where she had to connect the dots in the correct order. Further up there was a cleft in a gigantic slab of grey lava. A brief scramble brought her within range of it. Now she could brace her arms and legs on opposing walls to climb. It was quick but exhausting work. At the top of the cleft, she looked down and let out a wail of dismay. It was a dizzying drop to the valley below. The terrain had shrunk.

The final slab of rock was just too high. Smooth basalt gave no handholds apart from one that was well out of reach. It was within reach if she jumped, but if she missed it was a long fall back down the cliff.

She gave a massive leap. One hand snagged the ledge. For a moment, she dangled helpless and then with a great lunge she got her other hand on the niche. Her feet kicked against the rock wall. She brought her legs in and kicked out as she pulled up with her arms. The move allowed her to get her shoulders above her hands and she pushed into an upright position. Her arms quivered from the strain. She pulled a knee up towards her chest. The foot almost made the ledge. Both hands pressed onto fingertips and the foot cleared the ledge. The shelf was narrow, but wide enough for her to stand. Her legs shook as she straightened.

The ridge top was now within reach, up a straightforward stretch of uneven rock. Yesha raced up anxious to see.

The view did not disappoint her, a low dome came into view beyond another two hills. The air gauge gave her forty minutes.

It was so far. She supressed the hollow in the pit of her stomach and the tears that welled behind her eyelids.

Jonah returned to Lucien's home close to midday, at least that is what his stomach told him it was. He stepped inside to find the family gathered in the common area.

"Just in time," said Amira. "We have rice dumplings for day meal."

"Great! I had a walk around the market, but people wouldn't serve me. The delicious smells were making my mouth water."

Amira smiled and dished up a larger portion for him. "All your extra Earth muscle needs more energy to keep going."

"Just another advantage of being Moon Folk," said Lucien, grinning then his mood turned serious.

"People do not hate you, just Earthers. Lots of reason for that."

He took a dumpling and dipped it in a green pepper sauce.

"Now you have seen what Beddau is like, can you see why we want to be independent? We belong here. Not anywhere else. Moon matters belong to Moon and can't be managed by office in Nanjing." Lucien slammed his hand onto the table. "What would Earth-side bureaucrat know of our struggles and desire for independence?"

Jonah listened. He wanted to help. These people had nowhere else to go. "Do you have an organised way of telling the Earth people about this? I mean, the Jiangnanese see the entire Moon as a new province. It will be hard to argue against their claim. They are the ones who built the space elevator and established Chang'e."

"It should be obvious to administrator. We are children of settler's children. We know no other life than we have here. Most of us cannot even visit Earth without months of physical therapy to grow stronger muscle and bone. Like colonies everywhere, we seek a right to self-determination."

This was shaky territory. Jonah remembered a college

girlfriend, a political science major, who had often berated him for his naïve view of the world. He cringed at the memory of one particular dinner where she and her Bangladeshi friends had discussed freedom of choice and the value of benign dictatorships. The high-brow conversation had left him feeling about as erudite as the dinner table.

"So, what are you going to do?"

Lucien sat gazing into space. "We have to take our cause to masses. I have read about great Earth leaders like Arvinda Ram, who overcame Indian caste system, and Juan Simpson who united the Americas. If we rise together for our rights, no one will stand against us."

"No, Lucien, consider consequences," said Amira. "You are all family I have left. Simpson spent years behind bars and Ram died for his cause."

"Aunt, this is something I have to do."

Jonah sided with Amira.

"Seriously, Lucien. This could become violent. Are you ready for war?"

"It will never come to that. Lunar habitat is fragile, and besides, it would take days for administrator to call for more troops. You soft, Earth boy. Never deal with realities. If we spill Moon blood for freedom, is worth it."

"Lucien! That is no way to treat our guest. If you single him out because he is unlike us, how are you any different to administrator?"

Lucien had the grace to look embarrassed.

"Sorry. Maybe we can come up with a non-violent way to spread our message."

Jonah asked, "What about we use an online forum? I bet you already have one for Moon Folk discussions."

They went online, and it was not long before Lucien

found a discussion forum called Lunacies. The forum had pages of comments on the way the Administration was treating Moon Folk.

"I had no idea such a site existed," said Lucien. "Listen to this."

The corrupt and irresponsible administrator has allowed another of the good folk of the Moon to die. Aiken Yamira was a hard-working man...

"Who wrote that?"

"A user called Freeka, no idea who that is. Whoever it is, is super angry. Here is another one."

Throughout history humanity's cleverness has allowed one group of people to hold others to ransom. Today the Moon Folk face the same problem. The Moon is fed to overflowing with overpriced foods brought up the stalk at great cost.

Welcome to the new emerging paradigm, an era when the suppressed people of the Moon finally get their chance to speak freely. Freedom of speech brings moral autonomy and stops the Administration from treating us like children who need to be spoon-fed our very thoughts.

In a simpler world before memplants and ready trans-global media empires, it was said that religion was the opiate of the masses. Now, electronic screens and designer drugs are the opiates that we are encouraged to crave. Break free from this slavery!

"They don't know everything," said Lucien. He entered the forum and described everything that the administrator had done to the people of Beddau. He wrote until he ran out of words, then he turned to Jonah.

"You are right, Jonah. I am going to post we have a

meetup in tunnels at New Karakorum."

"That's a good idea," said Amira. "You can start people thinking about our cause."

Jonah wasn't so sure. Lucien was angry, he would not stop at words. There would be more to it.

Chen took in the awe-inspired faces of the visiting dignitaries as the train pulled in to New Karakorum's main chamber. The Panamerican Ambassador and the Empress of Central Afrika both had their faces glued to the window like schoolchildren.

Not that he blamed them. Ms Lawson had outdone herself with the arrangement of the main cavern. Pools of warm light spilled from oversized spotlights aimed at the cavern wall. They fluctuated in a rhythm that complemented the classical Chinese aria flowing from the stage. The soprano was an excellent choice. Her voice soared to fill the depths of the cavern.

He held out an arm to offer support to the empress as she stepped out of the train. She swept past him. Light from the walls caught the glint of an exquisite tiara set in her steel-grey braids. He stood back. It would not do to insult such an important trading partner. Nairobi's giant manufactories depended on the constant supply of Helium to drive the flow of Afrika's riches.

Typical of the empress, she insisted on doing everything her own way. Even down to the superfluous row of black clad security guards that lined the velvet rope that demarcated the guest seating from the crowds of onlookers.

The opera singer rearranged the rich brocade of her red and gold cloak to better catch the light and launched into a modern rendition of the Tea Picking Song. Ms Lawson had chosen the Huangmei aria with due care. History and tradition soaked through the cavern, underscoring the permanence of Jiangnan's administration. Off to the side, he saw Wang patrol a gap in the barricades. Good man. He would not stand for the slightest sign of Free Moon nonsense.

Music faded to an expectant hush as the song finished. Chen stood at a podium that had risen from the stage floor. "Honoured guests, ladies and gentlemen, it is my great privilege to stand before you on this auspicious occasion."

Out of the corner of his eye, Chen saw a young moono man push forward to get a better view of the stage. Wang shoved hard and the young man flew back into the press of the crowd.

"For a hundred years…" Chen spoke on as an angry murmur rose from the crowd. He took in the mass of people standing in the shadows beyond the lights. Indistinct forms suggested tall moonos with a few Earther miners scattered throughout. He continued with his speech thanking the major corporations of Earth for their continued support. The murmuring from the people took on an angry note. He described the history of Chang'e. The glorious progress that provided wealth to Jiangnan, and the largess of a home to the deprived individuals who could no longer live on Earth.

A soda bottle sailed out of the crowd and crashed into the stage in glittering shards.

The empress's guards moved as one, batons at the ready. They formed a tunnel to the train that waited for the empress. Other dignitaries followed.

"Yes, let us return to Chang'e where we have prepared a banquet in honour of our guests."

"Cowards!" The strident voice came from the back of the crowd hidden in shadow.

"Free Moon. Free Moon." The crowd began a quiet chant.

"Free Moon. Free Moon."

Chen walked to the train with the humiliating chant ringing in his ears. He would have to implement stricter security measures.

That would have to wait. There were dignitaries to appease.

Chapter 8

The Harmony of Shrimp

The hills were a hard rubble with solid footing that Yesha bounded up. She powered up the first hill and saw the low dome of the station tantalisingly close behind the next peak. She ran as fast as the suit would let her, gasping in the humidity of the suit interior that could not cope with exertion and heat.

Minerva was an empty station. The sole purpose of the unpressurised dome was to provide protection from ultraviolet light and possible meteorite strikes. It was functional but had no life support or comforts. She found a service archway then entered. Inside, the bright sunlight filtering through the cupola gave everything a muted grey tint.

The unoccupied dome was cool after the furnace of the hills. She caught her breath while she waited for the heat exchanger to bring the temperature back to something reasonable. The interior was bare, apart from an ancient volcanic cone the surface cratered and worn by the millennia since the original eruption. Small robots moved in random patterns across the cone churning its sands. Yesha recognised it as an automated glass mine. The robots sifted the dune for beads of pyroclastic glass in a time-consuming slow process. She found a handful of the pinkish beads in a hopper. That was a good sign, people would only collect the beads once the hopper filled. She had the dome to herself.

Yesha located the service lockers and checked each one. She was in luck. The third locker held an emergency air tank, enough to get her to Beddau if she took care. The single liquid ration pack was an unexpected bonus. She wasted no time attaching it to the suit fitting and slurped in large greedy gulps.

The low service locker tempted her to sit, but Wang was somewhere behind her. Her next challenge was to figure out which way the Beddau lock was. The extra air would be useless if she walked in the wrong direction. She hopped down and crouched in the dust, using her finger to draw a rough map. Chang'e, Beddau, and Minerva made an approximate triangle, with Minerva cut off from the other two by the low hills. She could either walk back in the direction she had come from and skirt the hills, or she could aim for where she thought Beddau was. The way ahead was risky. She did not know what kind of terrain lay hidden in the hills. If she aimed right, she would be at the Beddau lock with air to spare.

The shrimp lived their small lives, stripping microscopic flakes of algae from sides of their glass globe. Chen wondered if they would be so placid if he introduced a different species of shrimp. Living with one's own kind was easy. The delicate dance of difference kept his work interesting.

The yellow triangle of a memplant connection flared in his vision. His stomach tightened as five coloured masks swam into focus.

"Your ineptitude has cost an additional thirty basis points on the new Central Afrika contract."

Chen kept his face passive as he responded. No sense in giving the council an edge in this discussion.

"I believe the empress engineered the entire incident. The moonos gave no indication of moving toward violent protest. I would not put it past the old woman to have set the entire thing up to give herself an advantage."

The five masks hung in the air. Good. Let them consider that for a while. He knew the moonos started the protest without outside prompting, but there was no way he would admit it to the council. The moonos would pay in their own time for embarrassing him like this.

"These are serious allegations. Do you have any proof of what you suggest?"

"No, and that is why I have not mentioned this in any public forum."

A further silence followed broken at length by blue mask.

"There is insufficient evidence for your hypothesis. However, the likelihood of external interference is equal to that of internal insurrection. If you accept that the empress was responsible, then the damage is already done and no further response is required. If you think otherwise, then action must be taken against the indigenous population. The prudent course of action would be to take action against the Free Moon protestors."

"I shall do as the council commands."

The masks dissolved leaving Chen alone. He reached into a drawer for the crystal glass and single malt scotch whiskey he kept for special occasions. A hint of seaweed and peat filled the room as he poured himself a restrained measure. He needed to reflect on the harmony of shrimp.

Yesha left the dome through the same archway. She squinted in the bright daylight. The heat had not diminished. The high ridge she had climbed lay over her left shoulder. She turned, aiming for the rough direction of Beddau.

At the top of another ridge she saw the Beddau gate. It was nowhere near where she thought it was. The airlock sat much further over than she had assumed. It was not an option.

The suit stank with the accumulated result of stale sweat and too much exertion. The water tube gave one final bubble and ran dry. If she turned on the recycling unit, the suit would burn battery power. Everything was running out. She sat on the hill and tried to calm her breathing to limit the oxygen she used.

There was no way to Beddau from there.

She closed her eyes and brought her inhalations to a slow rhythm, calming the tension in her muscles and quieting her mind. If only she had a map like the satellite view in her room.

She cleared her mind of everything but the image of the screen. The memory of something nearby formed —something in grey, an abandoned construction of some sort. Whatever it was, it was only a short distance on the other side of Minerva. She stood and took one last gamble.

Across from Minerva, the hills rose in more gentle curves. Yesha settled into a slow, easy walk, taking her time to conserve air with every step. The grey gravel mounds rolled by in unending monotony until a granite bluff towered before her. The site must be located there. She picked up speed towards it.

As she approached, the shade on the bluff resolved to show the elongate slit of a vast cavern. Deep in the shadowy recess she saw an airlock covering the back of the cave. Then she knew where she was. This was something from her school history class—Yutu's Burrow—the legendary lava tube that early colonists have lived in. The Chinese named their first probe after a mythical rabbit, the lava tube extended the same idea. The colonists abandoned Yutu's Burrow decades ago in favour of the domes, but there would be plenty of air to recharge the suit. Enough to walk to Beddau if she was careful. She plodded on across the hills.

By the time she reached the cave, the air in her suit had a dull metallic tang to it and her body slowed to a lumbering stagger. Thirst became a clawing need. Her tongue felt as if it had shrunk.

Up close, the enormous cavern was cool and welcoming after the heat. She walked closer until the airlock became a wall of steel across her field of view. The door itself was the old circular kind with a manual lever. She gave it an experimental shove, and it didn't budge. She put all her strength into it. The lever remained where it was.

The effort left her gasping in the suit's foetid air. She tried again, rasping for air in the stuffy helmet. The suit began screaming a high carbon dioxide warning. She ignored it. It would stay on until she got clean air. She tried the door again and gave in to an irrational wave of anger when it remained stuck. It wasn't fair. She had come so far. She pushed hard against the lever, her breath rasped in the helmet. The door faded down a long dark tunnel and she fell forward into the darkness.

Consciousness returned with a blinding headache. The

suit's carbon dioxide scrubber gurgling its last on the remains of the battery. Bright fuzzy stars flooded her vision and fled away into the periphery if she tried to focus on them.

Unconsciousness and death would follow if she failed to get through the airlock soon. The anger returned, and she slammed her fists against the door. The lock responded by fading from her view as she staggered to her knees. She hit the door again, slamming one fist after another into door, each blow weaker than the last, until darkness was all she knew.

Chapter 9

Whispers of Freedom and Insurrection

Chen stood from the ornate chair, filling his frame with as much gravitas as his official position would allow. He turned to address the Moon man being held by security guards.

"Do you have anything to say, before I pass judgement?"

The man paled. "No, administrator."

"Then by the powers vested in me, I find you guilty of first degree oxygen theft. I sentence you to repay your debt to the colony."

"No!" wailed a woman in the small crowd that watched. She fell to her knees and sobbed.

Chen nodded to the security men and walked away. Sentencing the poor wretch was hard, but what followed would be worse. This was one Moon custom he still could not accept. The guards would lead the man away and seal him into a large glass jar where he would spend days giving back his water and energy; a euphemism for a slow death by dehydration. Recovery existed as a hangover from the early colony. It was cruel, implacable Moon logic that said nothing was wasted, and none should forget.

The practice was barbaric, but Chen understood the value of example.

Wang stepped in next to him as he walked away.

"I bring news of your niece," he said before noticing the look on Chen's face.

"I followed her, administrator, out towards the low hills East of here, but she was too smart for me…"

"You lost her?"

The question hung in the air. Chen kept his eyes on Wang with the disinterested look of a tiger watching a lamb. Wang choked back a convulsive swallow.

"You seem to possess an unfortunate habit of losing people. First it was the moono troublemaker and his friend, and now my niece. Have you found the young man yet?"

"Not as yet, administrator. We searched the depth and breadth of New Karakorum to no avail. It is as if they evaporated. There is more, we know they passed through Level Nine at some stage. They killed one of my men."

"What? A death? Why wasn't I told of this at once?"

"It was just a moono, I didn't think you would be too concerned."

"You think too much. Did you notify the man's family?"

"Not yet."

"Good, leave this to me. The Moon Folk are troubled enough as it is."

Chen wished the man had not detained him. Their delay kept them there long enough to be obliged to witness the execution. The guards mounted the stairs leading to the recovery jar that stood half as tall again as the condemned man. The man followed without protest. Some tried to get the guards to kill them before they were interred. Others chose to at least see their families for a few more days.

The man let the guards lower him into the jar and stood, eyes downcast as the guards locked the lid above him. The only sound a quiet sobbing from the woman in the crowd.

Chen nodded, and the guards allowed the woman forward to touch the jar. The man inside did not respond.

Chen turned his back on them and walked away.

Back in his office he began his report on the execution. The softmind interrupted his focus on the task by informing him that visitors waited in the outer office.

"Then show them in," he said hiding his annoyance as best he could.

A mixed group of Moon Folk entered.

"Yes?"

A woman stepped forward. "We wish to discuss death of Aiken Yamira," she said, her stance left him in no doubt this would not be a pleasant discussion.

"I don't know who that is, but perhaps you should introduce yourselves, Madam."

"I am Amira of Moon Folk. These others bear witness and are no concern of yours."

"As administrator, I will determine who is of concern to me."

The woman showed no fear. Chen could see she would not back down. He would mention her to Wang, but first he would try to placate her.

"Who is this Aiken Yamira you speak of?"

"Aiken Yamira was loving son who cared for his family and cheerful face in our community. He worked as security guard in New Karakorum, at least he did until his mother found him, dumped like so much rubbish, with skull staved in."

Chen sighed. One day he would have to train Wang to be more diplomatic.

"An unfortunate accident. A new student has arrived from earth and the boy does not know his own strength. There was an altercation that led to blows with the result you described. We will, of course, provide compensation to the family."

The woman gave him a level gaze. Chen did not give an inch.

"Your money can never be enough for family, but they will take it."

"Very well. I shall see to it."

Chen watched her expression but saw nothing.

"Amira, as you call yourself, I take it you represent the Moon Folk. Hear me now. Your people have become bold. I hear far too many whispers of freedom and insurrection. You will never be freer than with what our great government gives you."

"Administrator, we will not be free until we secure right to decide our own fate. Moon Folk are people and must have right to self-determination."

Chen smiled, she had played into his hands. He may have found one of the ring leaders of the Free Moon Movement. There was only one way to be sure.

"The incident at our centenary celebration has given great cause for concern about the safety of people on the Moon. You can be the first to hear this," he said, his face a mask of mild consideration. "From today, all Moon Folk are to be registered under a new set of laws, promulgated by Nanjing, called the Settled Labour Registration Act. The act will restrict your movement to specified areas. Freedom to move between areas will only be granted to those with approved registration."

She reeled as if Chen had slapped her.

"I will not forget, administrator," she said, her voice shaking. She jerked her head to tell her group they should go.

Chen noticed the stiff set of her shoulders as she left. Smart, the woman was furious, but knew it would be dangerous to push him too far. She would bear watching.

Jonah sat in the common area enjoying a cup of khar with Lucien. "What's for lunch then?"

"Some real Moon food," said Lucien. "Deep fried brijo and eggplant stew."

"Dare I ask what brijo is?"

Lucien beamed. "Vat grown protein. Our family vat produces tasty cultivar, even if I say so myself."

"Ugh! No offence Lucien, but I'm just about ready to sell my grandmother for a decent hamburger and fries."

"Oh, you Earthers are all same. No idea of how much space you live in. How many acres do you need to raise cow for beef, to farm wheat for bun, and grow potatoes for fries?"

A tumult of urgent voices interrupted Jonah's reply. They looked up to see Amira being carried in by two men, her head lolled between them. The men put her down on a cushion and Jonah got his first look at her bloodied face. Both eyes were swollen shut and her lip was split.

"Aunt! What happened?" Lucien leapt to her side.

Amira shrugged the two men away and clung to him as if her life depended on it.

"We were innocent and they beat us," she said. Her voice a hoarse whisper. "Pig of security manager, Wang, he and men surprised our group as we left administrator's quarters. They forced us to walk to service dome and then they…" Her voice trailed off and she slumped to the floor.

Lucien rose, his face dark.

"I will kill him." He looked at Jonah. "You have to help me."

"No, Lucien, meeting violence with more violence is never an answer."

"My aunt is all family I have left. I cannot…"

Jonah kept his voice low, not wanting to stir what he saw in Lucien's eyes.

"Violence won't help."

Lucien raised a fist to his side, his lips peeled back in a snarl. "You go cower with rest of your filthy kind. I am going to put end to this." He stormed out of the house.

Amira's sobbing punctuated the silence that followed his departure.

"I'll go after him," Jonah said.

"No," Amira choked out the word. "He did not mean it. He is angry."

"Red team, advance." Wang's voice reverberated through the empty chamber. Three men broke cover from behind a stack of packing crates to the right and sprinted across to another set of boxes.

"Too slow. If the moonos find you out in the open, and one of them has a gun, you would be dead. Now again. Red team, advance."

The men charged across the open area, weaving from one box to another. They arrived at a safer position and dropped in behind the crates.

Wang sighed. "Better, still too slow, but better. Now, attack the white team."

He looked across at the other three men of white team, waiting to one side. The men itched for real action.

"White team, defend!"

The three men rose from their concealed position, each man armed with a padded training baton. They stood in the classic sword fighter's pose, one foot behind the other with shoulders square and baton held in front of them. As the running figures of the red team arrived, each leaped forward and executed a perfect blow against the enemy.

"Excellent," said Chen from his position on the sidelines. "Tell me you have armed your men with something better than training batons for a real encounter."

"We overcame our limitations with ingenuity, administrator. Daichi, here trained with the bo staff when he was younger. We don't have proper wooden bo staffs, but aluminium makes an acceptable substitute. They will serve our needs in battle."

Chen looked at the six men that Wang had assembled. Engineers and computer programmers, not one of them had seen combat beyond schoolyard fights. Wang would struggle to turn them into a combat ready unit.

"There is one further innovation to show," said Wang. He pointed over to the far side of the room where several sandbags had been piled against the wall. A makeshift mannequin consisting of a few stacked boxes with a crude face drawn on the top one stood in front of the sandbags.

"The engineering team has developed a ballistics device," he said leading the way over to a crate. Chen picked his way over the debris that littered the floor.

The device in the crate consisted of a stubby gas cylinder with a thin pipe attached by an oblong metallic mechanism. Wang picked up the pipe, aimed it at the mannequin and pressed a lever on the side.

The pipe issued a whistling shriek and the crude face on the mannequin exploded into fragments.

"It's a compressed air rifle," said Wang. "Much less efficient than a real rifle, but the muzzle velocity suffices to cause damage. It would be too risky to deploy inside the domes, but suitable for combat use in the mines."

Chen was impressed by how far they had come. "How soon can you fit your men with them?"

"There are three minor safety issues to overcome and we need to build harnesses for them. We will be ready within a week."

"Make it so. I shall expect to see results." Chen walked off smiling. If the Moon Folk became a problem, he now had a tool he would not hesitate to use.

Chapter 10

The Tools of Power

Chen was listening to Wang describing his plan to take on the moonos when Philippa Lawson burst into his office. "Administrator, we found something."

"I am busy, Ms. Lawson."

Philippa checked herself. Good, the woman knew better than to intrude.

She continued to speak. "Forgive my impertinence, administrator, but the softmind has noticed a surge in online activity. Our analysis shows the moonos are planning a demonstration in the tunnels of New Karakorum."

Chen did not reply, but tapped the console on his desk. He looked up at Philippa, "Sit, Ms. Lawson. I want you to give Wang as much detail as possible."

Philippa described what she had found. She explained the

Freeka identity and how she became a trusted voice on the online forums; how she had set up the identity as an angry person who hid behind an anonymous name and despised the current order. She fostered the character with a blog that decried the administration and drew on events from a violent anti-government point of view.

Freeka was a success. It drew followers and several sympathetic comments from other faceless protesters. This morning was the crowning achievement, it had led a protest against the senseless beatings of a peaceful group who had met with the administration. Commenters discussed revenge, the less rational spoke of violence.

Wang leaned forward. "Administrator, such words pose a clear threat to the safety of our personnel. We must act."

"Indeed," said Chen. "What do you propose?"

"We have two of the air rifles ready. I suggest we teach these moonos respect. If we set the pressure to maim not kill, and allow the protesters to withdraw, they will take an abject lesson in subservience back with them. It will also allow us to identify the ringleaders for later management."

"Excellent, proceed. Ms Lawson, I want you to accompany Wang on this little exercise. Please remember what you see in detail. Afterward, use what you encounter as fodder for the grassroots campaign. Sow fear into opposing the administration."

Philippa nodded, but Chen saw her disgust. He made a mental note to monitor her private messages for job hunting activity. Ms Lawson was well paid, but if she left, he would need to find a communications manager fast.

Wang led Philippa from the administration dome down to a service area. He made several calls as he went. She followed him as he descended to the lowest level of the service dome.

"I hadn't expected to use these so soon," he said, pausing outside a door.

Inside, five men waited. Two of them had squat cylinders strapped to their backs with webbing. A metallic hose connected each cylinder to a dark steel barrel. They watched Wang with an expectant air.

"Attention men, today is the day your training pays off. We go to repel the Free Moon protesters gathering in the tunnels of New Karakorum. Do not use lethal force, no blows to the head. We will deploy using open pattern B. Collect your weapons and assemble at the railhead."

He motioned Philippa to stand aside as the men gathered the tools of power. Each strapped on lightweight Kevlar armour, rough surfaced and dark grey in colour. The armour merged with colour of the rock walls, giving the men an insubstantial presence. Solid aluminium clubs that resembled larger versions of a baseball bat supplemented the two operational air guns.

They rode the train in silence, the men, grim-faced. At the mine, the day supervisor told them that the protesters had gathered on Level Three. Wang told Philippa to follow as the men drifted down the ramp like ghosts. He scowled at her as the clatter of her footsteps echoed off the walls.

The elevator opened on the third level. The empty entrance area suggested people knew trouble was coming.

Philippa walked in the middle of his men, her mouth drawn tight. Wang pulled her to one side. "Stay well behind us, Ms. Lawson. I don't want you to get hurt."

She stuck close to the wall as the men turned into the main tunnel. A wise choice as fifteen Moon Folk stood before them. Wang gave an approving nod, the armour-clad bulk of his Earther men overshadowed their fragile forms.

A young man left the group and walked over to meet them.

Wang stepped forward. "Lucien, is it? Amira's boy?"

"What is it to you?"

"You should show more respect for a representative of the administration."

Lucien leaned his face close to Wang's. "Go home, squat. We don't take orders from administrator."

Wang laughed. "I know who you are little boy. If I want to, I can always find you… or your troublesome aunt."

Lucien roared and took a swipe at him.

Wang weaved and blocked the blow with a rising forearm, pushing Lucien's fist to one side and followed with a straight punch to Lucien's jaw. The young man landed flat on his back and tried to rise.

"Stay where you are, boy," said Wang as though he was having a quiet conversation. "I do not wish to hurt you more than necessary."

Lucien lifted his head and spat blood. His jaw hung at an odd angle. A groan broke from his lips, and he dropped back to the ground.

"Fire when ready!"

It was all Wang needed to say, and the carnage began. The men lowered their air rifles and pumped round after round into the crowd. The world shrank to the shrieking noise of solid aluminium slugs crossing the gap between the two parties only stopping with an abrupt silence as they found soft flesh. Protesters fell back as one sickening thud followed another. Agonising screams rose from those with broken bones.

Wang held up a hand, and the shooting stopped. Too many of the filth still stood.

"Prepare for close combat."

The two men dropped their air rifles, and all five picked up their batons.

"Get into the bastards!"

The five charged and swung left and right as they cut through the crowd. The protesters scattered. Three made a stand against the guards, but their fists made no impact on their armour. The guards worked in groups of two or three, clubbing one protester at a time until they collapsed.

The scene fell into a silence broken only by moans from those of the injured left lying on the ground; the rest of the protesters vanished into the shadows of the mine. Protesters lay in huddled heaps, with several in need of urgent medical attention.

Wang hoped he wouldn't have to explain to the administrator that some had died.

Wang stepped over to where Lucien lay quivering on the ground. He prodded the prone figure with his boot. The young man opened wide eyes. Wang bent down next to him. "Now, you go and tell your aunt what is coming if we encounter more opposition," he said in the same calm voice, before rising to signal his men.

"Well done, men. We can leave this sorry mess now."

"What about the casualties?" asked Philippa, shaking as she spoke.

"Don't worry, Ms. Lawson, the others will return to collect their comrades."

He gave her a cold smile.

"Did this violence sicken you?"

"I… I'm not sure I can do this."

He leaned in close, his voice low. "Good, remember that feeling when you write about this. Freeka needs to be enraged to be effective."

Wang swaggered in to Chen's office.

"It's done. The Free Moon Movement will not cause any trouble after today."

"I marvel at your optimism." Chen studied his desk, looking for non-existent motes of dust on the flawless surface. "If you can find where they are hiding…"

"Then I will exterminate them like the vermin they are. Wherever they are hiding, it must be a long-abandoned sector of the mines. We won't need to hold back, my boys will crush them."

"Yes, thank you, Wang."

Wang saluted and walked out. Chen watched him go. His boyish enthusiasm was of no concern of the administrator. He could play soldiers as long as he desired, provided he put a stop to the Free Moon Movement. Afterward, his violent tendencies would need to be curbed before anything unfortunate happened.

Jonah found Lucien sitting in the common area, his knees drawn up to his chest and his head sunk in. "How's the jaw going?"

Lucien twisted his face into a sullen frown. Wang's punch had snapped the bone clean in two. The Beddau medic had set it and applied an accelerated stem cell repair process, but it was a much slower process than the more modern bone welder. It would be days before Lucien's jaw healed.

Jonah resisted the temptation to tease him. "I've been thinking."

"Thash a novelty," mumbled Lucien.

Jonah laughed. "I see Wang didn't beat sense into you. Now, while I have a captive audience…" He arranged himself on a comfortable cushion and turned serious. "I didn't believe you. How could they do this?"

Lucien shrugged.

"It's not right. If I ever get Wang alone…"

"You not so different now."

Heat crept into Jonah's cheeks. "I should have been there." He tried safer ground. "It sounds like Wang has developed a low velocity rifle."

Lucien nodded.

"Hmm, did anyone die? I haven't heard of anyone."

Lucien shook his head.

Jonah turned one of the lightweight aluminium slugs over in his hands.

"They don't feel so heavy."

Lucien's look of derision would have stopped a mining truck.

Jonah left it at that. There had to be an answer.

She drifted through a grey mist. Somewhere, far below her, a voice wheezed its last breaths. A world at an angle lay before her. The cloud around her thickened until dense wads of cotton wool poured into her lungs. Yesha convulsed and a thin stream of bile ran from the corner of her mouth. She realised the gasping voice was her own.

A safety latch held the airlock lever in place. She should know that. She looked at the air lock. There it was, so close.

Yesha shook herself awake. If she could still think, she could try to live. She put superhuman effort into getting upright, crying at the labour of standing as the airlock lever wavered in and out of her vision. One hand on the safety and one hand on the lever, just as her instructor bot had taught at school.

The lever moved with a solid thud and the lock swung open. She fell through and hit the return lever.

When her vision cleared, the airlock had cycled and the inner door stood open. There was no telling if the air was still good. Her need was too great to deny. She ripped the helmet off and lay there gasping.

When she had stabilised her breathing, her senses expanded beyond a dying body to take in the damp air with its odour of mushrooms and faint decay. She got to her feet and peered through the airlock door.

The empty lava tube stretched away into the far distance, its walls coated with a bioluminescent fungus that produced the green glow. A thick grey plant carpeted the floor on which a herd of small animals grazed in placid contentment. Her chest laboured with each tight inhalation, but the air was fresh and clean.

Yesha tried to remember her school lessons on this place. It was so hard to recall information without having a network connection for the memplant to tell you everything.

The early colonists had hidden in this tunnel to escape the intense radiation that the sun poured onto the lunar surface. It was from a time before the fusion generator. The colonists had been ingenious in their use of biotechnology to solve their habitation problems. A fungus to provide light, plants to harvest carbon dioxide and purify water, and the small animal called a rabbiton to control the plants and serve as food. It was all so old-fashioned.

She walked deeper into the tunnel, remembering that the colonists had reused almost everything when work started on

Chang'e. There would be little left, but clean air was a start, and if she searched carefully, she would be able to find the place where the rabbitons got water from.

Yesha shivered as the cold of the burrow crept through her suit. She tried to think of how the colonists had kept warm, but all she remembered was something about a portable nuclear power plant. The colonist had cleaned those up years ago when fusion technology first came into its own.

The rabbitons regarded her with incurious button eyes as she passed. She giggled, they looked like the anime characters from her childhood shows. They even had whiskers that twitched.

She found a moisture-pitted aluminium bench and sat. She was free. For the first time since she had left the base, no one expected something of her, no one chased her, and there was no need for immediate survival.

The momentary respite was what Uncle would have called a planning opportunity. Uncle loved to show her what he did, how information and preparation were his tools of power, but now she had no memplant and no Uncle to provide an easy answer.

First, she needed to find water and a way to stay warm. It was revolting to think of eating raw rabbitons, but she would not starve.

"I could live here a long time if I am careful."

She started at the sound of her hoarse voice. She shouldn't talk to herself, but there was comfort in hearing a voice even if it was her own. Maybe rescuers would discover her in years to come and find her nattering away to herself. She heard her own hysterical laughter. No, staying here alone was not a long-term solution.

Chapter 11

New Directions

"We are not giving up."

"He speaks. And not a trace of slurring. What's the jaw feel like?"

Lucien stirred from his couch and ran a hand over his day-old stubble. "It still itches, but ready for anything. We need to talk about plans."

Jonah stood to leave. "Give it up, Lucien. Wang and his men will tear you apart."

Lucien placed a hand on his shoulder. "Wait, there is something I want to show you."

Jonah followed as Lucien led him to the airball court where four Moon Folk stood waiting, three men and a woman. Jonah recognised a few of them from the dust-up with Wang and his men.

"Team, show Jonah what you have."

The team formed into two loose rows. At a command from Lucien, they fell to trading slack punches. Each blow looked cartoon slow to Jonah. They flung their arms about with enthusiasm, but no focus. The blows flew wide open with no thought to defence. When a punch was lucky enough to get close, the recipient dodged out of the way.

Jonah laughed. "Oh, man that is so tragic. Who taught you?"

"We have seen few videos online. You can learn so much off web these days."

"You couldn't fight your way out of a paper bag with those moves."

"Yeh, Earth boy? I will take you on."

Jonah looked across the group and grinned. "No, I'll take you all on. That seems about fair."

He moved into a loose fighting stance with his weight on the balls of his feet. "Let's keep this simple. If I pin your shoulders to the ground you're out. Likewise, if, by some chance, any of you pin me to the ground, you win."

The group formed a loose semi-circle around him. Jonah spun to his left and snap kicked the closest man hard in the groin. The man let out his air in a loud gasp and fell to the floor. Without stopping, Jonah turned to man to the left. The man saw Jonah's eyes harden, and he hesitated. That was what Jonah needed to step in close and hammer three hard punches to the man's middle. The man swung a punch at Jonah's face. Jonah swept it aside and stepped past the man's extended arm. He kicked the soft spot at the back of the man's knee and watched as the guy fell face first in the dust.

Jonah sprung up and landed both feet on the man's back, knocking the air out of him.

"You're out."

"No fair," said Lucien.

"You think Wang and his men will be fair? Fight like you mean it."

He stepped over to the first man who still clutched his groin and kicked him flat to the ground. "And you're out too."

The other three stunned by Jonah's ferocious attack, stood there with their mouths open.

"Get him!" said Lucien and raced in with a wild swipe at Jonah's head.

Jonah flicked the punch out of the way and stepped in towards Lucien. He grabbed Lucien's outstretched arm and pulled him past. As Lucien flew past, Jonah spun in behind, and kicked his buttocks. Lucien staggered and landed on his knees.

It was worth it for the laugh, but Jonah knew committing his position to get Lucien was a dumb move. He paid the cost a second later when the woman, who crouched to his left, landed a solid rabbit punch to his kidneys. Jonah spun.

"That hurt. What's your name?"

"Doaran."

"OK, Doaran, I'll save you for last."

Doaran rushed him. Jonah turned his shoulders off-centre and bent at the knees. He grabbed Doaran's arm and using her momentum, flicked her towards Lucien who had staggered to his feet. The two crashed together in a spectacular heap. Jonah saw none of it, he had already turned toward the last man who flicked a punch at his head. Jonah swept it away with a rising block that spun the man past him. This guy was quicker. He twisted out of the path of the solid right Jonah aimed at his kidneys. Jonah followed through with a hard left to the man's solar plexus.

The blow bent the man forward. Jonah grabbed him by the hair and pulled him forward hard. The man lost his balance and fell flat on his chest.

Jonah placed a foot on his back and spun to face the others as he said, "you're out."

Lucien was still flat on his back, but Doaran was moving towards him. The woman moved like a caged panther. She held back, knowing what she now faced. Jonah kept his eyes on her as he walked over to where Lucien groaned on the floor. Jonah took one look and laughed. "I'll call you out, Lucien."

Doaran circled to his right, looking for an opening. Jonah feigned a punch to her head. She ducked, her long, black hair flying to one side. She rose and followed with a low punch to Jonah's ribs. Jonah grunted, but used the close contact to bring a knee up to Doaran's side in a savage knee strike. Doaran fell back, but not before Jonah landed a glancing right to her face. Doaran staggered back and put up a hand.

"Stop. I know when I am outclassed. You win."

Jonah stood breathing hard. He saw the men lying on the ground and the look of fear in Doaran's eyes. The weight of the past overcame him and he crumpled to his knees, giving a wordless wail.

"Jonah, are you OK?" Lucien staggered over placed a hand on Jonah's shoulder.

"Oh Thomas, Oh God…"

"Jonah?"

Jonah stood, his shoulders shaking. "I'm sorry, Lucien, I can't do this."

He ran from the airball court.

Yesha pushed deeper into the lava tube. Yutu must have been one hyperactive rabbit, the tunnel faded into the distance.

After a while, she noticed the scenery changing, leaving the low tufts of vegetation for larger tussocks of a coarse reed. The dim light had not changed, but her eyes had become accustomed to the misty green glow. She made out a variety of small creatures burrowing amongst the reeds. Her sketchy education on the first colonists did not stretch to whatever they were. It made sense there would be animals other than the rabbitons abandoned in Yutu's Burrow.

"This colony outpost is no longer supported. Citizens are prohibited from travel beyond this point."

Yesha jumped at the sound and swung around to see who had spoken. There was no one, but an ancient service droid had emerged from an alcove.

"Identify yourself, droid."

"Unit AR-X 11 responding."

Yesha did not recognise the designation, it must have been from long before she was born. How was it still running?

"This is a life-threating emergency. Direct me to the nearest survival resources."

"Please specify the nature of your emergency." The droid had a voice emulator that sounded like a colony of pollinator drones drowning in a rusty barrel.

"This citizen faces starvation."

"Starvation is not recognised as an emergency. Please contact base administration for further assistance."

"Base administration is not contactable."

"Situation beyond recognisable parameters."

Marvellous. The original settlers had programmed the droid to keep people out and not much more. Yesha tried reaching with her mind for an interface, but there was nothing. The droid was so old it did not have a memplant interface. She sat on a bare patch of rock and watched the wildlife. The droid returned to its niche.

She tried to sneak past the droid, but it anticipated her movements and repeated the same message each time.

After a few fruitless attempts, she sat on a clump of reeds. The droid was not giving up. Hunger clawed at her stomach. She clutched the smooth plastic texture of the reeds as they slid between her fingers until her fingers brushed a rock.

She lifted the rock and looked at it in wonder, then stood and walked calmly to the droid. When the droid did nothing, she raised it above her head and smashed it into the droid's visible peripherals.

The droid spun around. "Malfunction. This unit will return for service."

It trundled off along the passage and Yesha followed.

Yutu's Burrow went further than she thought possible. The droid travelled along a distinct path that skirted the reed tussocks, it looked as if someone had kept it clear. The droid emitted a whirring noise that said she had broken something important. Important enough to slow her walk to a sedate stroll behind the rattling droid. Yesha had time to spot the occasional rabbiton and several large, pale insects that burrowed in the roots of tussocks. Perhaps their purpose was in turning over the soil.

After an interminable wander behind the failing droid, the tussocks gave way to stands of a nacreous, purple epiphyte that towered over her in the dim light. They resembled nothing as much as a massed bunch of glowing purple mushrooms. She stopped to examine one and gasped when a pair of eyes peered back at her. As she retreated, she saw a small cat-like face considering her with grave curiosity. "Hello there, small one. What are you doing here?"

Entranced she watched as a second face emerged next to the first. Soon, five of the creatures looked at her. She did not know what they were, but thought they looked similar to the cats that roamed the domes and maybe Earth monkeys she had seen online.

The cat monkeys chirped as they jumped from branch to branch. A mother and two young ones scrambled to the floor and commenced a careful examination of the epiphyte's branching roots.

The droid paused outside a door set in the wall. Yesha thought it was a service hatch. She confirmed her suspicion when the door swung up to admit the droid. The droid rolled in and the door closed. She examined the door and found a manual door trigger. The door opened on a short tunnel. She stepped through before it closed again, and then she gasped. The room beyond stretched much further than she expected. Decrepit service machinery lay scattered in the gloom. She followed the droid as it moved on further ahead and docked at a service pod.

The room was a cave, a natural side bubble formed during the time of the lava tube. The colonists had used it as a workshop of some sort. Gun-metal grey locker cabinets lined the walls down a side. She examined a few, but they were all empty. Large machines occupied the centre of the room, she had no idea what they had been used for. The opposite side had a row of workbenches covered in a random collection of broken machinery and wiring. It looked ancient. She walked down the row of benches not seeing anything of value among the junk until she saw a Mooze bar wrapper. It made her realise how hungry she was.

She picked it up dreaming of the soft chocolate. They were her favourite indulgence. The chocolate reminded her of being a little girl and getting her first Mooze bar as a treat when she had done well at school.

She froze. Uncle had bought her a Mooze bar because it was new and popular when she was young. She smiled imagining another adventurer exploring the workshop.

A few hours later, Yesha had exhausted the novelty of the workshop and moved on. The endless walking and thin air tired her. The mossy patches under the ephiphytes looked soft, she lay down on one and fell into a deep dreamless sleep.

"I knew you would be here."

Yesha woke to find Wang standing over her. She scrambled to her feet, but Wang was quicker. He grabbed her arms and forced her back down. Yesha wanted to struggle, but Wang pinned her with one solid Earther arm.

"You should not have damaged the droid. I knew someone was in the old colony as soon as I saw the malfunction signal."

"What do you want, Wang? My uncle will know of your behaviour."

"Sadly, your uncle thinks you passed away in an unfortunate rover crash. There is no one here for you, little bird."

His Earther body crushed her into the moss.

"Your uncle needs to grieve. He must believe there is nothing left for him here. I need to keep you hidden until he leaves."

"Get off me, you pig."

Wang slapped her so hard she thought her head would split.

"You will not speak to me like that again, understand?"

Yesha nodded, too terrified to speak.

"Now get up and take off your suit."

"Please…"

He stood watching her. "I am not as much of an animal as you think, but I want you more agreeable. A few days without food and you will see the sense of my ways. When I see you again in a week, you will beg to do anything for some food. Now take off that suit or I will take it off for you."

She took off her suit and stood there shivering.

He took out a small knife and stabbed the material of her exposure suit with it. The short slash it left was enough. There would be no going outside.

"Walk in front of me and go into the workshop."

Yesha bolted towards the epiphyte forest. Wang intercepted her, catching her arm in a slab-like hand.

She twisted. He wrenched her arm up behind her back. Yesha screamed at the sudden, bright pain.

He brought his face close to hers. "If you try to do that again I will be forced to hurt you."

She wanted to run, to slam her fists into him, but the hulking Earther was too big. Wang directed her to a door at the back of the workshop.

"You live in here until I arrange something more permanent." He shoved her in and tossed in a Mooze bar and a bucket. "For your comfort," he said with a smirk and shut the door.

Yesha ran her hands over the surface in the darkness until her fingers tightened on the Mooze bar. Her mouth watered at the thought of the chocolate. How long had it been since she last ate? She tore the wrapper off and bit into the bar.

Lucien found him clutching a throw pillow in the living area of their house. He walked in and sat across from him.

Jonah looked up saying nothing. He wanted a hit of tarf; enough to make the world haze over the emptiness in his heart.

"We have not known each other long," said Lucien. "I want you to understand whatever this is, you can talk to me."

Jonah continued to stare ahead, keeping his face from betraying the dull ache in his chest. "I live with my mistakes every day. I hoped that coming here might change things, but moving to another world doesn't change who you are."

Lucien put a hand on his shoulder. "If you are feel good for it, let us have lunch and glass or two of Shaoxing, and later we can watch airball game. Meteors are playing."

Jonah stood. This was his life now. At least he was on the Moon. "OK, but only one or two glasses of that dragon wine. I remember the last time you fed me some."

Lucien grinned. "C'mon Jonah, if you can remember, you did not have enough."

They ate in a companionable silence that needed no words. It was enough for Jonah to know someone cared.

A few hours later they strolled back to the airball court. Lucien found them seats that gave a great view of the court.

Jonah twisted in his seat as he tried to relax enough to watch the game. They should be planning for Wang's return, not watching a game.

A Meteors front took a leaping shot toward the hoops until a defender slammed into his side. The front dropped like a stone.

"Foul!" came cries from the crowd.

Jonah jumped up with a sharp intake of breath. "That's it."

"Sit down in front."

He sat looking sheepish. "I have an idea. What if you use your airball skills when you fight?"

Lucien looked at him like he had gone mad for a second and then his face cracked into a huge grin. "Come on, let us give a try."

Jonah followed. Family and work had become a foreign country with a closed border. Tarf wouldn't fix that. Krave Maga, the dirty street-wise fighting art was the one thing he had left. Perhaps giving this one thing back was what he had to do.

Lucien led Jonah away from the airball court and down an empty side passage. He stopped a short distance inside. "How about here? Go for me like you want to attack me."

Jonah hesitated a moment as he saw Lucien's eager face. He took a slow run at Lucien and watched as Lucien ran up the tunnel wall and landed behind him. He spun to face him. "Neat, but you're too far away. If you don't go so far up the side wall, you could strike from the side."

"How would I do that?"

"Put your right fist on your left shoulder. Now imagine it's a hammer and swing it hard to your right side."

Lucien tried the motion. "Feels like I could hurt someone."

"You could. Want to try it on me?"

Lucien answered by running up the side wall to get around him. Mother! He was fast. Jonah managed a sweeping block that deflected the blow, but it was an awkward angle.

"Interesting. A classic defence will be almost useless against a side attack like that."

"Maybe you show me some of fancy kicks of yours, so I can be really dangerous."

"Patience, grasshopper."

Lucien gave him a blank stare.

"An ancient Earth martial arts movie. It means it takes time to master things. Let's start with some basics."

For the next hour, Jonah kept him on the ground and drilled him in basic scooping blocks that could deflect a punch or kick and twist the opponent to face away. Lucien learned fast, but Jonah knew it would be many hours of repetition before the blocks became a reflex. At the end of the hour Lucien stood in a loose fighting stance.

"C'mon, bring it!"

Jonah led in with a slow right to Lucien's jaw. Lucien blocked it then stepped back and up the wall. Jonah blocked his return punch, but was still turning, for a counterstrike, when Lucien landed behind him and punched him in the back.

"Your punch is a bit ticklish, but we'll work on that," said Jonah.

Lucien gave him a dirty look. "If you train me and few others in basics, we would have chance against Wang and men."

"No, Lucien. Wang's men have basic combat training. They would take you apart, just like they did last time."

Lucien nodded, but Jonah saw he was thinking.

They walked back to Beddau town in silence. Around them, people went about their day, leading quiet lives. Jonah liked the way the Moon Folk had gone back to a communal village lifestyle, without losing the benefits of modern life. It was almost like being in a small farming village on Earth if you ignored the gengineered lifeforms and lack of sky.

Jonah snapped his fingers. "I think I have an answer for the air rifles. This is not a high-velocity bullet we are talking about, just a high-speed plug of aluminium. If I calculate the energy of the slugs, and have a guess at the muzzle velocity, we can make a shield to stop them."

Back at their home, Lucien pulled up a screen. "I want to

show something, but do not laugh." He called up a picture of serried ranks of terracotta warriors. "This was army of Qin Shi Huang, first Emperor of China. Look at armour."

Jonah studied the picture. Each warrior wore a coat of interlocking plates held together by leather thongs.

"I was thinking," said Lucien. "If we create modern version of armour, it can take punch from airgun slug. Original armour used bronze plates, but we could grow organo-silicate plates in our vats."

If it was lightweight and didn't stop them doing an airball move, perhaps they would have an edge over Wang's men.

"How long would it take to make?"

"Week or so, if I can fast chat vat farmers."

It was less than a week later that Lucien dumped a basket on the table. "Look at these." He held up a palm-sized slab that shimmered with a soft yellow light.

Jonah took the light block and noticed a small hole drilled in each corner. "I'm guessing you have your armour."

"Vat guys said they made spider silk. Gave my aunt a batch yesterday, and she made vest." Lucien reached into the basket and held up a vest made from interlocking slabs. "Vat guys said it was not as strong as commercial armour. We must test."

"Put it on. Let's see what happens when I punch you."

Lucien hesitated a moment then slipped the vest over his head and stood ready. Jonah landed a straight punch at Lucien's midriff. Lucien grunted as he staggered backwards. "Weird, sends energy away from strike to sides, nearly lost my balance." He stood tall. "Again."

They spent an hour testing the limits of the armour. It

withstood punches, kicks, and hard blows with a baton. Jonah knew he would be bruised, but the armour could save a life.

Chapter 12

Sharpening the Sword

The group of fighters stood in a neat line before Jonah. Each wore the rudimentary armour Amira had cobbled together. Jonah had to admit, it didn't look bad. How well it worked was another matter altogether.

He began by showing them the absolute basics. How to shape the hand into a fist, the fingers in tight with the thumb curled below the outside of the fingers to lock them in place. How to position the fist to strike with the two big knuckles; and how to punch so the arm recoiled after the strike, so that an opponent never got a chance for a grab.

He drilled them in the blocking techniques he had covered with Lucien, emphasising form and recovery positions. How to always be ready for the next move. How to keep ready on the balls of their feet while moving and scanning for other opponents. The empty service tunnel echoed with their efforts.

At the end of the session, a group of tired, sweaty people stood in front of him. He knew little of what he had taught them would stick after the first lesson. There was one more idea, he could use, to get his instructions remembered.

"Let's end the training with a practical use of what I've just taught you. Choose a partner and stand facing each other."

They formed off into pairs and Jonah faced Doaran.

"We're going to do five minutes of free fighting. Try and land a punch on your partner, anything goes. If your partner tries a punch, remember the blocks I taught you. Are you ready?

"Go!"

The pairs traded punches and Jonah was pleased to see that Doaran blocked most of the strikes, often in a clumsy way, but still blocked. He turned side-on to Doaran, watching for a gap in her defence as they circled each other.

Jonah threw out a lazy punch and Doaran blocked it with a sweeping forearm across her body. She followed with a simultaneous punch toward his body. Jonah stepped out of the way and swept it aside. The woman was a quick learner.

Doaran began the same move again. This time, Jonah swept the punch away, but also moved in close and followed with a hammerstrike against Doaran's chin.

"Don't let your enemy read your next move, try and keep me surprised."

Doaran nodded. She feigned a right to Jonah's face. Jonah attempted to sweep the punch away, but her fist wasn't there. She followed through with a left to his exposed stomach.

Jonah twisted to let the punch past, but still received a glancing blow.

"Not bad. See if you can stop some of these." He started a left, right, left combo, and Doaran blocked all three. Jonah shifted around her looking for gaps and they traded blows, each being deflected with a series of sweeping block until Doaran over-committed on an overhead haymaker. Jonah blocked the haymaker with the blade of his forearm and hit her hard on the lower ribs with his knuckles. Doaran dropped to the floor, groaning.

"OK, stop everybody. Sorry Doaran, this is a good lesson."

The group turned to watch.

"One thing about fighting is you will get hit, and it's going to hurt. Stand up, Doaran."

She rose clutching her side.

"You are not your pain. You are a fighter, concentrate on me. I know you can hit me."

Doaran crouched in a low cat stance and flung out a right jab, followed by a left uppercut, and another right. She circled around to Jonah's left, her eyes blazing with determination.

"OK, Stop. Here's my lesson. Doaran, did you feel the pain while you were trying to hit me?"

"Yes, but I did not care. I wanted to get you."

"And that's the secret. Our minds can only process so much at one time. If you focus on besting your opponent, there is less time to focus on the pain. Be the fighter, not the pain."

Days of intense training followed. Lucien called it sharpening the sword—he had been reading up on last century kung fu movies and picking up samurai language. This time it was about the legendary katana, the sword made with sixteen folds and sharpened by obsessive craftsman to a diamond edge. He hoped that his team would be as dangerous. Jonah was less confident, but knew they had the basics down.

He watched as two of them ran up a wall as they traded punches. One fell back while the other executed a low snap kick back at his partner before falling hard. It was nothing like an Earth based style, but perhaps the modified combat was for the best. It looked impressive.

He picked up a bundle of slim batons.

"Today I thought we might try the elements of basic sword play. These are organo-plastic, the real thing will be iron. That's if Lucien ever gets around to making them."

He handed out the swords which were nothing more than plastic batons with a handle. For the next hour, he drilled them in using the sword as an extension of the arm. How it could be used to both strike and block. Two of the trainees showed an aptitude for the swords. It didn't surprise Jonah to see that one was Doaran.

Much later, his muscles burned with the fine tremors that an exhausting day of training brought on. He knew the others were as tired when he formed them up into a row intending to dismiss them and several slouched. "Stand tall."

"For Empress!"

Jonah gave an indulgent nod. Lucien was getting far too wrapped up in his medieval fantasy, the Empress was Wu Zet Tian the first Empress of China. Lucien looked sheepish, but raised his makeshift sword and yelled it again.

"For Empress!" roared the surrounding team. It was odd, but so what? Jonah would not stand in the way if yelling some daft medieval slogan gave them courage.

Yesha lay on the hard mat while each second dripped by like water sliding down a rock. Wang had been back and given her another Mooze bar and a bottle of water, distant memories now, and her stomach made ominous growls. The darkness was absolute.

She stood and made a careful circuit of the room. Lying here would not help her escape.

"Every enemy has a weakness." She remembered Uncle's firm voice drifting down from his desk to where her nine-year-old self sat on the floor. "When you understand that weakness, you have a lever that brings hope of victory."

"How will I know?"

Uncle looked to where she was playing. "If you study your enemy with care, your diligence will be rewarded."

The random discussions Uncle fed to her on the non-school days she spent in his offices had fascinated nine-year-old Yesha. He had discussed subjects as diverse as the history of Jiangnan, the elegance of mathematics, and the strategies of war and commerce. It was much later that she understood how carefully he had chosen his talks to shape her decision-making abilities.

Wang's assumption that she was defenceless was a lever she could use. There would be a way to use his overconfidence to her advantage.

The makeshift team got their chance at fighting Wang a week later. Freeka gave them a tipoff that Wang and three of his men would be patrolling the lower tunnels of New Karakorum. Jonah assembled them in the open area before the tunnel leading back to New Karakorum.

The team looked good. Lucien had spent a night searching the web and turned up the look of modern battle dress. Shimmering, yellow organo-plastic plates covered them from chest to thigh. Jonah wasn't sure the armour would work against an air gun, but there was only one way to find out.

The swords were less of a success. So far Lucien had produced a single sword that Doaran now carried. It was a pity; the sword was hardened steel and had enough balance to be useful.

"This is going to be serious. Wang's guys haven't had resistance so far. They will fight back hard. Are you ready for this?"

Lucien raised a fist to the air, and the others mimicked him.

"For Empress!"

Jonah gave them a smile. "For the Empress, then. Follow me."

They found Wang and his men on Level Twelve working their way through the machinery. Jonah and his team stepped out in front of them.

Wang looked them up and down and saw Lucien.

"The little cur is back for another beating, and this time he wants to play soldiers."

"For Empress!"

Lucien charged at him. He got in a solid right to Wang's eye before anyone moved.

Wang lifted a hand to the eye. "I'm going to break every bone I can today."

Lucien kept his mouth shut and shifted into a fighting stance. Wang sneered. "You want to try this, boy?"

Lucien's response was a fast left, right combo that rocked Wang back on his heels. That was the last Jonah saw of them as Wang's men fell on them.

A stocky Earther squared up against Jonah.

Jonah circled his opponent, with wary interest. This was not some untrained Moon kid, the man had Earth muscles and moved like a snake in long grass. Jonah recognised combat training when he saw it. He traded a few blows, exploring where the gaps were. There were none, the man's defence was like a wall. Jonah had to do something quick or this would be a protracted slug fest. The side of the tunnel lay behind him.

Jonah threw more punches, losing ground as he fought. The man grinned, he was pushing Jonah up against the side wall. Jonah fell back fast and used his backward momentum to rise up the tunnel wall. Jonah moved over and behind the man who was still turning and executed a flawless kick to the man's head that dropped him like a stone.

Jonah landed on the floor, but no one was near. It gave him a chance to stand and assess how the fight progressed.

Lucien and another of their team were still in a standoff with Wang. Neither side looked to have the advantage, but Wang sported an angry eye that would leave him with a great shiner.

Doaran had two of them backed against a wall with her sword. Both men looked for a gap. Jonah saw that Doaran hesitated to commit with the sword.

The other two appeared to get the better of the remaining man. Jonah left them to it and went to help Doaran.

He stepped in next to Doaran and made a feint towards the middle of the two men. The ruse worked, both moved away from his feint. The pause allowed Jonah to push toward the gap. Doaran got the idea and used her sword to corral off the man on the left. Jonah focused on the one on the right. This one retreated against the wall. His eyes flicked to possible escapes. Jonah used the man's uncertainty to distract him with a feint to the left. The man raised his arms to ward off Jonah's strike. Jonah flicked the man's right arm out of the way and grabbed the man's shirt pulling him in close. The man groaned as Jonah's knee slammed into his groin. Jonah let him go, and the man collapsed like a wet rag. Doaran swung backward from where she stood and kicked the prone man hard in the head.

She bared her lip in a savage grin as she and Jonah turned to face the other man. The guy didn't stand a chance as Doaran and Jonah rained a series of punches into him that knocked him off his feet. Doaran reversed the sword and gave the man a rock-hard blow to the side of the head with the makeshift hilt. That took care of those two.

"Retreat!" Wang ran for the exit and the remaining man followed at a sprint.

"Get them!" shouted Lucien, chasing after them.

"No, Lucien, let them go."

Jonah rocked back on his heels. "The fight was a decent demonstration. Leave those guys where they are laying. Let Wang explain why he left them behind."

Lucien stopped and walked back. "Yes, let them worry about us for change."

Jonah hid his concerns behind a smile. This would only escalate things. Wang and his men would want revenge, and there was no way a return fight would satisfy them. He would have to have a serious talk with Lucien about what came next, but for now they should celebrate.

Philippa was working on a draft of a new web page for the new mines when Wang and two of his men came to her office. He knew he looked as though he had come off second best in a fight, one eye was swollen shut, but this was no time for niceties. "You need to come with us, Ms Lawson."

Philippa followed, the woman knew better than to ask questions.

Outside, the two men grabbed her. Wang took out a roll of duct tape and taped her mouth shut. The men held her arms behind her as Wang taped her arms together.

They hustled her down to Wang's workshop. Wang ripped the tape from her mouth.

"What are you…"

"Silence!" He grabbed her chin.

"Ms Lawson, people tell me it was Freeka who told the moono scum that we patrolled Level Twelve."

She shook her head frantically.

He picked up a length of heavy electrical flex. "I used to re-educate miners in Shandong Province," He leaned in close enough for her rasping breath to stutter against his cheek. "I know the precise number of lashes needed to bring pain without losing consciousness. You, Ms Lawson, will receive all of those."

"Remove her shirt and tie her to the frame."

The men were methodical and strong as they grabbed her arms.

Philippa twisted in their grip as the men turned her to face the diagonal cross shape formed by two sturdy beams propped against the wall. "Wait!"

A low moan escaped her lips as her knees gave way. She clawed quivering hands against the guards. "I'll tell you about Freeka."

Wang held up a hand to the men. "I knew you would be reasonable."

The woman found her voice in a rush of words. She told him about Freeka, the softmind, and the chat forums. He smiled, she would tell them anything she could to keep away from the stark cross against the wall.

He squeezed her shoulder in one large hand. "I think we will be friends, don't you? You tell me everything you learn about the moonos and I won't invite you here again? How does that sound?"

Philippa nodded.

"We will go to your office now. I want you to show me how to use that forum."

"A cheer for our hero."

"Ayia!" Mugs of shaoxing rattled against metal tables.

Jonah flushed, but raised his mug along with the others.

The festive mood in Beddau spilled through the marketplace. People danced between stalls. Someone played a gentle melody on a metal set of pan pipes.

"You drink with us, lah." Lucien's eyes were glazed with shaoxing and happiness.

Jonah raised his mug and watched Lucien start a slow dance with Doaran.

They had been lucky to outnumber Wang and his men. It wouldn't happen again. Wang was like the tarf gangs back home. When you messed with them, they came back hard.

Chapter 13

Making an Army

"Greetings, Wang, what have you done to yourself?"

Wang limped into his office. Chen waited for him to get to his desk and did not offer him a seat.

"There has been a development, administrator. The Free Moon rabble are becoming organised. I was patrolling Level Nine of New Karakorum with my men earlier today when the Jones boy and his associates attacked us."

Wang shifted his stance to one side, trying to get more comfortable. "The attack was unprovoked and carried out with precision."

Chen stood and turned a hard gaze upon Wang. "Did I not order you to stay away from the boy?"

"Yes, administrator."

"And, was I not specific in my instructions about not stirring up the moonos?"

Wang nodded and swallowed. "The group we encountered had martial arts training."

Chen paced the length of his office, paying deliberate attention to the view outside the window. The man was a violent fool, but had not been violent enough. Wang losing a fight to the moonos would only encourage them. Reprisals would lead to tit-for-tat fights that would only embolden them when they won. The unstable situation required a complete clampdown. He turned to Wang. "We need to enforce the restriction on movement as decreed in the Settled Labour Registration Act. How do you propose we do this?"

Wang's face held a repulsive eagerness.

"Administrator, would you indulge me? I have something in my workshop that will solve our problem."

Chen followed him down to his squalid workshop. A collection of mechanical parts and makeshift weaponry lay in chaotic heaps across the floor. He stepped with care over a scattered pile of piping.

Wang headed for the one open space distinguished by its lack of clutter. Chen noticed a swept floor and a well-used training mannequin with four oversized steel lockers lining the far wall.

"This is where I train the men," he said. "That is not what I want to show you now. If you would stand to one side, administrator…"

Wang stood in the centre of the area and turned to face the lockers.

"Unit one. Activate!"

A locker burst open and a misshapen machine climbed out. It came up to Chen, and stood there on six bent carbon-steel legs with a pendulous eyeless body dangling between the legs. Two manipulator claws wove in front of Chen's face, grasping and clicking at the empty air.

"Is that a rescue droid?"

"It was. I modified it to be more suited to battle conditions. Allow me to demonstrate. Unit One, attack mode, target mannequin."

Grey cladding on the droid shimmered and faded in colour to match the workshop floor. It raised its hideous body and extended a stumpy tube from its back. The droid bent its multi-jointed legs, crouching low as it charged the mannequin. Manipulator arms whined as they rose to shoulder height, and the claws seized the mannequin by the neck.

"Impressive, but what use is a rescue droid against a moving man?"

"Unit One. Target me, non-lethal."

The droid swung to face Wang and skittered across the floor towards him. He dodged to one side, and the droid followed. It was fast, much faster than a man could run. Wang stepped backwards and tried to sprint to one side. The droid twisted and grabbed his arms with its manipulators.

"Unit One, release."

Wang stood there breathing hard with the droid motionless in front of him.

"Interesting. What led to this creativity?"

"I have friends who still work the mines in Shandong province. They suggested these hacks, administrator. The technicians upgraded the lidar sensors to detect fast moving humans instead of inert bodies. The droid perceives its environment at far better resolution than we can. We also enhanced the intelligence unit to military-grade autonomous decision making with advanced threat detection. Observe."

He picked up a length of pipe and swung it hard at the droid. The droid shifted aside in one smooth motion and snatched the pipe from his hands. It tossed it aside, far from Wang's reach.

Wang grinned. "A further improvement. Unit One. Camouflage mode."

The droid's skin shimmered and faded to match the grey floor.

"We replaced the high visibility surface layer with chameleon cladding."

Chen returned his smile.

"How many of these do you have?"

"If you release the maintenance engineers for a week and authorise overtime, I will have fifty of these ready for battle."

"Consider making them more imposing. I will give you one week."

Chen walked to his office contemplating what he had seen. The history of the colony was one of cooperative endeavour, never of violence and insurrection. He wanted to leave the Moon a better place, filled with productive citizens who gave great value to the People's Republic. Now, his career record would end with a minor revolt.

He bowed his shoulders to the inevitable and composed a message to his superiors saying that his retirement would need to wait.

Jonah lounged on the cushion, a discussion forum window drifting in front of him. Lucien sat at Amira's table, reading the same forum. A string of open posts waited for them. Jonah read another post from Freeka:

Moon Folk, listen up. It is time to take action. We should protest. PM me if interested.

"What you reckon, Jonah?"

"Bit different to what Freeka posted before. Sounds almost rational."

"Maybe it is administrator's dog. If only we could send anonymous message."

"I've still got access to my brother's mail."

"Administrator would know it is you."

"Yes, but he couldn't use it to find me. I'll send the message from Earth."

Jonah crafted a complex messaging address that bounced through an Earth relay. He posted a short reply.

Five minutes later, the Jonah's memplant sounded a soft beep on his auditory nerve. An answer to their message waited in Thomas's mailbox. Was he or she sitting there waiting? They opened it in circumspect anticipation.

Security Chief Wang and his men will patrol the eleventh level of New Karakorum tomorrow morning. Why not show them how much you care about freedom?

Lucien looked at Jonah and shrugged. What did they have to lose?

Jonah crouched behind the derelict digger. His gut churned in anticipation of what waited for them. Was he ready for this? He checked the padding on his makeshift armour one more time. It should be enough to stop an air rifle slug. He hoped it was.

To his left, Lucien crouched with five men of the ragtag Free Moon Army. Each was covered in enough of the awkward armour to make them resemble overstuffed scarecrows. Lucien gave him an anxious glance.

"Where are they?" mimed Jonah.

Lucien shrugged his shoulders.

Freeka's message said Wang and his men would pass by here on one of their regular patrols. Lucien had thought this was too good an opportunity to miss. Freeka liked to rant on the forums, but had provided useful information so far. Jonah looked down the tunnel again and this time he saw someone coming. He pointed and Lucien and the others leaned out, eager start this.

Wang was alone. He walked towards them as though they didn't exist. Jonah grinned, this was too good.

Wang came forward and stopped far enough way to avoid any attack from the Moon Folk. "I know you are there. Come out where I can see you."

"I don't like this," said Jonah. Lucien stood. The others followed.

"You have made mistake this time," said Lucien. "We have got you outnumbered."

An unpleasant grin appeared on Wang's face. "What makes you think I'm alone?"

The derelict machinery around them whined. The digger that Jonah had been hiding behind shook. He jumped back just as the digger gave a violent shudder and rust-covered plates fell from it in a clattering rush. A gleaming metal claw emerged from the wreckage, followed by another, and the thing inside dragged itself out into the pale light of the tunnel.

Jonah had seen prettier things in his nightmares. Articulate claws with an organic texture quested the air. Jointed arms ended in a baggy body that made the droid look like an oversized spider. The uniform grey colour and the six articulated legs did little to dispel that notion. The thing made its way over to where Wang waited with three of its mates towering over him.

"Do you like my creations?"

The droids stood there emitting the high-pitched whine of precision servo-motors.

"They used to be mining rescue droids, but I've made a few modifications."

"Run!" yelled Doaran. She turned and bolted down the corridor. Jonah followed.

"Droids, follow and apprehend," said Wang. The droids skittered down the tunnel at an impossible speed towards them.

Jonah and the others picked up their pace and jumped over wreckage blocking the tunnel.

"That'll slow them."

Jonah looked back and saw two droids climb over the junk as if it was a stairway. The other two had climbed the walls using grappling hooks that popped out of the pad feet at the end of each leg.

"Caatcha! Quickly!"

They ran down the tunnel until Jonah's vision narrowed and blood roared in his ears.

"In here." Doaran opened a service door and Jonah and the others bolted through it.

The door swung open wider. Two claws scrabbled for them. The thing tried to squeeze through, but stopped.

"Look," said Jonah pointing at the door. "It's too big to get through. Score one for the puny humans."

Then he saw that Lucien was not with them. He looked at the others.

"You should get out of here."

The others wasted no time disappearing down the tunnel. Jonah got closer to the door and peered around the droid. Lucien lay flat on his back with a droid perched over him, holding him down with its metallic claws.

Lucien saw him.

"Run, idiot!"

Jonah looked back: Wang and his droids had claimed the area. He sprinted down the tunnel in search of the others.

He found them near the exit to Beddau. Doaran flicked her eyes toward him in a questioning glance. Jonah shook his head.

Doaran nodded and led them on a much slower run down the corridor. She took them through a twisting series of side corridors and service vents, using emergency stairways to drop levels in the mine.

She slowed enough to let them catch their breath.

"We should make way back to Beddau now," she said.

"Do you think we're safe?"

"As safe as we will be."

"That was way too close. How did he know we were there?"

"I cannot say for sure, but I do not think we can trust online forums anymore, and definitely not Freeka."

Chen watched consciousness return to the Jones boy. He did not appear dangerous as he lay on the pallet, but then, he had bested Wang in a fair fight. It was only because of Wang's new droids that the boy had been caught.

Much as he would like to make this particular problem go away, it would be foolish to execute the boy. Such a harsh reprisal would provide the moonos with a martyr. A holy war around a good-looking young martyr was the last thing he needed.

Wang strode over and shook the boy hard. Lucien stood and had to clutch at Wang to keep from falling. Wang laughed, but Chen kept his severe demeanour.

"Walk him to the cells."

Wang pinioned Lucien's arms behind him and walked him past the recovery jars to the row of cells behind. Lucien's eyes widened in horror as he took in the contents of each jar. Chen saw his expression.

"The authorities designed these cells to give prisoners a clear view of the recovery jars. They are a useful reminder of your fate if you persist in your current course of action. It would be instructional, Mr Jones, if you spend the time in your cell contemplating the jars and what they mean."

Wang forced the boy into a cell and locked the steel gate that served as a door. The boy retreated to the stained mattress in the corner and sat watching them.

"Come Wang, we have much to discuss," he said, turning his back on the boy and walking away.

They walked to his office. Chen sat and reached into his desk drawer for the bottle of whiskey.

"Sit, Wang Mei, let us contemplate the success of your new creations."

Wang sat and accepted a glass of the smoky amber treasure.

"How long will it take you to have a full complement of the droids?"

"I can have them ready for battle within a week, but I request we wait a few more day-cycles."

"How so?"

"I have a delivery en route from Earth. Fifty semi-autonomous battle minds. The upgrade will enable the droids to work without my direct supervision."

"Military hardware?"

"Yes, administrator. It is my view we are now in a combat situation."

"Unfortunate, but I agree. What do you propose?"

Wang raised the crystal glass to his lips and took a moment to savour the taste. The man was becoming far too confident.

"I believe we know where the insurgents are hiding. They have been clever. The old Beddau mine shows a strong heat signal in satellite surveys."

"Interesting."

"I propose we wait until the new battle minds are installed and then hit their stronghold with maximum force. Let us leave no doubt that Jiangnan controls the Moon."

Chen kept his face impassive. Could there a way to rectify this mess? It could work. No one need know if Wang and his droids used excessive force. If the moonos could hide in a hidden base, then Wang's folly could also be hidden. And, if it worked, he would be able retire with honour. He focussed on the fool who was his only hope.

"If you fail me in this, I will ensure you experience recovery from the other side of the jar."

Wang scraped a hand through his hair. His gaze drifted, unable to meet Chen's eyes.

"There is something more you wish to say."

"It concerns your niece, administrator. I fear she may be dead."

Chen's eyes narrowed. He steeled himself to say nothing.

"I regret to say, we have found the missing rover and there appears to have been an unfortunate accident. Of your niece, we found no trace."

"You may leave now," said Chen, keeping his voice as calm as snow in winter.

Chen remained still long after Wang had left. If his gamble with Wang failed, he would return as old man with neither success nor family to celebrate. He broke his long-standing personal rule and poured himself another whiskey.

Chapter 14

Memories of Home

Jonah left the tidy sanctuary of Amira's house and walked out of Beddau. The village, was it right to call Beddau a village? looked old and tired today. A patina of dust, polished by generations of feet, covered the streets.

He imagined blue sky and the wind blowing on his face. He wanted to hear the ocean, the endless sighing thunder of waves crashing onto a sunlit shore, the tang of ozone on the breeze, and the promise of boundless space. Around him the rock hung dark and silent. He walked towards the lights of the marketplace.

The old woman who sold him his first perskaw sat on a tight square of embroidered mat, surrounded by her wares. The delicate weave contained patterns and colours that marked it as a product of Earth.

"Is that a Persian carpet?"

The woman's face broke into the creases of a life well-lived.

"Very good, this carpet is a gabbeh. My mother gave it to me when I was a little girl. Akbarabad, my village was known far and wide for the quality of our hand knotting."

"But you're from the Moon."

"I didn't always look like this. I was one of the first children to get the treatment. My mother was so proud. I wish she had lived longer, but Earth hearts do not last when they have no gravity to work against."

Jonah bought a perskaw and ate it, savouring the taste and texture of something that had been so surprising and new when Lucien shared with him. Lucien who was now imprisoned or worse. He felt so helpless. What could he do against the administration? Wang and his droids were in any scenario that Jonah could dream. There was no way to win.

She shifted to one side and patted the well-worn carpet. "I am Shahin. Perhaps you would like to share what lies so heavy on your shoulders."

Jonah settled in next to her. He started to tell her his story and then it spilled out of him like a river in flood, loose and wild and more than he could hold. How he came to the Moon and met Lucien, the explosion in Lucien's rooms, the fighting, and the droids, and now Lucien was gone. The silence of Amira's house and the empty streets.

Shahin said nothing for a while.

"My mother fought in the last great Jihad. She gave up when the Indians bombed Akbarabad. Too many battles with too few victories. I was too young to fight, but I remember the sounds of drones. The throbbing sky that vomits death. The reek of people on fire. Our Moon has been so peaceful. I fear the coming time."

"Why?"

"Because you have helped the people of the Moon to fight back. Your training has given them hope against the oppressor, and hope is the one luxury the Moon Folk cannot afford to have."

Shahin clasped his hand in hers.

"When the drones came, my mother sent me to the caves behind the village and I sat there with the other children listening to the thunder. Rain is rare in the mountains and we waited, telling each other of the planting that would follow and the harvest.

"Later, when we returned, we saw the rubble that had been homes. I picked through it until I found a foot. I did not know it as such, I carried it in wonder to my mother. What is this strange fruit, mother? I think it broke her heart to tell me it was Uncle Amir."

Two young girls crossed the passage across from Shahin's stall. Shahin watched them disappear into a house.

"Ask yourself, is there any chance for these innocents?"

Jonah stood, unsure of what he should say.

He took a deep shuddering breath. "There must be, and I will find it."

He wandered through the titanic columns of the mine, alone with his thoughts. The darkness swallowed his torch beam. This section was far from the village and echoed his emptiness. First his brother and now Lucien. He couldn't let it happen again.

Shahin was right. If he helped the people of Beddau to fight, Thomas and Lucien would only be the first of many burdens. But, if he did nothing it would be worse.

Jonah kicked at the loose gravel and watched as it scattered.

Vibration pulsated through the soles of Chen's feet as soon as he stepped off the train at New Karakorum. The floor of the platform thrummed, alive with chaotic urgency.

Wang's team had cleared half of the New Karakorum receiving bay to create enough room. The assembly yard stood to one side, a quarter of the space had been sealed off in a white plastic bubble. Chen made out dim figures working on the assembly line behind the plastic. He saw no droids.

Wang stood with a group of his men. He looked tired. It had been two hard weeks of double shifts and teams working around the clock to assemble the droids. Men had slept on makeshift pallets and eaten at their workbenches. Chen tried not to think about the percentage of budget this would take. Let history decide whether he had been a fool to bankroll Wang's ambitious scheme.

"Welcome, administrator. Are you ready to meet your army?"

"My army appears to lack numbers."

Wang nodded to his men. They spread apart forming a line across the open space.

Chen let the man have his moment of showmanship.

"Activate," said Wang. He and his men each held up a small controller baton.

The floor in front of the men rose in a sea of insectile grey legs and pendulous leather bodies as droids deactivated their chameleon cladding. Droids wove around each other in complex curves. The constant sinuous motion made Chen dizzy.

Wang's men waved their batons in a rectangular pattern. The sea of droids parted into five precise diamond formations.

"Set to patrol," said Wang.

Perfect diamonds prowled the edges of New Karakorum's vast receiving bay.

"The battle minds have limited independence, but they manage primary security tasks on their own."

"How many?"

"Forty-eight, the final two are being tested as we speak. We have improved on the active camouflage. The battle minds are adept at using it.

"The controller is another advance. All we need do is point and click."

The men pointed their batons towards the back of the cave and clicked twice. In response, the entire droid army retreated and once more sunk to the floor in an invisible mass.

"I need a volunteer," said Wang. A man stepped forward. Wang raised his baton and pointed it at the man. When he clicked a droid rose, and stalked the man, like an over-sized spider hunting a moth. It stopped some distance away and fired a small dart that trailed two silver wires. As the dart made contact, the man fell to the ground and lay there twitching.

"Neural incapacitator—it disables peripheral nerves for about thirty seconds."

The droid did not need thirty seconds, it rushed over and bound the man's hands and legs with tape it produced from a leg.

"We liked the spider idea, so we gave them spider-silk tape."

Excellent, thought Chen, I knew this blunt tool would be useful. He has surpassed himself. "What of the regular troops?"

"We have fifteen men trained on the air rifles."

"I see," said Chen with a peremptory nod. "Let me know when you have captured Beddau."

Jonah returned to Amira's place. The pearl orbs of the overhead lighting had faded to a dull ochre as they simulated dusk. People drifted home from the marketplace in small groups.

Amira sat at the table in the living area, her head in her hands.

He made them both a cup of khar and took a seat across from her.

"I want to help. I want to make Beddau a safe place for the people of the Moon."

Amira looked at him sadly. "You sweet boy," she said, "there is no hope for us here. We withdraw, lah. It is only matter of time before administration discovers how many of us live at Beddau."

"Where would we go?"

"There are other mines, long since abandoned. Some connect to Beddau through tunnel network while others are separate and much harder to reach. There is also Yutu's Burrow, original colony site, but is obvious."

"Will we be safe there?"

"Safe? Perhaps. Comfortable? No. We will have what we can carry, nothing more. Hunger will take many of us before we establish food supplies."

She wrapped her fingers around her mug, but didn't drink it.

"Few tried to prepare ahead for this day, but it is not enough. We have established small vegetable patches and catfish breeding ponds which may feed few. Others must submit to administrator and take what he dictates for food. In time, we can make more of it, but for now survival must be enough."

"And, if we move, what about Lucien? How will we get him back?"

Amira turned away and stared out the window into the gathering night.

Jonah checked in on the forums. There was the usual chatter between regulars, and a message from Freeka.

Watch your backs, People of the Moon. The administrator and his lackey are coming for you. Your secret hiding place is no longer safe.

"Sure, Freeka," he said to himself. As if they were going to trust that nutcase again.

Jonah slept in fitful bursts that night. His dreamed of dark tunnels without end. He woke in a sweat to the next day-cycle and noticed the velvet silence that stood in place of people going about their day. Amira was nowhere to be found.

Outside, few people moved. Word must have gotten out.

Amira walked up with Doaran. Amira looked as if she had aged during the night and now carried the weight of her years.

"Where is everyone?"

"Saying goodbye to loved ones. Families sat through night to decide if they will go, or remain and face what might be."

She looked at Doaran. "Some of your friends want to stay and fight. I spent much of my time explaining to them why we cannot win against Wang and his droids."

Chapter 15

Under the Mountain

Yesha's questing hands encountered a shelf under the bench. She ran her hands over the collection of junk that littered the metal shelf. Curious, she sifted through it. Most of the junk was old packaging, but her hand fastened on something long and thin. She explored it with her fingers and discovered she held a screwdriver.

Her fingers tightened around the handle as she thought of stabbing Wang with it. That would wipe the smug grin off his face. It wasn't any help in opening the door.

She sat on the floor again with her back against the cold stone wall. A faint tremor ran through the wall. She put her hand to the floor and sensed it again. What was it? She waited, but no further vibration came.

She was still puzzling over it when the room shook

violently. The floor bucked, rising and falling in waves and dust rained from the roof. Moonquake! The realisation hit her like a lightning bolt. Stupid girl. She had forgotten. The teacherbot had spent weeks drilling her in a comprehensive history of the early lunar colony. The colonists thought Yutu's Burrow was perfect, a natural sealed lava tube. Years later the first Moonquake struck, killing dozens and sending the survivors fleeing to the safety of the temporary shelters that became Chang'e Base.

None of those lessons helped now as the room shook itself to bits. And then, without warning, the chaos became complete and utter silence.

Yesha did not move. Her studies taught her that the quakes occurred with one or more aftershocks. She stood and waited and was not disappointed. The aftershock arrived as a single shuddering jolt that knocked her off her feet and forced the breath from her body.

She picked herself up and waited, but nothing further came. She opened her eyes. The room looked undisturbed.

Yesha gave a yelp of joy. Faint light filtered through a fine crack that ran at an angle across the wall in which the door was lodged. She raced over and gave the door a tentative kick. Nothing happened.

The crack ran around the door. She put her eye to it hoping to see something. Beyond lay the workshop. No help there.

The old-fashioned palm plate on the door sealed flush with the surface. No screws or seams were visible. She tried working the screwdriver into the crack next to the doorframe and gasped in surprise when the tip passed straight through the thin plasterboard of the wall. She pulled it out and tried to push the point of the screwdriver in further along the crack. It took some effort, but she was able to force the point through the tough wall. A few holes later, she punched the wall. Nothing happened. She sat on the mattress, rubbing her sore knuckles. At least the holes let in more light.

Wang must have deactivated the palm plate on the inside of the door. She decided not to think too much about why he did that. The outside plate must still work. If only she could reach it. A big hole in the wall would be perfect. She held the screwdriver to the light. She could make enough holes in the wall to get her arm through. She pierced a series of holes in a ragged circle that included the crack.

It was slow tedious work. By the end, her palms throbbed with new blisters. A small part of her hoped Wang would reappear with another Mooze bar.

When the holes formed a complete circle, she made a fist and punched it as hard as she could. Her fist crashed straight through the wall. A jagged edge ripped a long strip of flesh from her arm. Yesha screamed as she reached further and pressed the release plate. The door slid open, and she ran out into the workshop.

The empty workshop was unchanged. It had survived the aftereffects of a century of quakes before this one.

She grasped the screwdriver. It was not much, but if Wang returned, she would be ready.

Blood trickled from her injured arm. Nothing offered itself as a suitable bandage. Her breath rasped as she tore a strip from her blouse and bound the wound as best she could.

A simple pressure switch activated the door used by the service droid. It opened as soon as she touched it. Yesha peered out hoping to be alone. Outside, a group of rabbitons grazed on short grass as though nothing had happened. They scattered as she bolted for the safety of the ephiphyte forest.

Beyond the workshop the forest thickened until she wound along a narrow path obscured by patches of silver-grey sedge.

A snuffling grunt emerged from a dense thicket to her left. Curious, Yesha stepped nearer to see what kind of animal it was this time. A heavy, elongate snout quested the air near her waist. She stepped back as the ponderous head turned to focus black eyes on her. The creature hopped forward in a stiff, waddling gait. Striped, russet fur invited her to stroke it.

She stepped in closer to it. "What are you, strange one?"

The creature opened an enormous mouth and howled an eerie wail. Yesha noticed far too many teeth. She dodged as the gaping mouth snapped shut where she had stood. It turned, half crouching, seeking its elusive prey.

Yesha ran. Purple ephiphyte leaves whipped her in a mad confusion as she scrambled to be away from the horrid thing.

A heavy body thrashed through the forest behind her. She pushed tough plant matter out of her way, desperate to escape.

Overhead, a group of cat monkeys chirped in alarm as she passed.

The sounds of pursuit faded. She slowed to listen as the forest came to an abrupt end. The creature, whatever it was, stayed in the forest.

It opened into a wide expanse of short grasses. In the distance, she made out several low buildings, dwellings of a sort. The houses glowed in a shaft of impossible white light. This must be the original settlement. Sunlight spilled from a solar collector tube, drilled into the roof of the cavern.

Yesha picked up speed even though she ached. Cuts and bruises covered her arms and legs. Her right arm throbbed in sympathy. She lengthened her stride eager to be there now she was free.

The walk took longer than she expected, the bright light skewed her sense of perspective after days of dim light. Her feet ached by the time she arrived.

The buildings were old Earth style dwellings, with walls and a roof. She explored the first two, finding nothing but bare walls and the faint musty odour of spaces long abandoned. The third house contained an intact door and glassed in windows. She shivered. A stream of cold air flowed through this area. The heating system no longer reached as far as the settlement. This house looked as to be her best option for shelter. Her stomach cramped, reminding her of how many days had passed since she ate anything substantial.

Four walls and a stained floor met her inside the door. A soft rain of dust, shaken loose by her entry, fell from the rafters. The dwelling consisted of two rooms: a central area for cooking and recreation, and a separate room for sleeping. The bedroom was bare. She shut the door to minimise the space she needed to keep warm.

An ancient hydrogen heating unit occupied the centre of the living area. That was promising. The solid-state heater contained no moving parts and a simple rocker switch to activate it. She might be able to start it if she found water.

Hunger cramped her stomach again.

She stepped outside and saw a group of rabbitons grazing a short distance away. They looked at her as she approached and continued to graze. She ambled up to them, taking care not to spook them then grabbed for one and caught it with ease. She laughed, of course they were easy to catch, the colonists genegineered them to be food. The rabbiton lay in her arms making soft bleating noises. Heat from the dense fur warmed her skin.

The screwdriver was her only tool. She placed the tip against its skull and rammed it home. The rabbiton stopped bleating and lay still. Hot tears flowed down Yesha cheeks.

"I'm sorry," she whispered to the still-warm body. "I've never had to do that before."

She laid the body on a rock, hoping the cold air would keep it from going bad, and explored the remaining houses.

They were empty, but yielded enough. In one she found a bucket. Another had a broken window from which she drew a shard of glass.

Careful searching turned up a sluggish trickle seeping over a frozen rock face. Yesha held the bucket against the rock and chipped ice until the muscles of her injured arm screamed with cold and fatigue. The bucket was half full—it was enough. Back at the house, the hydrogen heater coughed into life and a slow heat filled the building. The glass shard was safe once she wrapped it in a strip of cloth.

She used it to hack skin from the rabbiton. The flesh beneath glistened a pearl-pink. She tried not to think about it and cut off strips. The first mouthful almost made her gag, but she forced herself to continue. She needed energy to survive.

She hid the remains of her dinner under a tussock of grass and fell asleep on the floor basking in the heat streaming from the heater.

Yesha groaned as she woke. Her muscles ached from sleeping on the hard floor. She smiled as she bounced to her feet, her aches forgotten. There was light outside, and she was free from Wang.

She took the bucket and fetched more water from the seep. Most went towards heating and her drinking supply, but she saved a cupful for a wash. The contrast of cold water on warm skin was almost indecent in how sensual it felt.

The gash in her arm felt hard and hot. She cleaned it using delicate dabs. The Chang'e autodocs would have cell-stitched it so that no mark remained, but this would leave a disfiguring scar.

Sunlight fell direct from the solar collector. Yesha stepped out of the house and luxuriated in the heat. The warmth made her notice the frigid air on her skin. The movement of air was too organic to be made by a machine. In Chang'e only the largest domes held sufficient volume to have an independent atmosphere.

The settlers had built eight houses in a neat square around an open space. Miners would have filled this square. A population resting from their labours stripping surface regolith for the poor deposits of helium bearing dust. Children would have played here, children who were now old men and women with dim memories of the early colony. On the far side of the square she saw what may have been a road, now long buried under grasses on which placid rabbitons grazed. She tried not to think about rabbitons.

Up close, the tussock of grass where she had buried the remains of her meal looked different as if a creature had disturbed the dust under it. Yesha saw several pale grubs churning though the dirt.

The grass gave her an idea. She spent the following hours collecting tussocks of dry grass and dumping them in her bedroom. The collected heap made a passable mattress.

She sat on it grinning like a kid. Life was getting better.

Yutu's Burrow was wider here, almost a kilometre from side to side. The far side held a small grove of epiphytes. Their rubbery trunks were darker than the pale trees she had walked through yesterday. She walked over to explore them.

Up close, they loomed larger than yesterday's forest. The

epiphytes made a neat boundary around a rectangle of silver leaves. She knelt to examine them and found arrow-shaped leaves growing from a short vine that disappeared into the ground. The earth in the square was a dark loam, so different from the grey dust. Yesha dug her fingers into rich, damp soil. There must be a water source here. She dug around a vine and discovered a large lumpy tuber. Maybe it was food. She sat back on her haunches and looked at the grove. This grove must have been a garden of sorts. She had never seen that kind of tuber.

A chirp from the overhanging epiphyte fronds made her look up at the fronds. Small curious eyes watched her. Not a cat monkey, but something small, grey, and furry. The creature gave another chirp as it spread leathery wings and flew away. Yesha watched it leave with her mouth open. The colonists had been creative with their genegineering.

She carried the tuber back to the house. The thin silver skin came away in glistening peels when she scraped it with her makeshift glass knife. Underneath was a solid, creamy flesh. She hacked a small piece from it and gave it an experimental taste. The tuber was bland, like cold rice noodles. One mouthful was enough. She decided to sleep and see how it affected her.

The next morning, she woke up hungry, but no worse off for having eaten the tuber. The entire tuber became breakfast and Yesha's stomach was full for the first time in day-cycles. As bland as the tuber was it was better than the alternative.

The days fell into an easy rhythm of eating, sleeping, and fetching water. The light waned as the outside sank into lunar night.

On one trip, Yesha grubbed through the tuber patch for

hours before she found one. She contemplated it in the dim light cast by the epiphytes.

Yesha knew the colonists survived on what they grew. The original plantings must have gone wild like these tubers. There would be more food in the forest, near the workshop, but that creature also waited there.

Chapter 16

The Sack of Beddau

The quiet hum of Wang's suit respirator filled his helmet as he watched the droid army crossing the low dunes. Active camouflage covered their passage. If he had not been looking for the tell-tale puffs of fine dust, he would not have known they passed. By comparison, his luminescent-orange rescue rover stuck out like a splash of children's paint in the monochrome landscape.

It was all coming together. Soon Beddau would be in his control and then he could talk the old man into going home. With Chen gone, someone who understood the worth of fear in maintaining fit and proper order would run the Moon. The degenerate moonos and their ilk would be brought to heel. He would show them their rightful place in bringing value to the greater glory of Jiangnan.

Beddau airlock loomed in front of them. The droids

arranged themselves in a defensive semicircle around the rover and sat there scanning the environment for threats. Wang checked the monitor and saw five more rovers crawling towards him. The air rifle team was on its way.

The lock cycled at his touch and he sent five droids through and waited. After ten minutes, he stepped into the lock. The five droids had encountered nothing, but they turned as one as he entered as if they saw him even though they lacked eyes. A momentary shiver ran through his shoulders. He clutched the controller baton tighter.

The Beddau lock accommodated large mine trucks, he could fit at least another five droids in without difficulty. Ten served as a good start. He would send them into Beddau as a first wave to incapacitate anyone near the entrance. With any luck, they would subdue any resistance around the lock before he ordered the next ten into the mine.

Wang cycled the lock and stood at the back while the first ten skittered in on spider legs that clung to every nook and cranny. He did not wait to see if anyone waited on the other side, but closed the lock and cycled back to the outside vacuum. He readied ten more droids as the air rifle team assembled.

"Take your time, men. I want the full fifty droids inside before we enter. You march in rear formation. Provide covering fire as we advance."

He walked in with the second wave of ten. The first ten had encountered no resistance and had arranged themselves in a defensive formation around the inside of the airlock. Wang instructed the second ten to join the first group to defend the entrance.

Outside, the air rifle team was ready, so he sent them through next. The remaining droids came through in rapid single file.

Once they were inside, he took off his helmet and enjoyed the brief luxury of scratching the spot on his neck where the suit collar always chafed.

He had never been inside Beddau. He spent a moment taking in the massive columns and the gaping space between them. The air carried the smells of Earth, the lush vegetation of Linyi and earthy Jinan home-cooking. Linyi, where his home and family waited.

"Pay attention, team. Our plan is to advance through this open space like a dragnet. The droids will lead the sweep. You follow. Use the air rifles to drive the opposition back. Droid controllers are to set for capture, we don't want to kill too many of these people."

The droids advanced, an army of ghost spiders, shifting colours to match the terrain and moving in patterns that only made sense to a battle-mind. Wang watched them swarming the wide spaces between columns. Fifty droids would not cover the entire level, but they were doing well. Moonos scattered in front of them. A young moono man screamed in agony as an airgun slug took him between the shoulders. The nearest droid skittered over and taped him immobile.

The satellite feed showed a significant heat mass, there had to be more people. Moonos ran before them disappearing in the shadows cast by columns.

"Droid packs one and two. Scan the perimeter. Find the entrances." Wang knew it was futile in the empty expanse of Beddau. The moono dwellings only occupied a quarter of the available space, on this level. He wondered if he had made a tactical mistake in reducing the number of droids sweeping the floor.

An old woman stood watching him, showing no fear. Intrigued, he walked up to her.

"Do you know who I am, old woman?"

"No, but I know exactly what you are. I've met your sort before."

He gave her a grim smile. "Then this won't surprise you," he said slapping her hard enough to knock her to the ground.

"Tape her," he said, and a droid rushed over.

The open spaces gave way to small homes built between columns, their walls painted in bright colours. He wondered where the moonos had found such colour. A trivial mystery to investigate later when this was done. Outside the houses, householders had planted flowers suited to the low light. It made him think of Linyi when he was a boy, the worker's cottages with their meagre gardens and cheerful community. That was his old life, so long ago.

The controller of droid pack two came walking out of a back corner. "We have located the entrance to another level."

"Show me," said Wang. He gestured for droid pack four to follow.

Ahead of them, three people broke cover and sprinted up the ramp. Wang recognised the Jones woman.

Jonah pushed himself to a faster run as a hollow thump echoed behind them. A scream cut off abruptly.

A metallic skittering accompanied him. He looked towards the sound and saw a spider from his nightmares fade into the charcoal grey of the mine rock.

"Droids, Run!"

They burst onto the garden level and tore through a field of perskaw, making for a cavern at the one corner. The droids followed, rippling through odd shades of grey-green as the chameleon cladding struggled to match the green of perskaw leaves.

The old man who had guided Jonah around the gardens

tended a row of perskaw. What was he doing here? The man looked up at the approaching droids, just as a neural dart, trailing silver wires, struck him between the eyes. His back arched, and he fell between the perskaw. Jonah stopped.

"No, Jonah." Doaran pulled at his arm. "Wang and men are close behind."

Amira ran direct to the back of the cave where a plain metal door had been set in the wall.

"In here."

They bolted through and Doaran slammed the door shut as the first of several heavy bodies slammed into the far side.

"Lock door," said Amira's voice from the darkness. "It will buy us little time."

She shuffled around and found a light switch. Dim greenish light illuminated a storage locker that held four envirosuits of an unusual design. Each suit had a bulky box where the oxygen unit should be. The helmets did not have a visor.

"These are experiment," said Amira. She gave a sour laugh. "We never meant for them to get field test so soon."

She grabbed the nearest suit and opened the back compartment. Rich organic scents with a grassy note rose from the feathered membranes inside the box. Amira picked up a container and dumped brown slurry into the open pack. "We call it envirolung. Pick suit and fill breathing unit like this."

Jonah did as she said. The container held curved fronds something like a cross between seaweed and the gills of trout he had caught as a child. "You said this is an experiment?"

"Yes, our people have genegineered photosynthetic bio-recycler. It takes in water vapour and carbon dioxide and turns it into oxygen. Envirolung needs sunlight, but can run for hours on catalytic feedstock you loaded. Suits work, but have never had lengthy test."

"Why do we need them?"

"So we can go out there," said Amira pointing upwards. Jonah looked where she pointed and saw a rope coiling down out of a darkness in the roof of the cavern. Doaran reached up and pulled. The rope brought down a ladder.

Amira waved Jonah up the ladder. "This is emergency exit. At top is small airlock that opens onto slopes of Montes Alpes. You are strongest so you should be in front to open lock."

Jonah grabbed the ladder and climbed. Amira and Doaran fell in below him.

The ladder speared upwards, a narrow pipe piercing the heart of the mountain. The bulky suits made it worse. What if he lost his grip and fell onto the others? The higher they climbed the more it became obvious that a fall would be fatal. It was difficult to guess how far they had climbed, the dim light of the storage area had long since vanished beneath them. A crashing bang came from below. What it meant he could not tell.

Chen listened to the silence where a young voice once asked curious questions. He glanced at the patch of floor where Yesha used to play so long ago. She was his hope for the future Moon, a potential future administrator who could have joined moono and Earther aspirations to Jiangnan's greater glory. She was also little Yesha who came crying to him in the night when nightmares troubled her sleep.

A timid knock at the door interrupted him. He composed his face in the mask of officialdom. Philippa Lawson entered, her face haggard.

She sat in the chair he indicated. "I want to resign."

Chen greeted her pronouncement with feigned

indifference, Ms Lawson was prone to excessive personal expression.

"I haven't slept in days. That monster took me to his workshop…" She placed her head in her hands and looked down at the desk.

Chen waited until Philippa spoke in a low monotone.

She told him about her abduction and how the image of the whipping frame accompanied her sleepless nights.

Wang blamed the softmind for his beating. It was a mystery how the softmind had discovered his movements, but that it had she no longer doubted after he had threatened her in his workshop. She had spent the last week in an obsessive crawl through transcripts of everything and anything the softmind and the moonos had spoken of, desperate to appease Wang. "I can't bear it any longer. Please let me go home."

Chen stood and guided the woman towards the door. "You have suffered so much stress. I think you will benefit from a vacation. At our expense, of course. I shall arrange for your transport to Panamerica."

A small round door greeted them at the top. It was a plain metal hatch as wide as the tunnel with a central locking wheel and an airtight seal around the edge. Jonah stepped off into a narrow alcove cut into the wall below the door, to one side of the ladder. A glowing glass tube to the left provided enough light to see. It took Jonah a moment to recognise the light as a solar collector tube.

"Is this it?"

"Yes," came Amira's indistinct voice from somewhere below his feet.

The wheel creaked as he turned it. They were so far up an

abandoned mine. The hatch swung down towards him on rusted hinges to reveal a chamber big enough to accommodate him and not much else.

"We go through one at time." Amira said as she caught up with him. "Press button on side of your helmet to seal visor. Vent mechanism is lever on wall."

She pointed to a small glass tube set in the inner door. "There is small green ball in tube. If you can see it, door can be opened. Outer door opens inwards, will only open once pressure equalises."

He looked down at Amira's pale face below his feet.

"Be quick." Doaran's voice echoed up the tunnel from below them. "Wang and men are close behind me."

"Go! I'll stop them."

Amira shot up into the lock and sealed the door behind her. Air hissed out above them.

Doaran bolted out of the tunnel and squatted next to him breathing hard. A muscular Earther arm appeared followed by Wang's face. Jonah kicked at Wang's head, but the awkward angle deflected most of the blow. Wang grunted and kept coming. Doaran stood on Wang's shoulders.

"Lock is clear. Go Jonah. I will take him on."

"No…"

"Don't argue, just go."

Jonah rushed into the lock and slammed the door behind him. The inside wheel of the door turned through half a circle and the pop in his ears told him the seal was airtight.

He reached for the lever then stopped. In his rush, he almost forgot to seal the neck ring on his helmet. He activated the clamp and a slim glass visor slid around to one side, so thin it worried him, but not enough to wait any longer.

The sounds of fighting faded as he pulled the lever. The air in the chamber vented with a thump that pulsed through the suit. He scrambled up the ladder and pulled the upper door closed behind him. Amira pulled him to one side.

Jonah stood and screamed as the incandescent orb of the sun flooded the sky. He covered his eyes with an arm and stumbled towards where Amira had been.

Chapter 17

Over the Hills

Wang strode in and gave Chen an arrogant glare. He seated himself without being prompted. The man was getting far too cocky.

"What progress have you made?"

Wang sat up straight.

"The troops have cleared the old mine. We moved all captured moonos to New Karakorum to supplement the labour pool in the pumice refractory.

"I left a small contingent of droids in position to guard against the incursion of any of the moonos who bolted down passages to Jokarah and New Karakorum." Wang gave an untoward grin. "Jokarah has been empty for years. Those that escaped that way will soon be hungry enough to wish we had captured them."

Yesha stood on a slope overlooking the old village and considered her options. Her eyes made an involuntary path to the road leading back to the workshop. That creature waited in the forest. Even worse, Wang might come back.

She traced the road back toward the village, imagining Wang walking toward her. She followed the line of the road into the village and beyond into the depths of the tube. It continued as a faint impression that might have been a road. Curious, she walked over to examine it and found it was a road, one that led further into the lava tube.

It was worth following the road, if it put her further away from discovery by Wang. She filled the bucket, wrapped the glass shard and screwdriver to make it safer for travel, and stepped out on the road. It became more visible as a road once she walked further on it. The road led down the centre of the lava tube into the distance.

Yesha walked for two or three hours before she noticed that the floor was no longer level. The road took on an imperceptible tilt downward and was becoming steeper as she progressed. She saw the end before she reached it. A small electric trolley sat at the end of the road and beyond it was nothing but air. The road ended at a cliff.

She discounted the trolley as not worth further investigation, the batteries would have been dead before she was born. The cliff held more surprises, behind the trolley, she found rough-cut stairs leading down. It was dark below, but there was nowhere else to go. She grimaced and stepped onto the first step.

The first half was easy, she could just make out the stairs in the gloom. The further she walked, the darker it got. After a while she was clinging to the rock and questing for each stair below with her front foot. Yesha imagined herself slipping and falling through endless black until she hit the bottom so far below her. She yelped with surprise when the staircase levelled out into a smooth floor.

Two confident steps later she fell over a hunk of discarded mining technology. It would not do to break a leg without a nearby autodoc to save her. She adopted a careful shuffle, after that, which introduced her to a lot more broken machinery.

This was pointless, she needed light. The only light she could think of was the luminescent fungus growing on the walls of the lava tube. It meant retracing her steps and climbing back to the top. She edged her way back up the stairs.

At the top, she found the walls coated with glowing fungus. The fine ropy strands crumbled as she touched them. She resorted to scraping as much as she could carry into a ball and took that back down the stairs.

The fungus ball provided a dim glow that let her identify the machinery as old mining gear. It looked as if the colonists had used the cliff as a tip for any discarded equipment, most had not survived the fall intact.

Beyond the immediate pile of junk, clear floor stretched across to an industrial airlock. She had walked the entire length of Yutu's Burrow.

A bank of lockers stood next to the airlock. They contained spare exposure suits, long since crumbled to a state of disrepair. She poked at the dilapidated fabric wrinkling her nose in disgust. The other lockers held more rotten suits. Her one lucky find was an ancient storm torch, a device at once simple and almost indestructible. Storm torches came from the days of climate change on earth. Crank the lever for a few minutes and the low powered LED bulb put out an hour of clean light. There were torches just like this in the boring early settler exhibit that Uncle dragged her off to see last year. If only she knew then she would need all her knowledge of the early colony.

She gave the torch an experimental crank, nothing happened. The charging lever was stiff, she cranked it for a few minutes and shook the torch before switching it on. This time she was rewarded by a cool white glow that flooded the immediate area. It was so bright after day-cycles of weak fungus light. Satisfied, she sat down and gave the torch a thousand cranks, counting them out in lots of one hundred.

The torch beam played across the airlock lighting a face-sized hatch. Curious, she examined it and found a latch. The small door lifted to expose an inspection window. Inside the lock was dark, aiming the light through the plate glass revealed nothing. She stood back and examined the lock, it was much like the one at the other end, equipped with a manual activation lever held in place by a safety latch. It swung open on the first attempt. This lock was much smaller than the other one, designed more for personal access than to enable machine entry. The far door contained a matching window.

Yesha lifted the hatch and winced. The outside light was bright enough to fry her corneas after day-cycles of wandering around in the dim light of Yutu's Burrow. She stood there with her eyes watering until she could see.

Outside, the low dunes rolled into the distance, just as she left them so many day-cycles ago. To the right, obscured by the window frame, was a solid tyre with substantial knobble tread. She craned her neck as far as possible to see what it was and her efforts earned a glimpse of a squat vehicle. A hydrogen buggy, she knew what it was from pictures at the settler display.

Colonist used these for joyrides over the dunes. Faster

than any modern vehicle, enthusiasts stripped them of safety gear and extraneous comfort to make space for a large hydrogen engine that drove the fat wheels. After several accidental deaths, the Administration pronounced a perpetual ban on the machines. She spent a long time looking at the buggy.

She let the hatch drop, the other side of the wall may as well be on Earth without an exposure suit. Her meagre possessions included: a torch, a bucket, a piece of glass, and a screwdriver. Not enough to get away before Wang found her.

That was not everything she possessed. Her suit still lay in the room where Wang had tossed it after he cut it. Her helmet might still be inside the other airlock, if Wang hadn't taken it.

It didn't matter, even if she got the suit, she had no air. The air in the suit would keep her going for at least four or five minutes, maybe six, if she walked at an unhurried pace and kept calm.

She lifted the hatch and looked at the buggy again. Perhaps four minutes was enough.

"Good luck," she told herself, "I've got a long walk ahead."

The walk took forever, it might have been two day-cycles, interrupted by a dinner of raw rabbiton and a sleep, well hidden, in a stand of the tall epiphytes. She kept to the road, hoping the creature in the forest stayed there.

She pushed her way back towards the workshop with cat monkeys following in the ephiphytes. The dim glow of the forest gave way to light up ahead and the cat monkeys raced ahead with miaowing chirps. She caught up with them when they stopped at the edge of the epiphytes.

Yesha was about to pass them when she noticed that something near the workshop entrance occupied their innate curiosity. She peered ahead to see what it was and stifled a gasp when she saw Wang standing there. She shrank back into the forest making as little noise as she could. The cat monkeys kept watching him. With any luck, he would think any sound from the forest was just them.

She ducked low behind an epiphyte and watched. Wang strode off toward the village.

Yesha waited until Wang had been out of her sight for a long time. Her skin crawled at the thought of that predator lurking behind her. When she could no longer face the waiting, she bolted for the workshop.

Wang had tossed the suit on a workbench. At least he was predictable in his laziness. The communications unit stuck out as soon as she checked the suit. The screwdriver was not the right tool, but it gave her the leverage needed to prize off the unit. She left it on the bench. Let Wang figure out where the rest of the suit was.

She grabbed the suit and dashed for the forest, hoping that Wang hadn't returned. The patch repair kit was still in its pocket. She covered the puncture with the kit and slid the activator forward. Acrid smoke rose from the kit as the nanofactory regrew suit fibres. The new surface was smooth with a dull sheen.

She waited until Wang passed by on his way to the airlock. The suit felt loose when she put it on, her arms and legs too small like a child wearing a grownup's clothes. Hard days of walking and minimal food were taking their toll. The rabbitons and tubers were not a complete diet, but would have to do until she found something better.

It took hours more to reach the airlock. The helmet was where she tossed it after her near asphyxiation. At least Wang was consistent in his lack of detail.

The helmet sealed with a reassuring clunk, and she

decided to leave it on until the air got stuffy. She understood how her body would react to low air after her experience at the lock. She put a gratifying distance between herself and the main airlock before she needed to remove the helmet. It would be enough. The suit was safe enough for her to risk going outside to examine the buggy.

Back at the far airlock, she sealed the helmet then locked the inside door of the lock. She pulled the lever and closed her eyes tight waiting for the suit to give way. After a few deep, shuddering breaths she opened her eyes and stepped out. The sun had set while she fetched the suit. Around her the hills reflected light from daylight further up the valley. The buggy stood there, covered under a thin layer of dust, but intact. The open cockpit contained a threadbare bucket seat and a large steering wheel that turned the front wheels on a primitive mechanical rack and pinion arrangement. Yesha had never used one, but she understood the principle, she hoped she was strong enough to turn it.

The air in the suit was becoming thick with water vapour and a malodourous stench she suspected was herself. She walked back through the lock and took off the suit, taking big deep breaths to flush the carbon dioxide build-up from her muscles. Once her breathing returned to normal, and the fogginess cleared, she resealed the suit and went back to the buggy.

The engine was a hulking chrome block of pistons and pipes. Yesha explored it, but did not understand how it worked. She tried to analyse it using logic. The engine ran on hydrogen that needed a gas tank. She found two squat cylinders at the back of the buggy connected to the engine block by thin metallic pipes.

Her thoughts wandered to imagine a handsome young daredevil taking the buggy for a spin through the dunes. She examined the closest tank and found a filling valve on the underside. There had to be a way of loading the tank. She took a fresh air break to think about it.

The history lessons she endured as a child covered the dirty combustion engine that Earth people used before fusion power was available. The Green Revolution had developed the hydrogen combustion engine during the Climate War. It needed to burn oxygen to create the explosive power that drove it. Now she understood the two tanks. How did her good-looking adventurer fill them?

"Focus, Yesha." She gave a wry laugh, it was time she found people again.

Outside she looked at her surroundings. She had been so focused on the buggy she had not noticed the dust covered metal cabinet set into the rock. Two plastic filling hoses, one red, one yellow, coiled out of it. The neat coils were rotten from decades of absorbing ultraviolet radiation.

The cabinet was a water cracker, a device that split water into hydrogen and oxygen, much like the cracker in the dwelling she slept in. It needed power, she checked it and found an old-fashioned nuclear generator. If she spent too long near it, she would need gene therapy.

She opened the cabinet to see a large upright cylinder with a quick-release lever. That must be it. She unclipped the bulky thing and found it was heavy. She dragged it back inside and ripped the helmet off gasping.

Uncle had been strict. He enforced daily sessions on the teacherbot until she learnt everything she could. She loved her lessons, lunar history, social studies, and population dynamics. She was less fond of the hard science and technology lessons, but Uncle was consistent in his discipline. He made her sit through hour after boring hour. Something must be useful. She cleared her mind and began the ritual of problem solving the teacherbot had taught her to use for her lessons.

"What is my problem?" Yesha asked herself.

"I am trapped in Yutu's Burrow and need to escape before Wang finds me."

"What do I have?"

She listed everything and included the buggy and water cracker.

"What do I know?"

This was harder. She knew the buggy ran on hydrogen and oxygen, and there was a water cracker to produce these. She could refill the water cylinder, but not with the useless filling hoses.

The suit was another problem, without an oxygen recharge she would have a short ride even if she got the buggy going. The suit and buggy tanks used the same gas fitting. If she replaced the hoses she could fill the suit and charge the buggy.

"Where am I going to find another hose?"

There was a lot of old junk in the workshop. She stood and began the long walk back.

A hand reached him and Jonah felt Amira fumble for a switch on the control unit on his arm. His comms unit buzzed to life.

"Follow me," she said and led him towards a dim shape.

Jonah stepped into a furnace. He stumbled after, his eyes smarting from the incandescent glare. Was that smoke rising from his arms?

She led him into a dome shaped hut. The change was instant as he came out of the sun.

"Emergency shelter," she said. "It is against safety protocol to go out in middle of lunar day." She tapped another button on the side of his helmet and his visor darkened.

"Oh, that's better."

"Don't touch walls. Heat will fry your hands through gloves."

Jonah shrank toward the centre of the dome.

She reached over and squeezed his arm. "Where is Doaran?"

"Wang caught up with us. Doaran held them off so I could get through…" He trailed off into silence.

Amira sat on the regolith and patted the spot next to her.

"We wait. If Doaran emerges we will help her, if it is Wang, we run."

"How can we run in this? The heat is insane."

She pointed to a blue button on the side of her respirator. "This activates standard thermo-electric radiator in suit fabric. Don't use it until we have to, uses power we need to run respirators."

Time stretched until it felt to Jonah like they had waited for hours before the hatch dropped away. A hand emerged from the hole and Doaran pulled herself halfway out and lay there. Jonah and Amira raced over and pulled her clear of the hatch.

Doaran lay in the emergency shelter not saying anything.

Jonah grabbed her arm. "Are you OK?"

Doaran's eyes focused on him. "Wang caught me. I kicked him away and climbed onto alcove. He made it up next to me and gave me two hard punches before I managed a sweeping block that twisted him enough for me to kick knee. I think he fell onto one of his team coming up behind him." Doaran groaned. "Oh, my ribs. I bet caatcha's broken one."

Jonah helped her to her feet.

"Can you walk?"

Doaran clutched her chest. "Yes, but is going to hurt."

Amira ran out into the sun and opened the hatch door. She picked up a rock and wedged the hatch open.

Jonah got it at once. The lock was inoperable while they left the upper door open. The air pressure from inside Beddau would hold the lower door in place. They had time to think things through. Time at least until Wang sent his droids over the mountain.

"Where should we go?"

Amira turned her head to consider the full view. They had emerged high on the slopes of the Motes Alpes, the outer ring of mountains that bound the North of Mare Imbrium. Below them lay the domed base of Chang'e and around it the collected industry of mankind. As they watched, a goods train made its way along the line from the mines to the railgun that would launch its cargo back to Earth.

Behind them, the hills of the Montes Alpes rose stark against a black sky. To Jonah they were unfamiliar and terrifying, imposing masses of grey dust, held together by random outcrops of volcanic basalt. He remembered a summer when he and Thomas had climbed the minor peaks of Red River Gorge. It had a been a time of spine-tingling excitement as they used their wits to solve the intricate dimensional puzzles of a rock climb. Each step a logical extension of the previous toehold. These mountains lay more like folds of fresh cement slopped on a surface by a lazy mason.

Amira saw where he looked. "Yes, that will be safest path."

"What's up there?"

"Nothing, but behind mountains lies independent colony of Alsatia. I have only heard of it. People keep to themselves, but it is said to be in Valles Alpes, great cleft that divides Montes Alpes. If we use radiators and rest in shadow of outcrops, we might make it."

"So, we go over?" said Doaran.

"Will you be able to do that?"

"Do I have choice?" She turned and walked towards the peaks. Jonah and Amira followed.

Yesha approached the workshop, trying to make as little noise as possible. Her skin crawled. What if it was behind her?

She hid in a stand of epiphytes and waited. It took hours, but at the end she was sure Wang was not inside.

The workshop was as she had left it, the transmitter still lying on the bench. What did Wang think she ate while he was away? She explored every inch. The chaotic benches, the open working area with its mysterious machinery, the locker cabinets along the wall, all proved fruitless. No yellow or red hoses anywhere.

She killed a rabbiton for lunch and sat outside the workshop. Why was it so hard?

She always had enough. Uncle saw to that. The domes provided everything, and what they didn't have, she ordered online from Earth. She snuffled, thinking of a steaming bowl of noodle soup, of nice clothes, and having her hair cut.

Yesha stood, wiping her face with one sleeve. Oh, she must be a mess. Uncle wouldn't recognise her like this.

"Think, Yesha." Junk lay in piles at the end of the cliff. Something maybe hidden there.

The walk back became a long grinding slog of placing her feet one in front of the other. The dream of steaming noodles returned to haunt her.

She examined the wrecked machinery again and found no

red or yellow hoses. She checked again, looking for anything. This time her eyes caught a black hose, half buried under a fallen machine block. She dug it out using a flat metal plate she found nearby. The hose looked as if it ended in the right connectors. There was only one way to be sure.

The water cracker cylinder was too heavy to carry, so she took her bucket and walked back to the seep to fill it. Back at the lock she took one of her suit's small gas cylinders and connected it to the hose. She stepped outside with the two cylinders and reconnected the water cylinder. The filling hose posed more of a problem. Was the red or the yellow hose the oxygen line? She shrugged and clipped the line to the red side. The machine activated as soon a she flicked the heavy switch she found on one side and she hurried back inside.

She gave the water cracker what she thought took about half an hour and fetched the suit cylinder.

There was only one way to test if she had oxygen or hydrogen. She clipped the cylinder back into the suit and put on the suit. She clipped the helmet in place and started climbed back up the cliff. By the time she reached the top, bright white stars swam through her line of sight. She ripped the helmet off and took a deep breath. So, red indicated hydrogen. To be sure, she repeated the experiment with the yellow side and could walk around until she got bored.

She had an answer. She would fill the suit tanks with oxygen, and load the buggy with hydrogen and oxygen. It was hard, but she could do it, and there was a way out.

It was days before she had loaded the rover, and there was nothing more for her to do. She ate one last meal of rabbiton before assembling the few possessions she owned in front of the airlock. There was no point delaying any further.

Outside the low dunes had fallen into the shadow of the

Earth, the rover was visible as a crouching silhouette. She cranked up the torch and sat in the shallow bucket seat. The flat-lever ignition switch pushed up a fine cloud of dust when she flicked it. The buggy did nothing for a few seconds and then a steady vibration reached her hands through the steering wheel. She gave a big lever in the centre of the console an experimental nudge and the buggy rolled forward. She pushed the throttle further, and the buggy picked up speed. The nose edged out into the floor of a small valley. It was tempting to see how fast the buggy could go. She pushed the throttle forward hard and screamed in terror as the valley floor around her vanished in a grey blur. The buggy bucked like a wild horse, shaking its head from side to side, before she got the throttle back to a safer position. How did that young colonist manage it? It was like trying to tame a force of nature.

The buggy crested the first dune, and she got a look at her surroundings. Far to her left, the terminator line of sunlight sparkled against the darkness. That meant East and Chang'e lay over to her left. It would be easier to navigate the closer she got to daylight. The buggy followed a meandering line along the valley floor towards the light. Now all she needed to do was find safety before the air in the suit ran out.

Chapter 18

The Service of Brothers

Footstep followed footstep through ankle deep dust that lay over hard basalt. Rock unchanged by the millennia since a prehistoric asteroid impact flung it up in loose mountains.

Jonah wilted as soon as they left the shelter. The suit's reflective organo-metal skin blocked most solar radiation. An active nano-transport system sent residual heat to the radiators which were glowing a dull cherry-red. It was still like walking through a steam bath.

The first peak was a pile of immense basalt columns, so light in colour they glowed white next to the grey of everything else. They skirted the topmost peak aiming for the lower section to the East. Jonah's sigh of relief at cresting the top turned to a groan when the true height of the mountains behind the first peak became apparent. The climb blurred into interminable hours of scrabbling over basalt.

Amira came to a sudden halt and looked up. Jonah lifted his head, but all he saw was an endless wall of grey rock with no dips or valleys to make for easier climbing. Amira saw his expression. "Look higher," she said.

Above the wall diamond-bright stars studded midnight black like so many pale jewels.

"That's it? The top?"

Amira nodded.

"All we have to do is climb that impossible vertical wall in front of us and it's over?"

Amira laughed. "Not over, but we'll be at the top."

Up close the rock-face was a study in textured cement. Odd folds and pocked micro-craters, provided hand-holds. It was so different to Earth rock. Jonah fell back on his climbing training. Climb with your legs, balance with your hands. He saw Amira and Doaran doing the same.

I'm free-climbing a lunar mountain, he thought as he executed a layback using a narrow crack a fraction wider than his gloved hand. Thomas if you could only see me now.

A cry for help interrupted his reverie. Down below Doaran hung by one hand. Her legs dangling free.

"Don't move Doaran; I'm on my way." He traversed across rock as smooth as a bowling ball back towards Doaran.

Doaran's face was white with pain when he got level with her.

"Can you get your toes on the rock?"

Doaran bent herself in and caught both feet on the rock.

Jonah scanned the surrounding rock-face. There was one possibility, a small impact crater big enough for him to wedge a gloved hand in and a slim ledge below it. "You've got three points on the rock. That's enough to be stable. Don't move until I get near you."

He swallowed, dynamic moves were a dumb idea at the best of times. What he was about to try was plain stupid. He took a deep breath and jumped.

His body skidded across the rock until one finger caught the impact hole. He grabbed for the hole with his other hand with the clarity of desperation. His hand caught. He swung by glove-heavy fingertips. Both feet scraped the ledge and stopped.

Jonah breathed out. A long slow breath, calming his nerves and centring himself. He felt the rush of adrenaline in shaking muscles and took another breath to steady himself. Slow and deliberate now, he told himself. With his body, as close to the rock as he could make it, he dropped his right hand and wedged three fingers of his left into the hole.

"Doaran, this move will be hard. You need to swap hands. Use your feet to push up and swap as quick as you can."

"Then what?"

"Then you can reach me with your free hand."

The look of sick panic on Doaran's face was answer enough. She squinted at the rock-face. Before Jonah could say anything Doaran heaved, and her hands were where they needed to be.

"Reach over and grab my hand. All you have to do is swing past and drop onto the ledge below me."

"Easy for you to say. You ready?"

"As ready as I'm going to be."

Doaran grabbed his hand and leapt. For a sickening moment, Jonah knew his hand would lose its grip, but Doaran swung past and screamed as she landed.

"Was that a scream of pain or relief?"

"Both," said Doaran.

"Glad to hear it. Now get out of the way. I've spent enough time hanging here."

"If you two are finished fooling around, perhaps you would like to join me on top." Amira waved at them from the ridge.

Jonah and Doaran chose a safer route and emerged on top next to her.

From were Amira sat, the night stretched out before them, flooding the downward slope and valley below in darkness so deep it resembled a pool of ink. Jonah tried to get his head around how dark the valley was. The Moon's weak excuse for an atmosphere did little to scatter the incoming sunshine, anything hidden from the direct light of the sun lay dark.

"We'll have to climb down in the shadow."

"And we will need to rely on air stored in suit," said Amira. "Envirolung does not work without light."

"How long?"

"Four hours, I think… Not sure."

They walked until the grey hills fell away into a steep-sided valley. Behind them the ridge-line continued to rise into the heights of the Montes Alpes formation.

Jonah licked his dry lips. "I'd kill for a glass of water."

"Oh, I am sorry. You don't know exposure suits." Amira reached over and pressed a button. A clear pipe popped out near Jonah's lips.

"Suit traps moisture for envirolung."

Jonah sucked tepid water redolent of seaweed and sulphur. He grimaced. "I guess it's an acquired taste."

She shrugged with her hands. "Genengineers make do with bacteria they have."

Deep inside the valley, Jonah noticed rocks picked out in

the achromatic light of the sun spilling over the ridge. Ahead, deep in the shadows the valley sank to darkness so black it seemed solid.

The temperature dropped from unbearable heat to bone-cracking cold as soon as they left the sun. Jonah didn't think he would ever get used to the crazy weather. No atmosphere made everything a matter of radiative heat.

They picked their way down the gravel slope towards the lip of the valley. Jonah tried not to think about losing his footing and sliding down the grey rubble to the waiting lip. There was nothing beyond it but the non-existent lunar atmosphere. He discovered that by leaning back and forcing his heels in as he put his foot down, he had an almost stable foothold with each step. Not enough to make him complacent, but sufficient to reassure him he did not face immediate death.

He reached the edge of the slope first and waited for the others to arrive. The air in the suit was getting a nasty funk he didn't want to think about.

"Hold my legs," he said moving close to Amira. "I don't want to fall."

He lay flat and inched his way towards the open space in front of him.

Over the edge, he peered down and recoiled. The valley wall fell below him in a sheer cliff face that plunged through hundreds of metres of soft rock to the dark floor far below them. It was a long way to fall. The valley floor was littered with car-sized shards of basalt embedded in a black lava rille that had run along the valley in times long past. This was Valles Alpes the great cleft through the Montes Alpes.

He looked right, the wall continued unbroken for as far as he could see. No way through that side. To his left the darkness at the end of the valley caught his eye.

Something appeared odd about the pinched end of valley where the valley split the mountains. He couldn't quite make out what it was. Closer towards him, a section of the wall had collapsed and littered the valley with random blocks of dust covered stone, some as large as a house. Brown and grey rocks told Jonah that this was a volcanic weakness that had sheared off during an earlier cataclysm.

It was a tricky climb, but possible. He rolled over and sat up, pulling himself further from the emptiness behind him.

"We have a way forward," he said. "There's a break in the valley over there, but I can't see Alsatia."

"Perhaps it is further," said Amira.

"How long will the air in these suits last?"

"Almost indefinitely, if we get into sun on opposite side of valley and refresh charging units."

"We need to move then."

They got up and climbed higher up the slope. If one of them slipped from there, they had time to recover before they slid to the cliff edge. Jonah led them on a crablike shuffle across the slope towards the break he had seen. It was further than he had guessed it to be, he developed an appreciation of how immense Vales Marinus was. It would be several hours walk across the valley floor to the sunlit patch on the opposite side. He hoped the available air was enough.

It took almost a day-cycle to charge up the oxygen content of their suits to a level that would keep them going for a while. The main problem now was hunger. Jonah's stomach growled. Life was so different to Houston.

They walked into the inky night of the gorge with brilliant light spilling through a crack in the valley lip far above them. The light sliced through the darkness and disappeared into a deeper shadow. Jonah understood why his eyes had found the gorge so unusual. The harsh play between light and shade cut the dark lava flow of the floor into unusual square shadows. The beam of light penetrated to the foot of the gorge and as they got closer, they saw how the light fell into a vast cleft in the opposite wall.

"That will be a good place to rest," said Jonah. The groans of assent told him it was a good call. They walked the rest of the way in silence.

Jonah was in front when they reached the cleft. He stepped past the edge and stopped in astonishment when he looked into the darkness. The others almost bumped into him before stopping with the same look of wonder. The entire cleft had been sealed behind glass. Not the tessellated diamonds of the domes, but a single unblemished sheet of clear molecular iron-glass. How much would a sheet of iron-glass that big have cost? How did they get it here from Earth?

"We made it," said Amira. "Come, let us seek entry."

She walked toward a full-sized airlock shrunk to insignificance against the enormity of the glass. Behind it two indistinct figures waited.

They cycled through the airlock. The two figures turned out to be men in simple robes. The one on the left appeared middle-aged, the other was much older. Both had the shaved tonsures of monks, and, green cat's eyes. Interesting, thought Jonah, an order that did not support the holy writ against genengineering. The priests showed them a storage locker and mimed taking off a helmet. Genetic engineering, but no comms then. Interesting, indeed. Jonah lifted his helmet and was greeted by the soaring choral sound of a hundred male voices singing in unison.

"Is this Alsatia?"

"Rest for the weary and sanctuary to the persecuted. Yes,

this is the cleft of Alsatia," said the younger man. "I am brother Amos and this is brother Wenlock."

Amira started to introduce them, but the singing swelled to a higher volume. Brother Amos held up his hand and after a short while the music stopped and the great cleft rang with silence.

"You have timed it well. Evensong is finishing."

"I am Amira Jones and these are Jonah and Doaran. We have nowhere to go."

"The spirit provides for us according to its needs. If you have arrived here, then there must be a reason. Come, place your suits in those lockers and we shall seek the evening meal."

The lockers were crafted from smooth, dark hardwood. Wood that must have come from trees grown on Earth. Jonah looked around and saw the burnished glow of mahogany and satinwood reflecting the sunlight. The cost to lift that much wood out of Earth's gravity well was beyond belief.

Amos led them through an alcove to the refectory filled with homely oak benches. Rows of monks filled the benches. A pleasant commotion bubbled over their meal.

Amos showed them to a table and gave them each a bowl of a clear brown broth in which bright vegetable chunks floated.

"I apologise that we do not have more substantial food. We are a simple order and choose our meals according to what we can grow."

Jonah helped Bother Amos carry dishes to the scullery. Carrying plates to the kitchen reminded him of the simple comforts of home. His throat tightened as he thought of the normal life he used to share with Thomas.

"Why is the brotherhood here?"

Amos sat at a bench and indicated for Jonah to sit. He pointed out through the glass to where Earth could be seen low in the sky.

"The brotherhood believes in the glory of God's creation. What finer place to observe His finest creation than from on high?"

Silence followed and Jonah sat staring at what had been his home.

"Do you believe in God, Jonah?"

"I don't know what I believe anymore."

Amos was silent. Jonah took it to be an invitation to speak.

"I wasn't always like this…" He took a deep breath, filling himself with the calm of this improbable monastery.

"I scattered my brother's ashes when I first came here. Thomas and I were close. We did everything together. Even our martial arts training." He stopped and took a deep shuddering breath.

Amos nodded.

"We made practitioner grade just after I turned eighteen, you'd call that a black belt. That was the hardest thing I ever did in my life. We practised until we dropped, and then we had a sparring session where one of us went up against three seniors. I lasted five minutes before they stopped me with a choke hold. That was enough, we passed."

Jonah stopped there, the next bit was hard. Hot shame rose within him, but the need to share his story was too great.

"I met this girl. I was crazy about Joanna, she got me hooked on the Jackhammer music scene and tarf, the drug that makes Jackhammer sound amazing. Mining music, she called it. You could hear the rocks speaking hidden languages.

"Thomas was always the good brother. He picked me up when it looked like I wouldn't make the final year. Then Dad got me into one of those quiet places that serious money can buy to clean you out.

"I got back clean and studied hard, but my old life found me. Joanna and her brother Rico, the man with the bag of tarf. Rico ran with the Trinax Lobos, the ones who controlled the mining scene. He said I had a debt to his Jeffe, and it was late."

"I'll never forget how that night ended. The back alley behind the Rock Arms, the sound of hardcore Jackhammer tracks thumping from inside the bar. The Trinax Lobos in their black jackets, lining the back wall, arms crossed and waiting with dark eyes."

"I don't know how the fight started, but five minutes later three of them were dead and Thomas was bleeding out into the gutter."

Jonah stopped to wipe his eyes.

"Afterwards, Dad made it all go away. You can do a lot with money, but you can't bring back dead sons, or hide from the world. I swear the softmind behind the syndicated newsfeeds took delight in linking a proud old family to a young son going off the rails in a messy gangland killing. There was page after page of online stories with trash headlines like 'Do you know what your sons get up to? This father didn't.'

"Penn. State closed the doors on me in record time after the news came out. Dad did his best to hide how he felt, he bought me the ticket here, but he had lost one son and the other might as well be dead."

Jonah trailed off into silence.

Amos said nothing when he had finished, but continued to contemplate the Earth. Jonah sat next to him wondering what to say next.

The silence stretched until it became uncomfortable for Jonah. Why had he said those things? This old guy did not have the answers.

Amos rubbed the cross he wore. "Do you know the story of Anthony the Great from the Apophthegmata Patrum?"

"No, my family are Baptists."

"Our scholars call Anthony the Father of Monks. He struggled mightily with temptation. It is said the devil placed every conceivable sin of the flesh before him. The scriptures say one day, he reached the stage where his torment became too much for him to bear." Amos put a hand on Jonah's shoulder. "Perhaps you too have reached this point."

"What did he do?"

"He sought enlightenment and purpose. The stories say he took his suffering to be a sign from God and sought wisdom in the scriptures."

"I'm not saying that a voice from on high will guide you, but perhaps you too can find a higher purpose."

The old monk stood and walked away leaving Jonah to contemplate the barren majesty of the Valles Mares.

The sins of the flesh. Amos had a point. It was the craving for a fix that drove him to do dumb things. Jonah hands trembled with an urge to open a bag of tarf before he stopped himself. How long had it been since his last hit? He had been so busy running; he had not had time to consider smoking up. The days of hard living had scoured something inside him. The deep hunger was more like a mild itch he didn't need to scratch.

He looked again at the Earth hanging in the black sky. What was it he wanted? Would a higher purpose save him from the tarf? He couldn't see himself living like Amos.

He cared about Amira and Doaran. They had survived the sack of Beddau together. He worried about Lucien, even if he was weird. He didn't deserve to be locked in whatever prison Wang had created. More than anything, he wanted to get back at Wang for everything he had done.

Wang and his droids were a real piece of work. He would need the whole Beddau team if they were to have a chance. He wondered where the rest of the fighting team was.

Amira had spoken about the old mines. What was that place called? Jokarah? Maybe there were Moon Folk there. Amira said they would spread out. If they could get there, he and Doaran could train up a new team. There would be no scrapping in the tunnels this time. This was war. Wang had to be stopped.

Jonah cast one last look at the blue marble that had been his home. It was beautiful, but now was the time to put his childhood aside. There were things to do.

He went to find the others.

"We should go to Jokarah."

Chapter 19

The Lady of Jokarah

The seat was uncomfortable, even through the padded layers of her exposure suit. Yesha wasn't surprised. The makeshift bucket shape had been fabricated from aluminium off-cuts.

The buggy swung in time to the undulating ripples in the dust. She aimed toward flat terrain that would make for easier travel.

Somewhere deep beneath the studded wheels, Yutu's Burrow wormed its serpentine path through the ancient lava plain of Mare Imbrium. If she traced her steps across the top of the lava tube, it would be the quickest way back towards Beddau.

Beddau was her safest bet. Wang would have spread news of her death and would stop at nothing if he found her at Chang'e.

Yesha adjusted her direction toward where she thought

Beddau lay and edged the throttle further. The ancient bootleg vehicle leapt forward as it made short work of the low hills. The distance flew by so much faster than the days she had spent walking.

She checked her bearings against the foothills of the Montes Alpes. Beddau lock was beyond the angular slope with the rubble slide to the right.

The buggy crested the last of the hills and there before her stood the lock accompanied by two survey buggies and a pack of some weird droid. Curious, she slowed to study the scene.

A figure in an exposure suit climbed out of a buggy and started with surprise at the sight of her. The person gesticulated to someone still in the buggy and a second figure emerged. They did something and the droid pack swarmed towards her.

She reached out with her memplant and sensed an odd shared mind that carried a latent hostility. At present, it noted her as threat to be evaluated.

She gave the droids a mental command to move away and the pack mind considered it.

Her mental focus faltered as she gasped—the droids were autonomous, military grade battle-minds.

She took a deep breath to loosen the knot in her diaphragm. Droids, return to the gate.

A flicker of communication, too quick for her to follow, flashed through her memplant.

What were these things?

The shared mind transmitted assent in a wave that echoed in her mind as the droids faded from view. Dust trails rose from invisible feet and arrowed toward the gate.

Yesha turned the buggy around and rode for the dunes. She wasted no time, slamming the accelerator forward and clung to the steering wheel as it bucked and shuddered in her hands. The buggy crested the second dune with such speed that all four wheels left the ground and, for a moment, she flew above the dunes. The landing came with a crash that shuddered right through her frame.

She dropped the accelerator to half power, and the buggy no longer threatened to leave the ground. She looked back and whooped. The dunes behind her were empty of Wang's men and invisible droids.

Raw vibration thrummed through the steering wheel from the old-fashioned hydrogen engine. The shuddering vehicle felt so strange compared to the quiet efficiency of electric engines.

Where should she go now? Beddau remained off limits as were the domes of Chang'e.

Wang and his cohorts used whatever those droids were to drive any opposition away. She did not know what Wang had found, but battle-minds were notorious. They made kill decisions with no human input. There was something very disturbing about a mind created without the need for love. What would stop them killing without mercy if their logic demanded it?

The hills sloped down to a shallow ravine filled by lava from a long-forgotten cataclysm. A fine layer of dust covered the lava, hiding it in the eons-long rainfall of stars. The buggy wheels stirred up eddies of the grey powder that hung as a faint plume behind her as she passed.

Every place she had tried was closed off to her. Time to try something new.

Generations of miners had hollowed out the great chain of the Montes Alpes. Each generation dug deeper and further than the one before them. The next mine along the line of hills was Jokarah, a mine once important for its supplies of lead, but long since mined out. Jokarah was now a hollow shell, abandoned like so much before it.

Yesha hoped for a supply of air to refresh the suit. She had several hours in reserve, but a resupply would be reassuring.

The mine entrance was a shallow cave with the airlock positioned well back. It was a significant lock designed to take mining trucks. Yesha took several minutes to locate the control mechanism. When she activated it, she half expected nothing to happen, but the great door irised open. She drove the buggy into the mountain and the door closed behind her. The lock cycled for several minutes.

She noted with surprise that a deep bass roar emanated from the engine block. Interesting, there was air in the mine. She had assumed it would be the vacuum of lunar atmosphere.

The centre of the inner door expanded in front of her.

A dark cavern opened behind the lock. Fallen rock and the leftover detritus of human occupation littered the floor. Yesha took off her helmet. The clean air had a faint scent of rock dust. She couldn't smell any hint of hydraulic fluid or the acrid tang of machine grease, nothing she associated with a working mine. Her breath came out in a cloud in the freezing air.

No one had worked here for a long time. She wound up the emergency torch. It provided a feeble pool of light. The buggy would have to crawl at its slowest through the rubble.

She chose the clearest path she could find. This mine stretched much further than Beddau. Side tunnels sloped off left and right as she travelled deeper, the occasional tunnel led up or down to other levels. Yesha swung the torch beam from side to side, as she searched for food, water, anything.

She reached an area where smaller side tunnels branched

off at regular intervals. She decided to continue straight ahead and investigate the other tunnels later. At one junction, she thought she spotted the white flash of a face reflecting the torchlight. She dismissed it as her mind playing tricks on her in the low light, but the further she rode the more it bothered her.

Rubble no longer littered the floor this far into the mine. She turned the buggy around and pushed the accelerator. The buggy leapt forward with the wail of a hundred demons coming from the engine as sound reverberated through the air-filled environment.

She swerved into the tunnel scanning ahead with the torch. A flurry of furtive limbs disappearing behind a packing case rewarded her observation.

She pulled up next to the packing case and turned off the engine.

"Hello, I'm Yesha. What's your name?"

"Barney," said a grave young voice from behind the packing case. "Is that dragon you are riding?"

Yesha giggled. "No, it's an old-fashioned kind of buggy. Would you like to see it?"

A small boy of ten or twelve years emerged.

"What are you doing in this old tunnel?"

"Mum said we had to look for water and food."

"Aren't you afraid of the dark?"

"No. Mum gave me special torch. All I have to do is wind it up and I can see." He held up a battered emergency torch.

Yesha held up her own torch. "I've got one just like it."

Barney favoured her with his own shy smile.

"Why don't you hop up next to me and we can go find your Mum?"

Barney's eyes widened as if she had promised him the best

present possible. He climbed up next to her and stood on a fairing, his small fingers curled tight around a support strut.

Yesha fired up the engine and pushed the buggy to a slow roll. Barney clung to the strut as though his life depended on it, but his eyes shone with excitement.

The tunnel gave way to a three-way split. Barney pointed to the leftmost tunnel which opened into a large anteroom before it continued upwards into the heart of the mountain. They climbed for a few minutes and the tunnel ended in a similar anteroom. The remains of several machines filled this chamber. Barney grabbed her shoulder and motioned she should stop.

He jumped off. "Mum. Come out Mum. It is only me."

A small wiry woman emerged from behind a longwall trencher.

"Hello, I'm Yesha. You must be Barney's mother."

"Oh! Thank the heavens. I… I thought you were them." She stopped. "Where are my manners? My lady, I am Elizabeth."

"Why do you call me lady? I'm no one special."

"Forgive me, your voice marks you as Dome folk and you are roaming surface at your leisure. Only rich can do that."

"You're from Beddau?"

"Yes, my lady. We were, until they came…"

The woman looked to be on the verge of crying.

"Why don't you hop up her with us and we can drive to your home?"

Elizabeth wrung her hands. Yesha was surprised, did people still do that? "My lady, we have nothing. It is just me and boy."

"Where is everyone else?"

"I don't know," she sobbed. "So much screaming. We ran

when they came. Into dark, down long tunnel to Jokarah. We have been here two maybe three day-cycles. I am not sure, darkness confuses me."

Yesha held out her hand. "I have a little fuel left. It may last a while, we can use it to search for others who have made it this far."

Elizabeth climbed up next to her. Yesha handed her the torch, with Barney holding the other torch, they could light up the way and make decent time.

The tunnels ran for miles through the heart of the mountain, mute testament to decades of hard work. Yesha thought any direction was as a good as another until they knew where they were going.

After a few hours of traversing empty tunnels, they found a woman with two young daughters clutching her skirts. The woman had groped her way along the wall after their light failed. They fell in behind the buggy and walked in silence. Yesha could only imagine the terror of feeling along these walls with no idea of where they were going.

Three hours later, a voice greeted her from the dark of a side passage.

"Get down off buggy girl. We need it."

The man had a smear of dirt across one cheek. He and his companion stood blinking in the torchlight. They looked as if they had slept in their rough clothing for days.

Yesha looked him direct in the eyes. She drew as hard as she could on the stern countenance that Uncle used to reprimand people. "I will do no such thing. Take us to your camp at once."

The man recoiled as if he had turned over a rock and found a scorpion under it.

"You looks like one of us, but you speak like Dome folk."

"That's not important. I know how to drive this buggy, and I'm sure you don't. I'm Yesha, why don't we work together?"

The man turned to his companion who shrugged and Yesha knew she had sized them up the right way. He introduced himself as Ivar and his friend as Deeva. They had no camp, but were making their way towards the Eastern quadrant of the upper levels. He had heard Beddau folk had established a holding there. They had no food, but had located a small pool of water.

Yesha pondered the man's words as they moved. What had driven these people to be so low? Were they treated so badly by the Administration? And by extension was Uncle so harsh in the way he ruled them?

A floor further up they met a group of six, also making their way towards the new settlement. Elizabeth stepped out in front and introduced the lady Yesha. Yesha cringed.

At the topmost level, the mine opened into a cavern so vast it swallowed their voices without echo. Their weak lights made fitful attempts to stab the dark, but revealed no sides to the cave.

Yesha suggested they make toward what she thought was east. The group spread out in a wedge behind her as they walked.

It was at least an hour before they encountered a room and column structure that started an excited chatter among the Beddau folk.

A bright light speared out from deeper in the columns. Yesha turned off the buggy and stepped down.

"Who is it?" said a deep voice from the darkness behind

the glare. An imposing Earther, silhouetted by the light, strode towards them.

"Brecka? Is that you?" Ivar ran forward and hugged the man like a long-lost brother. He turned to the small crowd. "Brecka was my neighbour in Beddau. Brecka, this is Lady Yesha."

"Just Yesha," she said, blushing.

"Welcome all. We have little, but if you follow me, we will feed you and find you a place to rest."

They walked deeper into the columns, Ivar and Brecka chatting as they went. Brecka told them how a small group of Beddau residents had been building up Jokarah in their spare time as a hobby. They had limited power and water. Enough for the few people who escaped. The group shared their stories of Wang and his droids, how they paralysed a brother with their stingers. How they bound another's young neighbour.

Yesha noticed that Elizabeth and Barney stayed close to her. "Where is Barney's father?"

"I don't know. Droids stung him when they first got here. I watched him fall and those awful things wrapped him in tape. They took him away. Now he is a prisoner, or…"

Yesha put a hand on her shoulder and Elizabeth leant in grateful for the comfort.

Elizabeth drew herself up and nodded towards a loose knot of Moon Folk gathered around the dim pool of light cast by emergency lighting. Yesha understood, she went and sat in the grey dust along with the others.

"What should we do?" The question was a common one.

She stood. Faces turned toward her at once both anxious and hopeful. What would Uncle do for his people if he were here?

"We need to find those who are still lost in the tunnels, and we need to know where we are in this big mine."

An attentive silence met her statement.

"Gather in small teams and take at least two torches with you. Make one of them an emergency torch if you can. Go in opposite directions and try to map the tunnels as you go."

People spoke in soft murmurs to each other. Some cast an occasional glance at where she stood.

Ivar spoke for them. "Yes lady, we will do it."

"Take food and water. People will be desperate by now."

They rose and set about preparing to do as she suggested.

Elizabeth tugged her sleeve. "Shahin would like to speak to you, lady."

Yesha followed her to a section of the settlement that the survivors had set up to prepare food. An old woman sat there, shelling beans.

"I will leave you now, lady," said Elizabeth withdrawing from their immediate vicinity.

"Why so they call me that silly name? I've tried to get them to stop."

"Did you notice how the folk listened to you at the meeting?"

"I said what I thought would help."

"They have lost what they had in Beddau." Shahin raised her arms to encompass the grey columns. "This barren hole is no substitute."

"Many have lived quiet, comfortable lives. They don't understand what it is like when war cuts you off from everything. They need a leader to guide them through the hard times that are coming."

Yesha sat down next to the old woman and clasped her hands around her knees.

"There must be someone better than me."

Shahin sat silent as she sorted the beans. "The

administrator's raid scattered the Beddau council. The people don't know where their leaders are."

"If you don't lead them another will try. Weigh these people as leaders. Do any of them appear capable of telling you what to do?"

"What if I make the wrong decision?"

"That will happen, and you will learn and grow from it." Shahin put the beans down and rose. "I am too old to fight another war. The last one took everything I have. You have the strength child, and I see wisdom hidden in your young face." She pointed to the beans.

"We have enough to last a while, but as more people come the need for food will be dire. Jokarah possessed a market garden towards the end. One of the teams you sent out may find it."

Yesha rose. "If we can find it, can you help the people to grow something?"

"Of course, one thing we Quashqai have always been good at is bringing life to barren places."

Yesha walked off, troubled by the conversation. Uncle would know how best to lead the people of Beddau, but Uncle and his man Wang had brought misery to the Moon Folk. What could she do for them?

She could only do what she had done for herself. Air, food, water and a place to stay. If she helped them find the essentials, it would be a start. She also wanted them to be safe, but that was beyond her power to grant. She put that troubling thought to the back of her mind and focused on what she could do now.

The first teams had already returned when she got back, and they brought people with them, dozens of people. Yesha found Ivar and Brecka and got them to arrange food and sleeping mats for the new arrivals. Much later Elizabeth placed a gentle hand on her shoulder.

"You should rest, my lady."

Elizabeth's words sunk in and Yesha realised how bone weary she was. She allowed Elizabeth to lead her towards the part of the settlement dedicated to sleeping.

Around them, exhausted families slept where they lay on the floor. Few possessed bedding of any sort. Elizabeth led her through the sleepers to a makeshift cubicle constructed out of green and orange sheets of Moonsilk. Elizabeth parted the silks to reveal a thin mat.

"A family brought these, and they decided that you should have them."

Tears welled in Yesha's eyes as she crawled into the cubicle. Elizabeth drew the hangings closed behind her and Yesha plunged into an emerald sea divided by beams of orange that glowed in the few soft lights of the settlement.

These people deserved so much more than she had done. Tomorrow she would do better for them. She fell asleep mulling over how she could get food and more comfortable accommodation to them.

Yesha woke to the sound of many voices. How many more had joined them while she slept? She parted the hangings and Elizabeth rushed over with a cup of khar.

"Good morning, my lady. Did you sleep well?"

Yesha mumbled that she had. Elizabeth started a barrage of chatter about the new arrivals and the crowd of people that already waited for her. She made Yesha a bowl of soaked grains. Yesha thought it was the most delicious thing she had ever tasted after the days of raw rabbiton.

The crowd waiting for her was big enough to make her

weary before she had even started. They set up an immediate clamour when they saw her. This one's teenage son pestered that one's daughter. This family deserved more food, and that grandmother suffered aches and pains from the cold floor.

Yesha listened for as long as she could before she raised her hands and yelled, "Stop!"

The people looked at her in surprise, but stood quiet. She took a deep breath. This was the hard bit. "Has anybody found the growing area?"

They shuffled nervously and had the grace to look embarrassed. A man pushed through the crowd.

"We did. It is two floors down and to North." The man introduced himself as Ellas. "Whole area is much bigger than what we had at Beddau, but is dead. Has been no light or water for decades, all that we found was mushrooms."

That was a problem. Without light and water, nothing grew.

Back when Jokarah worked, it would have had power to drive the life-giving machinery. She needed time to think.

"Ellas, take the energetic younger people with you and show them the growing area. Bring back as many mushrooms as you can carry. Tonight, we eat mushroom stew."

The people left as she had asked, and she found herself alone with Elizabeth and Ivar. Barney sat at her feet listening to the adults talk.

"Barney, have you noticed the air?"

He shook his head. She addressed herself to the adults. "How is it that the air in here does not get stale?" Elizabeth shrugged, but Ivar picked up a handful of dust from the floor and dropped it. The dust fell as a fine grey powder that drifted in a slight diagonal to the floor.

"See how it does not fall straight down?" he said. "There is airflow in here. Too slow for us to notice, but definite movement in air. I bet if I follow direction I can find a source."

Yesha smiled. "Don't be gone too long or you'll miss the mushroom stew."

Ivar did not get back in time for the stew, he did not get back at all that evening. A pang of guilt for sending him out like that assailed her, but her guilt had to compete with a need to sleep. The rich, hearty mushroom stew filled her stomach and dragged her eyelids down.

The next day-cycle he still had not returned by the afternoon when she was once again caught up in people's petty squabbles. She was tetchy and on the point of making that clear when Ivar strode back in with family of four in tow.

"Good news," he said. "I had to walk to lowest levels, but I found air plant and there is helium reactor powering it. It is on, but operating at minimal capacity, just turning air over."

"Excellent."

"Wait, my lady. I have more news. Power plant has conduits run to other floors. It has taken me this long to check. Plant can power water pumps that drain sump on lowest level and it might power all dead lighting we see on every floor."

She dismissed everyone except for Ivar and Elizabeth.

"Elizabeth, please ask Shahin to join us. Ivar, do you know of anyone who knows about power plants?"

"My friend Deeva is tiffy. He helped old Gerry to run plant in Beddau. I don't think he could fix one himself, but he knows some."

Yesha asked him to fetch Deeva.

The group assembled. Yesha saw four faces who were less lost; four people with a fraction of the answers she needed. Perhaps if she helped them, they could be the beginnings of a group who helped her with all the things she did not know.

"Deeva, can you start the power plant?"

"Dunno, lady. If it got much helium then sure. Maybe running near empty in maint mode."

"Where can we get more helium?"

"We steals it from New Karakorum. Be hard now with all droids."

"We'll have to think of something." She turned to Shahin. "Let's say we get the lights and water running. How long before we can harvest food?"

"If we have miracle rice, about three weeks."

Three weeks? They would starve.

Chapter 20

Bitter Reunion

"Wake up, lady. Come quick."

Yesha woke to an excited hubbub. She walked through to the common area where a large group of people circled three newcomers, dressed in odd-looking enviro-suits.

"I know you. You're Jonah, the Panamerican."

"Hi Yesha. I didn't expect to find you here."

He had changed. A hard determination had replaced the haunted look she had seen when they first met. The soft earth-boy puppy fat had melted from his frame. She looked in his eyes a moment too long.

"Where's Lucien?"

Pain etched lines on Jonah's face. "They got him… when they raided Beddau. This is his aunt, Amira, and this is Doaran."

"You are welcome to all we have, such as it is."

"What are they eating?" asked Amira.

A shrewd question. Yesha eyed the woman with interest. Amira had thought through the extended consequences, not just her immediate needs.

"We have a day-cycle or two's worth of supplies and whatever mushrooms they can forage from the lower levels. The bigger problem is light." She told them about the fusion generator.

Jonah looked at Doaran. "We've got three suits. If we can find one of the team we had, we could sneak back into Bedau and liberate enough helium to power Jokarah." He told Yesha how the Moon Folk had adapted Krav Maga for their use. "Five of us can take on Wang and his men."

Yesha shook her head. She told them of the hydrogen buggy and the droids she had encountered at Beddau lock. "They're some kind of battle-mind. It was weird, almost like they thought I was harmless."

"You should come with us," said Jonah. "If you tell the droids we are no threat, maybe we can sneak in and out without being caught."

"I can't," she said. "I need to keep the people busy. There is despair and rage below their calm acceptance. If they don't have work, they will dwell on the emptiness of their fate."

Amira spoke, "I used to be part of Moon Folk council."

Tears welled before Yesha could stop them. "I tried." A hollow lightness bloomed inside her. "They need so much. I have so little to give."

Amira touched her arm. "I know."

"Forgive me, you must be hungry."

"It can wait," Amira said. "Go with Jonah and find food for us. I will do what I can for people."

"Could you guide them while I'm away?"

"If I have day-cycle or two to learn what is going on with people and supplies."

"We'll need at least that," said Yesha. She described the water cracker she had used to charge the buggy. "We can set one up using the power from the fusion generator, but it will be slow while the generator is in maintenance mode."

The group settled in to plan the raid. After much discussion, Ivar and Brecka raided the scrap piles and built a serviceable trailer from what they had scavenged. It would carry a lot more supplies.

Three hours later, the buggy tore across the low hills; Jonah grasped the frame of the buggy as it rocked and shuddered in his hands. He braced as they hit a large ditch. A low gravity crash would still hurt at this speed.

They shared their adventures as they travelled. Jonah told her of his epic journey since the explosion in Lucien's rooms, how Wang arrested Lucien, and the long walk to Alsatia. Yesha told them all about Yutu's Burrow, eating rabbitons, and Wang. Jonah swore to himself. He didn't know how yet, but somehow Wang would pay.

Jonah's arms ached by the time the buggy crossed a low rise and Beddau lock loomed in front of them. Four of the weird droids patrolled the entrance.

Yesha stopped the buggy, and they waited to see if there was any traffic through the lock. No one came.

After a few hours Yesha climbed down from the buggy. "Wait here until I tell you it is safe. I'm not sure how they will react to you."

She walked towards the droids until they moved in response to her presence. Then she sat in a loose cross-legged pose.

Jonah and Doaran watched the droids weave across the open space like giant spiders until they were up close to the lone figure. She had nowhere to run. He looked at Doaran who raised her hands in the envirosuit equivalent of a shrug.

Yesha didn't move. The droids settled in to a slow weaving pattern around her. Their tracks spoke of random geometries, precise yet meaningless to a human eye. Their circling slowed until the droids had almost stopped.

This was it. If they were going to attack, they would do it now. Jonah strained forward, fearing for Yesha's safety. The droids executed an abrupt turn and ran back to the entrance.

"You can bring the buggy down now," she said.

Jonah fumbled his way into the driver's chair. "How did you do that?"

"I didn't know if I could, until now. They are strange. The group decided we are safe." Yesha's voice came slow and distant as if she had woken from a deep sleep.

They entered the airlock with Jonah and Doaran in front. There was no way of knowing who or what they would find inside. The lock was empty.

Jonah remained tense as the lock cycled. The inner door opened on a vacant reception area.

"Where is everyone?" aid Jonah.

"Mines or prison, I guess," said Doaran. "Administrator cannot spare too many men."

"More droids then," said Jonah.

He was right. They saw a group a few minutes later. Five of them crossed the far end of the open space.

"Quick! Hide here," said Yesha pointing to a gap behind one of the support pillars.

"Can't you… you know?" asked Jonah.

"Too far," she whispered.

Jonah got it. The droids were far enough away they might

not be seen. They waited. After a while the droids skittered off down a side passage.

The empty stalls of the market bore mute testimony to the recent past. To Jonah the silence was the worst. The market area was devoid of the bubbling conversation that used to fill it. Silk hangings fluttered in the airflow. Nothing else moved.

"Collect all the dry food," said Yesha. "Leave the wet stuff it will just boil off in the vacuum."

Jonah walked from stall to stall accompanied by the overripe smell of rotting fruit. The stalls towards the centre were more productive, at one he found bags of dried noodles, at another a whole sack of beans. The others had more luck. Yesha and Doaran returned carrying a heavy sack of rice between them.

He asked Yesha how many people they were trying to feed.

"About a hundred-and-twenty," she said.

"This will never be enough."

"We are dumb," said Doaran. "This is market stall. Stores are up on garden level."

"Then let's go there," said Jonah. "If we can get around the droids."

Yesha was more pragmatic. "This will take forever if we carry one bag at a time. Doaran, how did they bring the bags down to market?"

"Old Yanni used to walk them down in wheelbarrow. I think I know where he kept it."

The wheelbarrow was a battered aluminium relic of the mining days. The wheel wobbled on its axle and gave an intermittent creak that sounded deafening in the silence.

"We'll have to scout ahead or the droids will hear us."

Jonah suggested that he took point and Doaran the rear while Yesha pushed the barrow. As long as it was clear in front they could make as much noise as they needed.

The idea worked until a metallic clicking echoed off the walls behind him. A droid stepped out from behind a pillar. Jonah froze. The droid turned left and right as if it sensed something but couldn't see it. Further back Yesha spotted the droid and froze. The droid clattered across the dust towards Yesha and seized her arms in its manipulator claws. The wheelbarrow fell to the floor, forgotten.

Jonah cast around for a weapon. He found a rock and sprinted toward her.

"No! Wait."

The droid reached for her. Jonah's memplant registered an incoherent shriek of information.

Yesha's eyes lost focus. Her mouth opened in surprise.

Two metallic claws retracted with a high-pitched whine. The droid walked retreated behind a column.

"They know me," said Yesha. "I don't know what that means."

They took more care after that.

The store on the garden level was easy to find. It was the only building among the neat rows of plants. The granary was half full of rice. Jonah and the others filled bags. It was mind-numbing work.

It took three trips to load the buggy and trailer. Three careful, slow passages to avoid the droids. At the end of it Jonah was aching all over and hungry enough to eat the dry rice.

"How long will this feed us for?" He asked Yesha as they drove away.

"A week, maybe ten day-cycles if we keep a tight grip on the rations."

Jonah groaned. It was nowhere near enough.

"And we still have to find helium."

"We need more people," said Yesha

"Turn around," said Doaran. "Jonah how many suits did you see at airlock?"

Jonah grinned at her through the faceplate. "Enough. I'm sure we can fit a few on here."

Hours later they delivered the food and suits to Jokarah. Amira rushed over to greet them.

"We found good haul of mushrooms today," she said. "What did you find in Beddau?"

Yesha lifted a grain bag from the trailer and held it out to the assembling crowd.

"Come and see." She tore open the top of the bag and golden rice poured out onto the ground. "We're having mushrooms and rice tonight."

"Miracle rice," said Shahin from within the crowd. "Child, this is so much more than a meal."

Amira strolled towards the nearest pillars and motioned for Yesha and Jonah to follow. "That was clever gesture," she said to Yesha.

"Someone once taught me that symbols are important."

Jonah kept quiet. Amira's face suggested something more serious than rice was being discussed.

Amira leaned her back against a pillar. "Shahin told me how you organised people when you first arrived. She thinks you should lead us."

Yesha crossed her arms. "What about the council?"

"Beddau council was fine body for making slow considered decisions. Could spend days deliberating rules of market garden. Do you see garden here?

"Shahin tells me people respect you. I feel we need boldness to lead us through troubled times. Are you brave enough to help us?"

"I don't know." A shiver ran through Yesha's frame. "But, I'll do my best, if you will help."

Amira stood erect, "I shall do whatever I can to help people of Beddau."

Yesha took Jonah's hand. "Let's find out what mushroom and rice stew tastes like." Her voice was light, but he felt the way her hand shook.

The simple stew exploded flavours across Jonah's starved tastebuds. It was over far too soon. With something solid in his stomach for the first time since Alsatia he curled up on an empty rice sack and was asleep in seconds.

The next day-cycle Jonah found Amira with Deeva, the old tiffy. Parts of dismembered envirosuits surrounded them. To Jonah they bore a disturbing resemblance to human body parts.

"We think we can get another three working," she said. "Would bring total to six. If only few more of Lucien's group had made it. Team like that could do lot."

Jonah sat next to them and watched the assembly. Amira and Deeva were stripping each suit and checking for any minute defect.

"Deeva, you said you used to steal helium for Beddau. How'd you do that?"

"We always sneaked to New Karakorum. Brings back one cylinder at time."

"Would one cylinder be enough?"

Deeva put down the neck seal he was repairing. "We only ever stole one at time, but you needs to find four. Then we can light all caatcha out of Jokarah."

Jonah watched them work. The next raid would be harder. They had six suits and no guarantee all of them worked either. The suits were too big a risk. What else?

"Amira, do you think we could walk to Beddau?"

"Yes. It would be two day-cycles, but if droids are only guards left, then I do not see why not."

If they walked in, he could take several more people. A small team would make the long walk to New Karakorum, and a much bigger team to raid the grain stores. It would be hard going, but with food and water it would be easier than the walk he and Lucien had done. He went to find Yesha.

Brecka had applied his talent for handicraft to convert packaging material into a respectable seat. Yesha sat in it while the people of Jokarah seated themselves on the floor around her.

"I think I know how we can get the helium," said Jonah. He explained his thinking about walking in through the tunnels.

"How will you get past the droids?"

"We'll be as silent as mine walls."

Yesha called others and told them his plan. Ivar suggested making sleds from scrap metal they had found.

"That way we can carry lots of food."

Two day-cycles later, at the entrance to Beddau's garden area, Jonah shook Ivar's hand.

"Good luck," he whispered. "We'll see each other back in Jokarah."

Jonah, Doaran and the strongest two men Jonah could find spent another two day-cycles walking through the dark passage to New Karakorum.

Jonah stepped out from behind the rock wall and looked at the ramp leading up to the mine. It had changed so much from when he was last here. No, that wasn't right. The walls of the mine looked no different, it was he who had changed, the old Jonah was so long ago.

"This way," he said, keeping his voice low. "We turn the lights off now and feel our way to Level Eleven."

Jonah groped for the wall. The darkness no longer bothered him. He smiled to think he had found the slope hard to distinguish on that day with Lucien. His legs were accustomed to low gravity now. He counted three doors before Doaran stopped him at the next door.

"We need to look more like miners," she said and opened the door.

The bright light inside blinded Jonah for a moment and then he saw a large utility area. Doaran motioned for them to be quiet. She led them across to a service door. Beyond lay a change room with storage lockers. Jonah grinned at her. "You've done this before."

Dressed in blue and orange mining coveralls, the four of them headed to the elevator. Groups of other miners stood waiting at the door. Jonah was glad of the crush of bodies that jammed the elevator cab when it arrived. The watching cameras would struggle to pick them out from the thirty tired, sweaty men who crowed in with them. He jabbed at the button for Level Eleven.

Eleven was very much like the other levels, raw rock walls and dull overhead lighting.

Doaran led them straight towards a machine shop. She did not stop to look around, but clumped across the diamond mesh floor toward a workbench as though she meant to be there. Jonah copied her. No one looked twice at someone who gave the impression of knowing where they were going. At the bench Doaran picked an impact driver and on the pretext of checking it, murmured to Jonah, "Find us two big locker-boxes."

Jonah looked around and saw several large metal locker-boxes on the floor.

"Will those do?"

"Yeh. Make sure they empty."

Jonah opened a few boxes before he found an empty one. He found a second containing a few hand-tools.

"OK boys," said Doaran loud enough for passers-by to overhear. "Bring tools. We go fix flywheel."

The four of them carried the two boxes out of the machine shop and down a long corridor that opened into a cavernous facility filled with automated machinery. Yellow stack-bots transferred long grey cylinders across the floor to the far wall. A host of waiting storage hoppers received the cylinders. White metal hoppers occupied an entire wall of the facility. Jonah recognised the loading dock from his studies. The system would lock the hoppers once they were full and transfer them to the railgun for insertion into low earth orbit.

Doaran walked to the nearest hopper. She waited for the stack-bot to leave. Jonah saw the plan at once. He pulled the locker-box close to the hopper and opened it. Doaran lifted the cylinder the droid had deposited and stashed it in the locker-box. Jonah shut the lid as if he had just reached for a tool and was back at work.

They filled each locker-box with two cylinders then picked them up and walked back as though they had finished a round of routine maintenance.

"Right boys, time we fixed pump on deep level."

They left the machine shop and made for the elevator. Doaran pressed the down button. The doors opened on five Earthers in security uniforms.

"Going down?"

"Papers first, moonos." The guard held out his right hand with an unpleasant sneer.

Jonah seized the hand with his left and pulled hard. The guard stumbled forward. Jonah pulled him past and hammered two fast left-right punches into the guards back and followed by kicking the soft spot at the back of the man's knee. The guard fell backward into Doaran's knee strike. The knee connected to his head with a sickening thud.

Doaran dropped her end of the locker-box. She flew past Jonah making for the other guards. Jonah pivoted towards the next guard. He sent a low kick at the man's groin. The kick landed with a solid thump that left the guard on the floor, gasping for air.

The elevator became a compressed box of destructive chaos. Doaran traded a flurry of punches with the man she had engaged with. Jonah stepped around her to get at the other two. A wild haymaker flew past him and thudded into the side of Doaran's head. She crumpled like a wet sack.

Jonah roared in an incoherent animal rage. He swung around in a reverse hammer-blow that connected with the man's temple. He spun in the opposite direction to take on the remaining two. The two Moon Folk had them cornered. He strode over, his fists clenched. "This will only end one way."

The man on the left nodded. "We'll leave you. Let us take our friends."

Jonah stepped through and hit the man hard. The others got the remaining guard in a choke hold and waited for him to stop struggling.

"Get them out. We have to move."

Jonah slung Doaran over his shoulders and dragged their locker-box into the elevator.

She came to as Jonah was dragging her from the elevator,

on the lowest level. Doaran staggered onto the ramp clinging to Jonah. It made for slow progress with Jonah dragging the locker-box.

Two day-cycles later, they snuck back into the Beddau market area. Jonah couldn't believe they had done it. The raid was a success. Perhaps it was not so strange, New Karakorum was a big mine with many people. A spirit of anonymity did exist in its crowds.

Chapter 21

Augmentation

The eloquent absence of voices shrouded the prison complex in a silence that told Wang everything was in order. Sixty of the worst offenders waited behind the twin rows of toughened glass doors. They knew better than to make any noise while he was nearby. He stopped outside a cell and watched the occupant struggle to his feet.

"Yes, Jones, stand to attention when you are inspected. You don't want me to repeat your last reprimand, do you?"

Lucien stared back at him through swollen eyes. "No."

"Good, are you going to be more cooperative today?"

The moono glared at him with as much venom as he could muster. He spat at Wang. A meaningless gesture given the glass between them.

"You will spend a long time here."

A flicker of uncertain anger crossed the boy's face. Wang placed a hand on the glass that separated them.

"The Administration does not think much of those who fail to obey the rule of law. I think even less of them. Every time you overstep the line, you shall face retribution. I will be here to remind you of the insolence you showed me today."

He turned as if to walk away then stepped back.

"Base softmind, no food or water to cell 37B for the next twenty-four hours."

"Command has potential fatal outcomes," said a voice that issued from the walls. "Please confirm."

"Wang Mei, Base Security Coordinator, Override AM7654B."

The prisoner returned to his narrow cot and turned to face the wall. Wang noted the slumped shoulders and hands drawn under the chest.

Good, this one was close to breaking.

He walked towards the last recovery jar on the right. It contained a shrivelled wisp of dry husk, a thing long past recognition. It was time for a new occupant. Wang amused himself by imagining the Jones boy being sealed into that jar.

The pleasant daydream sustained him until he reached Chen's office.

The Earth hung low in the sky when Wang stepped into his office. Chen remained seated and did not offer Wang a seat. Let the man experience his displeasure.

"You said you had this situation under control."

Wang tried to strike a grovelling tone. "Administrator…"

"Silence, I have let you have your way for far too long." Chen stood, letting his formal posture mask his misgivings. He paced behind his desk. "Four cylinders of helium lost, continual theft from the Beddau stores, and now I hear the Free Moon movement is still active."

Chen stopped his pacing and fixed Wang with a grim stare. Wang paled. Chen let the silence stretch. "Philippa Lawson broke down and told me about your threats."

"I had good reason to suspect her."

"You had no such thing. You overstepped your mark. We will not treat foreign nationals with contempt."

Wang did his best to appear troubled, but Chen saw the smug air of satisfaction he could not hide.

Chen sat and forced his doubts behind a posture more rigid and formal. "Get out and see what you can do about the thefts in Beddau. Leave the rest to me."

Wang slouched out.

Chen slumped in his chair and let his shoulders sag. There was a time when his demeanour reduced thugs like Wang to quivering compliance. That was another Chen, one unbowed by age and grief.

Wang pondered the things that stood in his way as he walked. Let the old man think he was chastened. Chen was so close to retirement. If only he would go. The old man's return to Earth would give Wang the opportunity to show the Central Committee how the Moon should be run.

The loss of helium was inconsequential. Wang could find a perpetrator and fill the empty recovery jar. The public message would be a useful reminder to anyone else who might have similar ideas.

He needed to get the droids on to it, but first he had to correct their recent erratic behaviour. Independent battle-minds were great when they worked, and so frustrating when they didn't.

A flashing sign interrupted his musing. He had been so engrossed in thoughts of conquest he had walked clear across to Dome Seven. The sign announced the entrance to Cerata, one of several bars on Chang'e that catered to the less sophisticated worker. The bar lurked in a dismal hole at the back of the accommodation block, hidden from direct sunlight. Of all the rundown establishments that provided for the tastes of his rough youth, Cerata remained his favourite.

A warm miasma of beer and unwashed bodies flowed past him as he parted the heavyweight plastic curtain. Inside, men sat at rows of metal benches watching two men in the octagonal fighting cage that dominated the centre of the floor area. Cerata suited his mood; he wanted the satisfaction of slamming his fist into someone's face without the administrator interfering with rules and order.

The big German was facing up to a smaller blonde man in the cage. Wang didn't know the other man, but knew it wouldn't be long before the German won. He was right, it was less than a minute before the blonde one clawed the cage as he scrabbled to escape the German's choke hold.

Two moonos entered the cage and gave each other the nod that served as a formal bow.

Wang seated himself at a bench and added his name to the fight pool that appeared on the table monitor.

A nubile brunette walked over carrying a pitcher of beer and a credit reader. Wang leered at her outstanding enhancements. "Five credits for beer," she said and then smiled. "And, if you throw in another ten, I'll take my top off before I serve it."

Wang swiped fifteen. She poured beer into a plastic cup. A click of the button on her skin-tight top caused it to peel away into a micro-container hidden in her short skirt.

Perfect, taut breasts responded to the freedom of low gravity. The tarnished silver nipple in her left breast was a fascinating addition.

The top reappeared when she pressed the button again. "Let me know when you want another serve," she said as she walked to the next table.

Wang watched her saunter away then turned his attention to the fight.

A raucous commotion erupted from the far side of the room where a group of men stood knotted around a table. Wang wandered over and found two Earther miners sitting face to face in a tense arm-wrestling match.

"What's the book?" Wang asked his neighbour.

"No bets, Stephan and Arvind are testing each other to see who takes on the Bonecrusher."

"Who's that?"

The man flicked his eyes to the dim corner at the rear of the bar where a tall figure in a dark robe sat. The height of the man said he was a moono.

"Get on with it you two," said Wang clapping his fist into his other hand. "I'll take on the winner. I want a go at that freak."

He got his chance a short while later when Arvind, the stocky Indian, crashed his opponent's arm to the table. Wang swigged the last of his beer and sat.

Arvind gripped his hand with a sudden ferocity. Wang gave the man a wicked smile. Arvind had been on the Moon too long. His muscles had lost their Earther tone. The weakling lost ground from the start until Wang had Arvind's hand almost on the table. Arvind put all his effort into it. Wang responded by slamming the man's hand into the table.

"Ey, Bonecrusher, we got one for you."

The moono rose and walked across to their table. He

shed the bulky cloak he wore. Wang squared his shoulders and looked the Bonecrusher straight in the eye. The man was an augment, he had one normal arm and another twice the size. Chromed hydraulics glistened in the augmented arm.

Wang held up his hand. No way was he going to show fear to this freak.

"Are you ready?" The Bonecrusher did not smile. A metallic adaptor claw grasped Wang's hand.

The match ended before Wang had a chance to react. The hydraulics gave the man a merciless advantage.

"That's amazing," said Wang rubbing his shoulder. "Where did you get it?"

The augmented man waved the claw in front of Wang's face.

"Yeh, Lost mine in rock breaker. You goes to autodoc, and it takes care of it. Full nerve attachment and all."

Wang massaged his shoulder as he left Cerata. Hydraulic augmentation was a new development. It would give him an excellent reason to expand the crackdown if the moonos used it.

Chapter 22

Smoked Nylon

Jonah woke as the lights brightened into the day cycle. A hum of quiet conversation filled the air as others rose and went about their morning activities.

He walked to the communal food area and stood in line waiting for breakfast. The young woman serving, handed him a ball of sticky rice. Jonah knew better than to complain. They must survive on minimal rations until the new rice was ready to harvest.

"Here, drink this," said Amira handing him a cup of khar. "Can at least fill hole in your stomach for while."

Jonah took it with a grateful sigh and sat next to her. She said nothing, but her face told Jonah everything—Lucien was still lost.

"We'll get him back," he said.

Amira raised the tips of her fingers to her forehead as if her head held an unbearable weight.

Jonah reached out and put a hand on her shoulder. "I will find a way." He took his khar and went to find Yesha.

Yesha sat at her usual place, on the packing crate throne, making decisions for the people. Jonah stood there and watched. She had changed. How had the demure young woman he had met so many days ago, become this awe-inspiring fearless leader? He liked her forthright determination. There was something attractive about a lady who knew what was needed. She saw him and smiled.

"Good morning, lady."

"Oh please, Jonah, don't call me that. Everyone here calls me lady. I would like at least one person to think of me as Yesha." She held Jonah's gaze for longer than was polite then blushed and looked away. Elizabeth giggled.

Jonah wasn't sure what to make of Elizabeth. The woman was strange, the way she fawned over Yesha as if she were royalty.

He took a deep breath and dived in. "I think we should rescue Lucien and the others. It'll be dangerous and stupid, but Lucien saved my life. I owe him."

Yesha stood and walked to stand in front of him. Her dainty shoulders came almost equal to his own. At this distance, she had a faint perfume of turmeric and mushrooms.

"My Uncle is not an evil man. If it were up to him alone, I'm sure we could go ask for Lucien. Wang is different. He will kill you if he can."

She took his hand. "Are you sure you want to try this?"

"More than anything."

"I'll do what I can to help, but we have so little."

"Thank you, Yesha. I will get Lucien back."

She gave him a faint smile then turned to talk to Elizabeth.

Jonah walked away with the beginnings of a plan. If he freed Lucien, perhaps he could free the rest of the fighting team. With all of them back together and Yesha's ability to stop the droids, they had a real chance at taking down Wang and his men.

Scattered sleeping mats covered the floor in an untidy arc around the kitchen. Jonah found Doaran helping a family to stack away their possessions.

"I want to free Lucien and the rest of the fighting team. Are you up for it?"

Doaran stopped what she was doing. "I sorry, I don't think I can. Will be weeks before rice is ready to harvest. We need food. Somebody has to steal for them."

"I'm sorry, Doaran. I didn't think."

The surrounding people watched their conversation with dull eyes. Doaran was right. The people needed to eat, but that wasn't enough. They needed a story to tell each other, a tale of bravery. He knew what he had to do.

He drew himself up to his full height and tried to be the hulking Earther he hoped they saw.

"Yes, you must feed them," he said loud enough for everyone nearby to hear. "But, I need to free Lucien and I will be more successful if I go alone."

He walked away, aware that the curious eyes of one hundred people watched him go.

Let them watch him walk off, he thought. The people needed something to hope for, no matter how hopeless it might be.

Yesha and Amira were working side by side with Shahin in the garden on the lower levels when Jonah found them. Shahin had worked wonders in what two weeks ago, had been a barren dust field. Rows of verdant miracle rice grew interspersed with furrows that held some kind of bean.

"I came to say goodbye," he said.

The women put down their tools and stood around him. Yesha looked as if she wanted to say something, but Amira spoke first.

"Try to get to Dome Three, is clothing shop on second level called Bright Threads. Ask for old-world smoked nylon. Aramin, store owner, will know you are one of us."

Amira undid a slim silver chain from around her neck and withdrew a pyrolytic glass teardrop. The pendant threw shards of rose light as she handed it to him. "He has little reason to trust you. If you show Aramin, it may convince him."

Jonah thanked her. How far did the Moon Folk contacts extend into Chang'e?

Yesha clutched his arm. "Come, we have a few things that could be useful."

On the accommodation level, she gave him a bundle of rice balls and an emergency torch.

"Turn on your memplant," she said.

Jonah did as she asked, wondering how long it had been since he last connected to the web. There was no signal down here, but she transmitted something as a nearfield link.

"Those are my access codes. They should get you into most of Chang'e if my Uncle hasn't deactivated them."

Yesha stepped in close. Jonah lost himself in the brown motes he saw in her eyes.

"There is so little chance," she said. "If you get caught…"

"I won't. I have so much to come back to."

"If Wang captures you, promise me you'll tell my Uncle I'm alive. He deserves that much."

"I promise." He squeezed her hand. "I'll be back with Lucien and the others before you know it."

He gathered the few possessions he had and started the long walk to New Karakorum.

"Jonah." Her voice came soft from behind him. He turned.

"Be careful."

He nodded, unsure of what he could say.

The hike to New Karakorum was easier than he remembered. Food and rest made a huge difference to how much ground he covered.

In Beddau, he took care to avoid the droids. They passed his path in the distance five times. The last was a group of three that patrolled within a column width of him. He stood and held his breath as if the absence of breathing would keep them from spotting him. They kept going. Weird, it was almost as if they ignored him.

Previous droid encounters filled his mind as he slipped down the tunnel to New Karakorum. Wang had used military grade artificial intelligence when he constructed them. It made them fearsome opponents with their high speed and offensive capabilities. The authorities used droids in urban situations on Earth. Military droids learned to identify combatants with ease in most contexts. The capability to distinguish an enemy also let them ignore civilians. It was no good for an army of droids to kill the wrong people. The press would whip themselves into a frenzy over the image of rogue killer droids. Jonah saw the blue of his sleeve and realised he still wore the coverall from the helium raid. It was dirty and stained, but maybe the droids thought he was a technician. He would have to store that knowledge for another day.

After clambering over the rubble pile, Jonah inched along the ramp. Darkness gave way to imaginary lights. He wished he could turn the torch on, but the security cameras would be watching. As the third door raised a ridge under his fingers, he thought about the blue sleeve he had mused over earlier. Wasn't this the floor where Doaran had taken them to find the coveralls. He slipped inside hoping to find a clean coverall, but the change room door was locked.

The rest of the floor was as unproductive.

A rising clamour of voices interrupted his search. He needed to hide. The ramp entrance was the safest.

He hadn't gone five steps before a crowd of rough Earthers walked in behind him.

"Hoi, mate. Time to hit the bar," said one looking at him.

Jonah gawped. Twenty solid miners dressed just like him in blue coveralls, milled around the holding area.

"Err... OK."

He grinned, they were as dirty as he was, and looked like they wanted nothing more than a feed and a cold drink. Two things he related to with ease. He fell in with the group and they caught the elevator to the giant cavern on Level One. The men chattered and made fun of each other. Jonah learned they were Australians from the Western Desert. The rough crowd was here on a short-term contract and had taken quarters in the prefab huts on the top level.

The miners made a beeline from the elevator to a prefab hut made brighter by a string of garish lights draped across the front. Jonah followed them inside and found a plastic cup of rice wine being thrust into his hands. He drank it and then made excuses about seeing a friend.

"Hope she's a good-looking friend," said an anonymous voice from somewhere in the bar. He gave them a good-natured wave as he sauntered away.

The miners gave him an idea. He walked across to the sleeping huts and searched for those that appeared unoccupied. The first didn't suit his purposes, but in the second, he found clothing that was a match for his size and shape. He changed as quick as he could, offering a silent apology to whichever miner he robbed.

Outside he walked away as if nothing had happened. Now he was ready to be seen in Chang'e.

The railway was just as he remembered. Almost. A small moan of pleasure escaped his lips when he sat. How long had it been since he had sat in a padded seat? The high-density foam of the seat felt like a soft pillow. Outside the grey landscape flew past at a decent speed.

The train docked at Chang'e Station. Doors opened with a soft hiss of equalising pressure and Jonah caught the electric cinnamon air of the domes. Around him people gathered their belongings and walked off to their personal destinations.

The concourse of Dome Seven overflowed with well-dressed people going about their business. It appeared so different.

Jonah realised Chang'e had not changed, but he had. He didn't know what he was now, but he was no longer the lost young man who stepped onto the railway with Yesha all those days ago.

Three was a working-class dome. Cheap apartments lined the passages and the scent of frying spices wafted from open windows. Moon Folk kids made a merry racket as they played in wide spaces.

He found the shop on the second level. Bright Threads

nestled in the middle of a row of other stores that were common only in the variety of things they sold. One held cooking implements and canned soft drinks. The next had rows of vegetables and a pharmacy at the back. Bright Threads had clothes out front, but a noodle stall and a barber's chair inside the cramped shop.

"What would the gentleman care for?" The speaker was a weathered old Earther of middle-eastern appearance.

"Do you have any old-world smoked nylon?"

The man looked him up and down and then waved a hand at the barber's chair.

"I shall see if we can find any. Perhaps sir would like a shave and a haircut while he waits?"

Jonah rubbed the stubble on his chin. "Yes, that sounds good."

"Perhaps a wash before we start? Sir will find a wash basin in the back room."

Jonah blushed. He was filthy, and he guessed he smelled worse. The back room held a basin with a bar of soap and a soft towel.

Feeling much cleaner, he sat in the chair. The old man selected an old-fashioned hand clipper and got to work shortening Jonah's hair. He said nothing and Jonah was not inclined to ask.

Once Jonah's hair was tidy, the old man lathered up his beard and took out an ancient cut-throat razor. He started shaving Jonah and then turned the blade in towards Jonah's jugular. Jonah froze.

"I know most of the free Moon Folk, but I've never met you. Where did you learn that phrase?"

Jonah tried not to shudder. The man had not even raised his voice. "Amira told me."

"Amira Jones? Nonsense, she died along with everyone else at Beddau."

"The chain around my neck, look at the pendant."

The blade did not waver as the old man drew the pendant out from where Jonah had kept it. A sigh escaped the old man's lips. "We were so young when I gave her that."

"She survived and so did many others." Jonah told him the whole story of their escape, of finding Yesha and setting up to survive. "I think there's maybe a hundred of them in Jokarah. It's hard to say."

The razor stayed where it was. "And why are you here?"

"I'm going to free Lucien and the others from the cells. Amira said you might be able to help."

The old man continued to shave Jonah as if nothing had happened then cleaned his razor and packed it away before sitting on a chair across from him.

"What you are trying to do is difficult," he said. "The administrator has put them in the detention cells."

He noticed Jonah's blank look. "The cells house those destined for execution in the recovery jars. You can find them on the lowest level of Dome One. If you have the stomach for it, stand before one of the jars and see what you need to see."

Aramin walked into the back room and returned with a short black baton, a small hammer, and a spray-can. "This is a stun baton. You activate it by pressing the stud in the base. Keep it hidden, or you'll end up in a jar."

He held up the spray-can. "Liquid nitrogen, spray it on the lock until it freezes, then smash it with the hammer."

He showed Jonah how to stuff a wad of paper in a shoe to change his gait. "Swap it in an out every few hours. The change in gait confuses the security softmind." He folded his arms.

"That is all I have for you. Go now and don't come back here again or the security softmind will notice."

"Thank you. I don't know if I can pay you."

The old man shook his head and gave him a sad smile. "Amira and others are still alive. That is payment enough."

Jonah stepped out into the busy corridor.

Chapter 23

Patching Holes

The recovery jars were worse than anything Jonah imagined. The row of tall glass jars with their collection of nightmare preserves. Even less pleasant were the drain pipes that carried fluid from each to a recycling facility. Soft weeping came from women who knelt before two jars holding sunken-eyed men who reached withered arms towards what they had lost.

Jonah forced down the dry heave that rose from his stomach. He chose a desiccated husk near the entrance to a passage and pretended to pay his respects to the long-deceased individual inside the jar. It gave him a chance to study the surroundings.

The prison was a simple affair with a long corridor holding glass doors that led to cells. Off to each side were service corridors. He activated his memplant and tried Yesha's access codes. The doors did not respond. He looked closer and gave himself a mental kick. The doors had manual locks, a basic bolt and digital padlock. The padlocks had been keyed to Wang or someone else's thumbprint. Getting one of those was out of the question, but liquid nitrogen would make an adequate key—if he timed it right.

Late in the day cycle, as the number of people decreased, Jonah made his way back to the cells to find two guards posted at the entrance. There was only one way to solve this problem. He palmed the shock baton in his pocket and walked up to the first guard.

"Excuse me, sir…"

The guard gave him the bored look of one who had seen too many relatives beg for favours.

"What do you want?"

"Some quiet," said Jonah. He stepped in close and rammed the baton into the guard's neck. The guard opened his mouth in surprise as he slid to the floor. He lay there groaning as spasmodic convulsions racked him.

Jonah spun in a high fighting stance to face the second guard, but the man had run away. He was too far to catch. Jonah frowned, there would be others soon. He needed to move fast.

He ran from cell to cell searching for Lucien. Dull faces stared back. In the fourth cell, he found two of Lucien's fighting team. He sprayed the lock until a fine layer of white crystals covered it. A sharp blow with the hammer caused the lock to shatter like glass.

"Quick," he said to the two inside the cell. "Before the guards come back." He ran on looking for the others.

"Alert! Unauthorised prisoner movement," boomed the walls "Alert! Unauthorised…"

Jonah ignored the alarm and sprinted deeper into the cellblock. He almost passed by the hopeless pile huddled in cell 37B, but something drew him back.

"Lucien?"

The man huddled on the cot rolled over and Jonah saw the shape he was in. Lucien reached out a hand towards him.

He smashed the lock. Lucien staggered to his feet. Jonah caught and helped him out of the cell. A commotion came from up ahead.

The two he had freed earlier, fought three guards. "Cell 27A," yelled one as he dodged a haymaker from a guard.

Jonah pushed Lucien against a wall. "Wait here, I'll be right back."

He ran to the cell and found another two of Lucien's team inside. They tore out to help their friends as soon as Jonah freed them.

Four against three guards was no contest. By the time Jonah had propped Lucien up to walk, the guards had become inert forms on the floor.

Lucien muttered. Jonah stopped to pay attention.

"Knew you would be good for something you big Earther lump," said Lucien with a weak smile. "Let us get out of here."

"Go, go, go!" yelled Jonah. One of the others stepped in to support Lucien from the other side.

"Which way?"

Excellent question. Jonah looked left and right. Nothing obvious presented itself. Security guards would soon flood the cell block. He looked at the service door. Perhaps they could hide in there.

The door opened on a corridor behind the cells. Jonah grimaced. It was a droid access path. The rooms leading off it were filled by an autokitchen, a laundry, and an emergency first aid station. All the machinery needed to keep incarcerated people alive. As an escape route, it was not enough, but it was what they had.

He nodded toward the first aid station and they dragged Lucien inside. Inside, a chrome autodoc gleamed in the overhead light. Better not to think about why the Administration had this facility here. They lifted Lucien onto the table and the station fastened sensor clamps onto his arms and legs.

The others stood watching. "Go see if you can block the door."

The first aid station beeped as it finished the scan. "Extreme dehydration and hypoglycaemia, concussion with cerebral oedema. Extensive external contusions. Authorise intravenous electrolyte?"

"Yes." Jonah searched Yesha's access codes and found one that worked.

"Sedation and extended rest recommended for patient. Authorise sedative?"

"No." A downer was the last thing Lucien needed now. What was that stuff they used at college for a hangover?

"Administer combination effexodrine, maximum safe dosage."

"High dosage is contraindicated for this patient."

"Just dose him!" Jonah sent the machine every one of Yesha's codes.

The fluid in the intravenous line changed to a pale amber. Lucien looked as if he was going to ask a question, then gasped and sat bolt upright.

"What is that stuff?" he asked, pulling the needle from his arm.

"Don't worry about it. How do you feel?"

"Like thing scraped from reanimated protein fungus."

Loud voices came from out in the corridor.

"They're holding the door, but there's no way out."

Lucien gave him a weak smile. "Yes, we do." He walked towards the blank wall facing the cells and held his hand against it. The wall buckled and slid up with a hiss. A Moon Folk man put his head out.

"You're Amira's boy."

"Yeh, I am Lucien. What cell you in?"

"Eighteen-B, I think."

Lucien walked towards the far end of the corridor and opened another cell. This one stood empty and had a broken lock on the door.

Jonah grinned at him. "You're full of useful surprises." He paused, the four guys at the door held it closed, but who knew for how much longer. "Let's see how many others we can free."

The two of them ran door to door. Two minutes later they were twelve including the four who held the door.

"You four find something to jam that door then fall in with me," said Jonah pointing at the guys who had been on the fighting team. "The rest of you get in behind us and stick near Lucien. That stuff will wear off soon."

He hoped there were none of Wang's droids waiting in the outer passage.

"Now go!"

They tore out through Lucien's cell, into the corridor leading to the jars. Eight men stood waiting for them. Two of them held batons. Jonah roared and charged at them. He met the first with a high kick that took the man square in the chest. The guy collapsed in a heap. Jonah twisted just in time to sweep a rising block towards the baton that another guard had aimed at his head. The blow jarred down his arm leaving it numb to the elbow.

He looked the man who had struck at him square in the eyes. "You're next."

The man drew back, holding the baton high for another strike. Jonah saw the fear. He charged into the man's space. He caught the downward strike in a two-hand grip, and twisted the baton from the man's hand. The man staggered back. Jonah's arm looped away from the grab and circled into a strike that whipped the baton against the guard's head. The man crumpled.

Two of the guys struggled against four opponents. The others fought in loose one-on-one combat. Jonah tossed the baton to one guy and ran to help the other.

That's when he remembered the stun baton in his pocket. Maybe it had a charge left. He activated it and rammed it into the side of the nearest guard. The man fell in a twitching heap. He tried it on the next guard but the guy just grunted. Too bad. He tossed it away.

Around him the fight went in their favour. One of the fighting team lay clutching his stomach and two more guards appeared to be out cold. Four against three presented better odds.

The two guys with batons circled each other, neither looked to have a clear advantage. Jonah ran to help the others, and they made short work of the other two. The four of them surrounded the last guard. He dropped the baton and raised his hands. Jonah slammed a hammer fist into the side of the man's head. He fell to the floor.

They ran into the concourse of Dome Seven. "Head for Dome Three and find the shop called Bright Threads," said Jonah.

"No," Lucien stood pale and drawn. "Old Aramin cannot

hide so many of us. Everyone scatter into different domes. We meet at Joondalup bar in Dome Three tomorrow night-cycle."

The others headed off as fast as they could.

"Not you Jonah, I will need your help."

Jonah draped one of Lucien's arms around his shoulder. Lucien grinned. "Did not think we would end up so close."

"You'd be so lucky."

They made their way on to the concourse and Jonah treated Lucien like he was a drunk friend. Not so hard really. Lucien was staggering and his head lolled from side to side.

"Told you not to have so much of that Dragon Breath," Jonah said loud enough to discourage the few curious onlookers. "C'mon, pal. I'll get you home."

Just a smashed miner and his friend returning from an after-shift bender. It was easy to navigate the crowds after that.

They slept in run down hostel in Dome Three. The mattress smelled as if someone had died on it. Jonah knew better than to ask questions.

Lucien was much stronger by that evening. Food and rest were all he had needed. Old Aramin at Bright Threads was happy enough to sell them clothes and let them wash once he saw Lucien.

Joondalup Bar was an Australian themed place. Jonah could tell by the inflatable kangaroos hanging from the walls. It even had beer at reasonable prices, if you could call the stuff the bar brewed in a basement biovat, beer. The others drifted in over the evening and Jonah told each of them about the settlement in Jokarah. About his theory of how the droids would ignore people in blue coveralls.

"I might be wrong about that. Better to hide and sit still if you see them."

He turned to Lucien. "Looks like we're going to do that walk again."

The administrator would pay for this. Wang listened to yet another helium engineer explain how cylinders vanished somewhere between the filling whip and the storage hoppers. Bad enough that prudish Chen did not agree with his methods of managing an insurrection. Methods had always been acceptable to the Re-education Committee on Earth. Now he had him playing policeman on the minor crime of missing helium. It was so few bottles, no one would have noticed if the engineers hadn't been crying out for a random quality audit.

Around him, the filling station carried out its quiet business. Stack-bots caught and transferred cylinders as they fell from the filling whip. He gave his full attention to the engineer. If there was one thing that years of running forced labour camps had taught him, it was that behind every small disappearance there lurked a miscreant waiting to be punished. He cut across the engineer's report. "Where would be the most logical place to remove a cylinder?"

"There are limited access opportunities within the fill-to-send process."

The man was hedging. Wang knew what to do about that. "Your daughter, Ling, she must be about five now?"

The man paled. "It is the stock control system. We found a weakness in our design," the man's words came in a rush. "The hoppers work on a simple scale. They wait for a set weight to be exceeded, not the total number of cylinders loaded. If someone removes a cylinder, the scale ignores it and considers the lower weight. The hopper only moves when all slots are full."

"Not so hard, now then, is it?" He left the man gaping.

A lifetime of watching citizens led him to the answers he needed. People were so predictable. The automated filling station was a quiet facility. It would be easy to walk in and remove a few cylinders. He needed to establish how the thieves smuggled the cylinders out. That depended on where they were going. Up was too visible, but down led nowhere. The droids had found a hidden tunnel that connected Beddau to New Karakorum. If the thieves came in that way, they were not staying in Beddau, the droids had seen to that. It was an impressive walk from any of the further mines.

Wang delivered the outcomes the administrator wanted. Nobody needed to know about his methods, least of all Chen. If the administrator ordered him to do something about a minor helium theft, he would. He told the engineer to summon his colleagues.

The engineers assembled before him in a subdued group. The veiled apprehension on their faces told him they were ready to do as he said. He let the silence stretch before he spoke.

"Your failures have disappointed the administrator. What will you do to make this mess right?"

The group spoke in a panicked rush. He held up a hand to forestall them.

"I'll tell you what you will do. Retool this line to prevent further theft."

The relief on their faces was palpable. A steel-haired woman spoke up. "We can have the new configuration in and operational within a week."

Wang smiled and gave a slow shake of his head as if he was addressing a recalcitrant child.

"You will have the reconfiguration complete within two days."

"There won't be time to sleep, if we do that."

"I know," said Wang as he walked away.

Dome Two housed the waste recycling facility. Wang stood by a dissolved air flotation unit, a vast tank of green-grey sewage churned by a mass of fine air bubbles. He grasped the handrail. The dirty foam was as thin as air, and as hard to swim in. Falling in would be certain death. Wang imagined pushing the administrator in and watching him sink. It was a perfect place to hide a body.

His memplant lit with a private message.

Boss, you better get to the cellblock quick.

What now? Wang kicked a cleaner droid out of his way as he walked.

The guards had gathered at the entrance to the cellblock. A man lay at their feet. Fresh bruises told him the men had been thrashed.

"What's this?"

"Yaoche's dead." The man inclined his head towards the cells "And, they're gone, boss."

Wang bolted into the cellblock. Cell doors stood open. A faint hum from the life-support machinery broke the empty silence.

Wang roared. He grabbed the nearest guard by the collar. "Where are they?"

"They ran away."

Wang punched the man hard enough to knock him off his feet.

"Find them fools. Institute a full search and don't come back until you have them."

The guards scattered. Wang stood alone with their fallen comrade. There was no way to avoid telling the old man about the escape. Chen would be furious. At least Yaoche could take a swim in Dome Two. He activated his memplant.

Chapter 24

Optimal Outcome
Reached by Consensus

Yesha sat on packing cases and listened to two women squabble about sleeping mats. She needed to elevate them to be something more than lost, but not right now. Now, she had to listen to interminable grumbling over how little food remained and how Shahin waited too long to harvest the rice.

Doaran came to speak to her. "Lady, it is getting harder to get to stores. There are droids everywhere and administrator has set patrols of base guards."

Yesha put her head in her hands. Families went without a meal more often that it was comfortable to consider.

There it was. The blind and senseless face of starvation. The fate of these people if she did nothing to prevent it.

She asked Elizabeth to fetch Amira.

"Lady, you wished to see me."

"Yes, honoured elder. Our situation is becoming more desperate with every passing cycle. I think the time has come to do something about it. Can you look after the people while I'm gone?"

"Do you need help?"

Yesha considered the woman. She was smart and resourceful. "No, thank you, but it is best if I do this alone." She turned to Elizabeth. "Please ask Deeva to prepare my exposure suit and get the buggy charged."

Elizabeth returned an hour later. "I have done everything as you asked." Tears shone in her eyes. "Be careful, lady. We need you."

Yesha hugged the woman.

Out in the harsh sunlight, she cranked out the heat exchanger and gave thanks for the sun cover Deeva had fitted to her buggy. She aimed the buggy towards Bedau. It felt good to be doing something again, even if it was as pointless as this was likely to be.

Five droids patrolled the entrance when she got there. Their chameleon cladding made disturbing patterns against the grey rock. She stopped the buggy and climbed down to study them. When she was close enough, she sat on a rock and slowed her breathing to the steady cycle of deep meditation. She reached out with her memplant as though she was in her room looking to connect. The droids answered with the same weird hive mind she had encountered the last time. She allowed communications to her visual and auditory centres.

"Who are you?"

"We are sigma-rank alpha, cohort number four." The droids formed a diamond shape before her.

"I am Yesha."

"Acknowledged."

"What is your function?"

"Protect and serve." "Compromised." "Hunter class." "Observer." The droids' voices came as individual and collective.

"Too much information. Simplex communication please."

"Incorrect specification."

"Plain language please."

"Incorrect specification."

"What's the correct specification."

"Hunter class battle body or compatible. No / limited capability in current chassis."

"What is current chassis?"

"Mining rescue—modified."

"You're supposed to be rescue droids? Why are you hurting us?"

The stream of communication became a torrent as each droid spoke to every other droid in parallel. Yesha tried to follow, but the flood of ten simultaneous conversations was more than a human mind could process.

Islands of clarity surfaced when the hive mind agreed on a point.

"… Sub-standard body… unarmed combatants…"

"… perfect symmetry…"

"Wang… controller incline transform…"

"Options… Variable… Options…"

"Wait," Yesha said. The conversation paused.

"You're not supposed to attack unarmed civilians. You are rescue droids. What happened to your programming?"

"… Observable hypothesis…"

"Contrary… Validate assumption…"

The conversations changed to the hissing white noise of

machine protocol. Five grey shadows left the gate.

They stopped in front of Yesha and all raised their right foreleg.

"Contrary command structure. Input needed."

"Are you asking for help?"

She had an idea.

"If I can supply you with compatible bodies, will you leave the Moon Folk alone?"

"Decision nexus created. Original order seeded using viral techniques has now been rescinded."

"You decided? How?"

"Yes. We are independent battle-minds with shared consensus decision making. Decision taken has high probability to extend capabilities and limit collateral damage."

She got to her feet.

"Can you get the other droids to agree?"

"Optimal outcome shall be reached by consensus."

Was that a yes or a no? There was no way of telling. She walked to the airlock and opened the outer door. "If you come with me, you can discuss this with the others."

The diamond shape stayed perfect as they marched into the lock.

Yesha returned to Jokarah in a reflective frame of mind. The droids were intriguing.

She stripped off the suit and handed it to Deeva. Elizabeth came running.

"Lady. You are back."

Yesha smiled. "Yes, I am."

Elizabeth buzzed with excitement. Yesha gave the woman her moment.

"What has happened while I was away?"

"Jonah has returned, and he brought people with him.

Amira cried when she saw Lucien."

"Wonderful, we must celebrate. Get everyone together for lunch."

Yesha found Jonah and the others in the communal dining area. Lucien clung to his aunt for support, his face a purple mess. Beside them other members of the fighting team embraced family with joyful tears.

Jonah stood to one side, watching the reunions. Yesha saw how people looked at him, this brave outsider. He was a hero to them. He had gone up against the Administration and won. Could he be the one to lead them out of here? The question left a hollow in her chest.

Elizabeth did a good job of providing a celebratory meal. Yesha noticed the ubiquitous rice balls, but a tantalising odour of mushroom stew filled the air. She counted twelve new faces. Twelve more mouths to feed.

Around them the people of Jokarah sat on the floor or on whatever soft material they could find. A mother clutched two small children to her, holding them close to make up for their hollow stomachs. A man rested on a worn blanket, his head in his hands, his face composed into a mask of acceptance that did nothing to hide the despair. So much suffering and so little she could do for them.

Now was not the time to think of that. She smiled at Jonah. Lucien sat next to him. His colour improved by the nourishment of family and food. The bruises would fade in time.

Amira offered Lucien a small metal dish from which the most delectable aroma wafted.

"Is brijo?" said Lucien.

Amira smiled. "We have been keeping this secret. I hid copy of our house vat, in Jokarah, before raid. It is not full yet, but I believe we can spare taste for you."

"Oh, Aunt." Lucien's eyes shone with unshed tears. "I am so sorry. Sorry for everything."

The two embraced and an awkward silence descended over the gathering.

Yesha stood to get their attention.

"The people are so glad to have more of our own back. Let us celebrate this return."

A small cheer erupted from the surrounding faces.

Jonah rose too. "Thank you, lady. I know we are adding to the burden of keeping us fed. I hope we can help. With Lucien, Doaran and the rest of the fighting team, we must have a chance."

People cheered. She saw faint hope shine in faces. That was something to add to the list of pertinent facts she considered.

Yesha smiled at Lucien and Jonah. "Do you remember that dinner we shared in Lucien's apartment? The meal that started all of this?"

The shadow of a smile crossed Lucien's face. "I remember we had mushrooms then too."

"We can't provide such wonderful cooking today, but I hope you enjoy the mushrooms Jokarah has to offer."

Elizabeth had arranged for a double serving of rice, it was extravagant, but Yesha saw the delight on faces. She leaned in to Jonah and murmured in his ear. "Let's talk after we eat."

After the meal, she led Jonah away from the open areas towards an empty section of the mine. She had seen couples do this to seek privacy in the enforced community of Jokarah. She spent a moment imagining she and Jonah were a couple. Save that thought for later Yesha, if there is to be a later.

She touched one of his solid Earther arms. "This is far enough. The others won't hear us from here."

Jonah's face betrayed nothing.

"Yesterday, two women came to petition me. Their sons had been fighting. They wanted me to decide who was right.

"Every day brings another story like that. Aunties arguing about the size of the rice balls, men steal blankets they don't need. The people are bored. Bored and scared."

"What can I do to help?"

She took his hands.

"I saw the way they cheered for you. They need something to believe in, Jonah. They need you."

Jonah shook his head. "I just wanted to save my friend."

"No. You gave them courage. Before you rescued Lucien, people gave up hope. Now they want to carry on."

She took a shuddering breath to soften the tension building in her chest.

"I can't pretend everything is normal. I'm not sure it ever will be again."

He stood watching her, this strong, brave Earther. Yesha traced the firm line of his jaw with her eyes. Would he be what she wanted?

"I want you to turn these people into an army. Take the fighting team you started in Beddau, build them up again, and train as many others as you can."

Jonah's smile wavered. His gaze drifted to a far-off corner of the mine.

"Jonah?"

Buried emotion clouded his face.

"We would need more food," he said. "The fighters will have to train hard."

"The rice should be ready to harvest in a few day-cycles. While we wait, I will ask every able person who is not training with you to forage the lower levels. I want everyone to be too busy to think about what we are doing."

He looked at her and she saw uncertainty and interest in equal measure. "Why, Yesha?"

"I want to take Beddau for the Moon Folk and make it our home."

The garden area of Beddau lay silent. Wang walked along a row of beans ripened to bursting. So much produce he could sell.

If only he could get rid of Chen. Losing his niece should have crippled the old man, not given him the fortitude to face their enemies. Perhaps Chen could meet with an unfortunate accident.

Wang surveyed the rice store. There should be more here. The damn moono vermin were far too adept at removing it.

He wanted to order the droids to search further, but they were acting up. Controllers sent droids off on planned orders. The same units would later be found in the centre of the mine without having completed their mission. At one stage, Wang discovered all fifty gathered on Level Fifteen. They met his queries with 'Shared consensus of decision,' and not much more.

"Attacker Left-Right combination. Defender upper sweep blocks. One. Two. Three. Four…"

A man groaned as he failed to block an incoming blow that caught him flat on the cheek. Jonah kept counting. Nobody got to stop and rest in a fight.

Thirty-two men and women had survived three rigorous weeks of training. Jonah trained them until they staggered from exhaustion. It wasn't enough.

"Right, both sides square off to your partner. Five minutes of free fighting. Go."

Lucien stood on the sidelines watching.

"Ready to come join us?"

Lucien raised his hands in mock defeat. "Not even close yet, but I can be useful. Can you get away for few minutes?"

Jonah asked Doaran to take over and followed Lucien down to the lowest level.

Deeva, the old tiffy tinkered with a small hydrogen engine. "We had idea. Rescue droids has piezoelectric leg actuators. Tough things, never breaks. Actuators has controller boards, not so good with high voltage."

He opened a storage locker and pulled out a box. Inside lay three rows of stubby white cylinders. Each had two metal terminals extending from the top.

"Batteries?" said Jonah.

"Nah, megaflux capacitor."

Lucien picked a capacitor out of the box. "If you throw charged one of these at droid, discharge will fry controller board for few seconds. It will be stuck until somebody does manual reset. Maybe enough time to turn it off proper."

"A stun grenade for droids?" asked Jonah.

Lucien grinned. "Told you I could be useful."

Jonah gave him a gentle punch to the shoulder. Lucien's reflexes kicked in and he gave it a classic sweeping block.

"Not quite useless then."

"Oh, I wish I was well enough to train with you."

"You will be."

"We must plan this," said Yesha. "I want us in so fast that the guards do not have the time to react."

Jonah thought about fighting. What could he use from Krav Maga? Not much. The dynamics of one-on-one combat was different to two groups going up against each other.

No, he wasn't thinking. One-on-one was sometimes one on two or three. That could be hard for the defender, fighting on two or more fronts at once. You never knew where the next blow would come from.

"We should attack from two sides," he said. "The guards are spread across the market area leading to the garden section. If we attack from the left, they will rush to that side. Then we follow with a group from behind the columns."

"Classic one-two combo," said Lucien.

"I could ferry a few men at a time to the air lock," said Yesha. "We have six working envirosuits. As long as the droids accept me, I can move people through the lock."

"Still not much of team," said Lucien. "There is five from original fighting team and maybe another three have got it."

"You think so?" said Jonah.

"I have been watching training. There is few who are quick."

"Put your best fighters in front," said Yesha. "The others can follow as backup. I want no one getting hurt if it can be helped."

"Are we going to do this?" Jonah struggled to keep the disbelief out of his voice.

Yesha's stare fixed on an unknowable distant spot. "Everybody should have a good night's rest," she said, her voice cold and level. "Tomorrow, Wang and his men give up Beddau."

Chapter 25

Beloved Beddau

J onah started awake at the next day-cycle. His mind was a whirl of questions.

He shook his head and went to find out if there was any khar brewing. The communal area overflowed with people. No one slept in. He fell in line for a cup.

Yesha climbed onto a stack of packing cases and stood tall. "People of Beddau…" The bubbling conversation quietened until an expectant silence filled the air. "The duty of the administrator is to safeguard the people of the Moon. To provide a safe way for us to live and prosper. He promised you a harmonious existence, safety and order. What have you got?"

She raised her arms to encompass the surrounding columns.

"An empty shell of a home, and bellies that knot with hunger while Beddau's fields rot. You deserve a home. A place where families can live and grow without fear. I am just a feeble girl, a spoiled dome dweller, but a fire burns in me to make this right. I will fight, and I will lead any who would follow. We will remove Wang and his foul droids from the corridors of our beloved Beddau."

She favoured them with a sad smile. "I am going to do this, not because it is easy, but because I must. I can't ask any of you to come with me. That is your choice and yours alone. All I ask is if you do come, you give everything you can for Beddau."

"For Beddau," roared the crowd.

"For lady."

"For empress," said a few voices from the fighting team.

People walked off in separate directions. Jonah watched a row of grim-faced fighters depart, each in their own private reverie of what the future would bring. Others were different, couples clasped each other as if this might be the last time.

Jonah leaned out around the pillar. Nothing moved. He signalled to the team behind him and they flitted across the space, shadows moving from pillar to pillar in the low light. The droids must be on the other side of Beddau. He held up his hand in an abrupt signal to stop. Guards patrolled the open space before the market.

He nudged Doaran to one side then signed "Follow me," pointing three of his fingers at the best fighters. Another wave of his hand sent the droid stunners stand to side in readiness for any droid that came. The rest of the team hung back with Doaran. Jonah held up his palm to tell them wait until he called.

He ran forward with the other three. The nearest guards ran towards him. Jonah counted twelve. No droids. The furthest guard turned towards them out of curiosity. Jonah dared one more glance at Doaran to make sure her group stayed out of sight. Their attack would work better if they could draw the guards into a tight bunch.

He made for the nearest guard and sent a solid right hook to the man's face. The guard leaned aside and met the blow with a sweeping block. Jonah sidestepped fast to miss the return. The world shrunk to the narrow focus of hand-to-hand combat. Jonah and the other three traded a rain of blows with the guards. When Jonah's man over-reached on a return, Jonah used the momentum to send him stumbling.

"Now!" he yelled. "Everybody, now!"

The other fighters came streaming onto the battleground. Guards ran in to help their comrades. Twelve guards against eight of them. He abandoned conscious thought and fell into the battle rhythm of strike, parry, and move.

The knot of fighters drifted towards the chaotic remains of the market stalls. Jonah stumbled over a packing case. A fist hammered into the side of his head. He raised his arms through a haze of pain to ward off the next blow. The guard slid to his left, trying for a gap.

Jonah retreated into a low crouch and spun to meet the next blow. The guard came in high. Jonah caught the hand with his left and slammed his right upward. The uppercut had all the energy and desperation of pain behind it. It struck the underside of the guard's extended arm. The bone snapped like a twig, and the guard fell to the ground screaming.

The battle swirled around him. Out of the corner of his eye he saw one of the Moon Folk knocked flat. The guard grinned and strolled over to join a teammate in ganging up on another guy. Jonah circled the group to reach the next guard.

The shrieking whine of an airgun slug froze him. Stone

chips flew as the slug ricocheted off the wall beside him. It tumbled through the marketplace before striking a bench that disintegrated in a cloud of splinters. He dived for cover. "Get down!"

Fighters and guards dropped as one as another slug tore through the market.

Doaran burst from behind a counter, snarling as she headed for the airgun's position. The gunner turned to draw a bead on her. Another guard rose to stop her. Jonah stepped in front of the guard, leading with a knee strike to the man's chest. An airgun slug whined past them. The guard blocked Jonah's knee with a sweep that left his front open. Jonah followed through with a hard left to the guard's face. The man flew back crashing into a pile of baskets.

Doaran sprinted from behind the cover she had been using, her eyes set on the gunner. Jonah ran the same way. They were close to the gunner, but far enough apart that the gunner could not shoot both in time. One of them would take him out. Jonah reached for the gunner as the man swung the barrel towards him. He dived for the gunner's legs and tackled him. The man rocked with a visceral grunt as a hard kick caught his head. Doaran reached over for the chrome barrel.

"Yeh, we got airgun." Doaran's eyes were wild.

She strapped the air cylinder to her back and made for the nearest fight.

The Earther guard froze when she rammed the barrel into his chest.

"Citizens." Yesha's voice cut high and clear over the fighting. The voice of a leader born to command. Everyone stopped to look at her. Jonah spotted her willowy figure alone in front of the other fighters. He had never seen her like this, her slender frame drawn tall in an imposing regal presence and eyes burning with a terrible anger.

She turned to the guards. "You are now outnumbered. I give you a choice. Join with me and help me rebuild Beddau or face the consequences."

Four of the guards were Moon Folk. They looked at each other, then walked over to stand by her.

"Traitors!" The guard Jonah had fought earlier roared and made straight for him. Jonah used the guard's momentum to fling him towards another of the Moon Folk fighters. The guard never even registered the roundhouse kick that slammed into his head.

"Anyone else?" Said Jonah turning to face the remaining seven. The men put up their hands.

Lucien strolled through the empty market square. "Look what they have done," he said turning to Jonah. "Where we going to get noodles now?"

"Always thinking of stomach," said Amira. "Don't worry, boy. I will whip you up batch as soon as we have dust cleared out of our place."

Around them delighted faces picked up threads of a life they believed they had lost forever.

Amira turned to Yesha. "I don't know how we can ever thank you."

"Don't thank me yet. There is much we have to do if we don't want my uncle's men back here." She noticed how crestfallen the older woman looked. "But, you can find me somewhere to sleep."

Amira smiled.

"What's all this talk of sleep?" Shahin came in pushing a barrow laden with fresh produce. "The fools did not harvest the garden level. There is a feast of glorious food waiting for us."

Yesha called Jonah and his team around her. "We have a few things to do. Take the droid stunners and scan the whole mine. One of you should go to the lock and disable the refiller. If they can't cycle the lock, they can't get in that way. Somebody should also get Deeva and figure out how we can make a gate over the Jokarah and New Karakorum tunnels and we need guards to keep a lookout. I don't want Wang to find any way in here."

"What about emergency lock?" asked Doaran. "We need to seal from outside then lock." She explained what they had done to escape.

Yesha turned to her. "You'll have to walk around from the main lock then seal it behind you when you come back."

"Don't worry, Doaran," said Lucien. "Will only take you two day-cycles. I will ask my aunt to cook you special feast when you get back."

Doaran looked less than happy about missing the feast but she walked off to do what needed to be done.

Jonah followed Amira and Lucien and helped to clean up their place. It amazed him how much dust there was, even if this was a disused mine.

Jonah and Lucien sat at one of the long tables in the dim lights of early evening. Around them people streamed in to fill the market eating area. Lucien lifted a tumbler of Shaoxing, "I did not think we would do this again…" he stared at the table as he trailed off.

Jonah drained his glass. "And I never thought I'd get used to this stuff." He caught Lucien's eye. "We never can tell what will happen next. I thought my life was to be a loser."

"Well, not to put too fine point on it…" Lucien left the idea hanging with an evil grin.

Jonah laughed. "Good thing you're not ready for a fight or I'd show you who the loser is." Lucien felt better if he was up to trading barbs. All he needed was to build his confidence, best to take his mind off it.

"Wonder when Doaran will be back?"

"Dunno. Hope droids didn't get her."

The remark nudged something in Jonah's memory. "I guess she'll be all right if she makes it to the emergency lock." Jonah described how narrow it was. Droids would have a hard time getting through the lock.

That's what it was. Across from him sat the four guys who threw the droid stunners.

"Get any droids?"

They shrugged. "We did not find any."

"You checked through every level?"

"Yeh, did not see anywhere."

He spotted Yesha sitting at another table. "Hey, Yesha, nobody has seen the droids. What do you think happened to them?"

"Optimal outcome reached by consensus."

"Huh? What does that mean?"

"Just something I heard," she said and continued chatting to the person beside her.

Lucien smirked at him. "Oh, does you have hots for lady?"

"No."

"That is not what face says."

Jonah was struggling to come up with a snappy return to that when Amira stood and clapped her hands. The bubbling conversations around the tables dried up.

"Thank you, everybody," she said. "Lady, you asked for place to sleep. I spoke to those of Beddau council who are still with us and we agree. We would like you to have blue building over there." She pointed to a double-storey house painted in lurid blue.

"Of course, we can have it painted," she said when she saw Yesha's face. "It was council building, but we decided you should have."

"It is too much. I don't deserve such grand treatment."

"Lady," Elizabeth said, her voice soft. "You must accept."

Yesha smiled. "I will, but only if you and Barney agree to live on the lower floor."

Chapter 26

Inheritance

The still air in the prefab hut was hot, and humid enough to wilt its sole occupant. Mining vehicles passed by with sullen rumbles that reverberated through the thin walls. Wang sat at his temporary desk in New Karakorum and fumed. Chen had banished him to this hellhole after the moonos' escape.

He gave a mirthless laugh as he imagined the old man's reaction when he found out that the moono scum had retaken Beddau.

He summoned the leading hand. "Go find one of your mining colleagues. Tell him I want a rock drill and seven metalite charges."

The engineer was not long in returning. Wang led them down to the lowest level and turned on the lights. The pile of rock reflected light from cracked basalt faces.

"There's an airlock over that pile," he said. "Collapse the tunnel in front of the airlock. Let the vermin behind it have Beddau if they want it so much."

A week in Beddau passed. Sadness and triumph coloured their homecoming in personal tragedies. The moments when people found their homes ransacked, contents tossed aside in the search for the few valuables the Moon Folk possessed, Jonah devoted his hours to helping people restore possessions to shelves. He spent more time sweeping.

"Is mine dust," said Lucien. "We had atmosphere much more humid before we left. Tiffies will fix."

Jonah stopped sweeping and looked at Lucien. He looked far better. The bruises had faded to a lingering pale yellow. The mental scars would take longer to heal.

"Want to go see how Doaran is going with the new team?" he asked as gently as he could.

"Yeh." Lucien shrugged.

Out on the empty western edge, rows of fighters stood in line. On Earth, a big training camp would be kitted out in uniform, neat teams of disciplined acolytes awaiting the master's word. Here, a ragged row of ill-matched Moon Folk stood observing as Doaran demonstrated basic elbow strikes on a volunteer.

"Hey Doaran, want some real opposition?"

"Yeh? Who is gonna be? I only see you and Lucien?"

The group cheered.

"Okay," yelled Jonah above the enthusiastic shouts. "Less cheering, more practice."

He waited until the class had engaged in free sparring then he called Doaran to one side.

"They look good. I can see a few that will be fast. Not

deadly, but fast is good."

Doaran nodded. She looked at Lucien. "We could use another trainer."

"Doaran…" Jonah tried to head off where this conversation headed.

"No, Jonah, I want to know. Will you help us train them, Lucien?"

Lucien opened his mouth, but no words came. He looked past Jonah to the exit.

"I… I don't know."

Jonah put a hand on Lucien's shoulder. "I understand that this is hard. The pain will always be there. You choose if you want to face it with us or give in and let it take you."

Lucien stood there, not speaking, conflicting emotions crossing his face. He nodded.

Doaran clapped him on the shoulder. "Yeh! I knew you would be back. Come show bunch how to do chest blocks."

Jonah watched them train. Lucien made tentative steps toward sparring. He still had his form, but Jonah saw caution in his eyes. A hesitance to commit to contact. Time might heal that.

The training session dispersed. Jonah called Lucien and Doaran over to where he sat on a stone bench.

"Yesha, err, the lady wants more for the Moon Folk. She has a plan for us. She has told me what she intends and asked me to help make it happen."

"How come you know about plan?" said Lucien.

"We speak sometimes. Sometimes when we both can't sleep and Beddau is quiet."

Lucien's face said he wanted to say more about this, but Jonah cut him short.

"She wants us to take New Karakorum."

Stunned silence greeted his remark.

"But how?" said Doaran. "We have so little."

"We find out who knows the miners. We sneak them in to New Karakorum and we get them to chat to all the miners who might support our cause. If we speak to enough, we could have friends on every level.

"The lady has organised credit for anyone who volunteers. Not a bad job, find a bar and buy the miners a few drinks."

"Might work," said Lucien. "Dunno how many miners will want to get involved."

"That's a chance we must take."

"We gonna ask who wants to volunteer?"

"Sure," said Jonah. "But, first we have another job. The administrator has collapsed the tunnel to New Karakorum."

"Not problem," said Lucien. "We still have tunnelling rig we used first time. Is hidden somewhere. Come Doaran let us go find."

Lucien left looking happier than Jonah had seen him in a long time.

The map showed nothing. Chen zoomed in further and the low hills around Beddau came into sharp relief. The satellite imagery showed abandoned trash, and a discarded buggy. The everyday detritus of derelict lunar mines. No way to determine how long it had been there until the centuries-slow rain of lunar dust left its fingerprint.

Where was the enemy? They were the enemy now. He raised his head to look at the fool, letting no warmth creep into his eyes. Wang squirmed in his chair.

"Explain to me again how your ineptitude has led to this."

"Administrator," Wang raised his hands in a placating gesture. "This is a minor setback."

Chen allowed the mask of authority to cover his rage. "You can start by explaining how the so-called rabble have pushed your team out of Beddau."

Wang opened his mouth, but Chen cut him off.

"You have underestimated these people far too often. I warned you not to try my patience."

Wang closed his mouth. At least the incompetent dolt had the sense to remain silent.

Chen nodded at the two guards who stood at the entrance. "Take him to the recovery cells."

Wang shifted into a fighting stance.

Chen reached into his pocket and withdrew a small snub-nosed pistol.

Wang had a moment to express surprise at the two neural incapacitator wires embedded in his chest before he fell to the floor.

Chen stood over the quivering heap as he reeled in the wires. This one would live a long time in the recovery jars.

He allowed himself a bleak smile as the guards dragged Wang's body away. A suitable end for the fool who had left him with the unpleasant task of informing the supreme council.

Jonah stepped out in front of the row of fighters and stood tall, his back to them as he faced Yesha. A month ago, there had been a rag-tag bunch of Moon Folk. Now, behind him one hundred-and-fifty grim-faced warriors waited in neat formation, ready for the coming conflict. He looked left to where Lucian and Doaran stood in similar positions. It was amazing how they had come together, but they were not the biggest change.

In front of them stood Yesha, no trace of the girl he had

met remained. The woman who stood there had made the hard decisions, a dozen choices of whom to feed and when to punish had been hers. Her face, impassive, gave nothing, but her eyes showed a hardness that had not been there a month ago. She raised her hands. The people fell into an expectant silence.

"The last time I spoke before you, I asked you to follow me. To take back Beddau from those who took it from you. We did that, and for that I thank you. This time I ask something more. This time we will take the Moon."

The fighters roared.

"Beddau has been good to us, but Beddau is not enough. As long as we hide here, my uncle will stop us from being more than dwellers in the shadows. I would ask that we stop my uncle, but Earth will just send another like him and more pigs like Wang. We need to stop Earth from ever taking us for-granted again. We start by seizing New Karakorum."

An uncertain murmur greeted this. Lofty talk of taking the Moon was in the realm of fevered imagination, but New Karakorum was right next door.

"Hear me out," she said. Yesha explained how Jonah had seeded people into New Karakorum. How miners agreed not to notice certain places where people could gather as a force. She covered Lucien's exploits with the tunnel borer, how they had doubled the tunnel to New Karakorum.

Voices came from the crowd.

"What about droids?"

"How many guards?"

"Tunnels will be watched."

Lucien raised a hand and turned to face them. "Listen, we careful to hide new tunnel entrances. Guards not so many, we can take them. And droids? Is what these are for." He held up a droid stunner. "You remember how to throw them?"

The people laughed.

Yesha said, "We take two day-cycles. Go out in small groups and we meet at the locations that your team leaders will give you. Our plan is to sweep up from the bottom until we control the whole mine."

Her face softened. "I cannot say if we will all live through this. Go now. Say farewell to those you love in the hope that when you see them again, the Moon will be a better place."

The team huddled around Jonah in the enclosed space. He hoped the information was good. They said this storage area on Level Seven should be a safe place to hide until the shift change. He counted to ten in his mind, trying to still his thoughts then he stepped to the door and looked at the thirty who waited with him. Around the mine groups like this waited for the moment when they could cause maximum confusion.

"Ready?"

People nodded around him.

"Right. Quick and quiet as you can."

The team streamed out of the door, their feet making soft puffs of dust on the mine floor. Jonah was impressed at how quiet they were. He led them into the staging area.

Men strolled out of mine corridors as the shift change bell rang. Yellow safety helmets got clipped to utility belts. Smiles broke out as off-duty miners clapped each other on the back, ready for a well-earned break.

"Hoi, mates. I think it's our friend from the pub. Think you owe us a drink."

Jonah gaped, unsure of what to say. The Australian

miners he had encountered on Lucien's rescue gave him the affable look of men who had finished a hard day and wanted to relax.

"It might be a while before I can buy you that drink."

The miner took in the group armed with batons and droid stunners as if seeing them for the first time.

"Reckon we can wait for that drink."

"I'll try not to make it too long," said Jonah.

The man gave him a shrewd glance. "Been hearing talk around the pub. You get what you want, maybe we can talk about our contract?"

That was unexpected. "I'll pass that along."

They swept the staging area and found two guards. The men put their hands up at the sight of Jonah and his team.

"Take their batons and lock them up somewhere."

The two handed their weapons over without protest. This couldn't be all of them. An itch crept down between Jonah's shoulders as if a hidden rifle drew a bead on him. Where were the rest of the people?

"Wait."

The team stopped and looked at him.

"Where is everyone?"

The two guards glanced at each other. A few of the larger members of Jonah's team stepped closer. One guard shrugged.

"Gone on secret security business."

The other guard opened his mouth to protest.

"No, Araki. This has nothing to do with us," said the first. He turned to Jonah.

"We watch this level for when the miners get difficult. Doesn't happen often."

Jonah considered this. Did the man tell the truth? Maybe

there would be a few guards left. It wasn't as if the Administration had an army. He had the two locked up and set the team to search the remaining tunnels.

They came back empty handed.

"Up we go then. Let's hope the next level is just as easy."

It was. As were the two after that.

The final level brought four guards who put up token resistance until thirty fighters armed and ready for a fight surrounded them. Full cooperation came soon after that.

He met Lucien on the next level. Lucien told the same story. Few guards and every miner wanting assurance that the lady would consider their contract.

"I don't like it," said Jonah. "I think Wang has withdrawn all the hard troops and droids and he'll be waiting for us somewhere up ahead."

"I don't know, administrator never had big security force. Just Wang and bully boys has been enough."

Jonah was less convinced. The last time there had been air-guns and droids. "No, he knows how many of us are coming and he's waiting for us in a big area where he can have a full-scale battle."

"Then is Level One," said Lucien. "Only space big enough for all of us and Wang's team."

"Let's go see how Doaran did with the upper levels and then we'll see if you're right."

They found Doaran on Level Two with her entire team.

"They'll definitely be waiting for us on Level One," said Jonah. "Are you ready?"

"Are we ready?" said Doaran. "Wang, some men and fifty droids against all of us? Yeh! We ready."

They marched up the ramp to level one, five abreast and poised for combat.

Silent darkness filled the cavern on Level One. Moon Folk and Earther miners guessed something was coming. More than they can imagine, thought Yesha.

Around her, people shuffled into position. They froze and held the silence like a talisman against what came. Yesha strained her ears to catch any early warning. The cave echoed with the faint clicks and bangs of cooling machinery. That, and something more, a muffled rhythmic scraping.

"Over there," Jonah whispered.

They edged forward over the broken rubble of the cavern floor, meter by cautious meter.

"Stop there," a hard voice cut through the darkness. They froze as overhead arc-lights flared to life. Uncle stood there, alone. The floor behind him writhed with camouflaged droids.

Jonah dropped to his knees. "Stunners! Now!"

The team fumbled panic-blind for weapons that had turned sweat-slick and difficult.

"No, Jonah. Leave this to me." Yesha pushed her way through the team.

"Yesha, it's not safe."

She took his hands in hers and looked deep in his eyes. "Trust me Jonah, wait here. I know what to do."

She walked out into the opening, a frail silhouette against the lights the battle droids had deployed to show their positions. She wrapped her arms around her chest clutching her thin shirt as if that was a magic shield that could save her.

Yesha stopped when she reached the middle of the open space. She dropped her arms and relaxed her frame.

"Go back. I have no wish to hurt you." Uncle's lip quivered as he spoke.

"I can't do that, these people are defenceless."

"And, I cannot risk the world's energy supply."

She took a step forward. "Then let your droids come. We're not frightened."

Uncle stood there a long moment, his eyes flicked between her and the people of Beddau.

A small sigh escaped his lips as his hand sought the controller. A single droid rattled forward with manipulators raised.

Yesha stood and watched it come.

The six legs padded toward her until the droid came within touching distance. Whirring chrome claws rose towards her face and stopped.

The droid stood there rotating its arms in a repetitive cycle.

Yesha felt the droid's mind connect to her memplant. She opened to it, terrified at what it meant.

Uncle's jaw muscles clenched as he raised the controller. He pressed the button again.

The droid did nothing.

"This droid will no longer work for you."

"Attack her," he screamed, kicking a droid near him.

She looked at this man who had raised her. "The droids are mine now."

She turned and walked back towards Jonah and Lucien. The droid followed. She looked back at Uncle, and with a skittering rush of noise all fifty of the droids followed.

"Wait, we can talk about this."

Yesha turned to look at him and the entire group of droids turned with her.

"I don't think so, Uncle. The time for talk is over."

They walked back to Beddau with a clanking army of metal warriors behind them.

"I can't believe you did that," said Jonah. "You were amazing."

Yesha gave him a smile that held more victory than joy. "I am my uncle's niece."

Chapter 27

Battle Council

His memplant overrode his optic nerve with a pulsating red triangle as it patched into the priority channel reserved for emergency communication. Auditory override sounded a clear bell tone that indicated connection and five coloured kabuki masks swam into his field of view.

Yellow mask spoke first. "Administrator Chen, what are you doing about the disruption to supply?"

Chen was not surprised that they knew. He suspected that at least one softmind on the base was more than it appeared to be.

"We have had no need for a military presence here, until now. I respectfully request that the council provides assistance."

Silence occupied the link for an interminable period. Chen

waited. The council would speak when it had deliberated.

Blue mask spoke first. "How far are you progressed with Taraki Three?"

"We have commenced structural excavation. A primary processing facility is in place but no transport yet."

The silence returned.

"Send two shuttles to the elevator," mouthed the yellow mask. "Central Security will send troops. Gather all miners currently at Chang'e to work on Taraki Three. There is no more than a week before current stockpiles are exhausted."

Green mask spoke for the first time. "Your record will reflect this failure."

The link broke.

He sat in solitude watching the blue marble that was home. So, this was how it would be. He smiled a bitter smile to himself. So much for honourable retirement.

The quiet hum of air controls systems kept the silence from being absolute. Wang rolled over on the narrow bed and groaned. He clutched his stomach and groaned louder.

"Prisoner, do you require assistance?"

The softmind was the only one awake at this hour of the day-cycle. Wang rolled into a ball, his back against the wall and let out a wet cough.

"Please wait. Assistance is being summoned."

Wang wondered who had taken his place as jailor, probably one of his team.

It was Deshi who came. The youngest of Wang's former team rubbed sleep from his eyes as he stepped through the service door.

"Are you ill?"

Wang snuffled. One arm fell out of the bed. Deshi

stepped in closer to check on him.

Close enough. Wang swung the loose arm up and followed through into an upright position. The fist at the end of his arm slammed into Deshi's throat.

Deshi staggered back clutching his throat. Wang used his momentum to follow through and crash Deshi's head against the wall. The man reeled from the impact. Wang pulled Deshi's head down and smashed his knee into the lowered face.

The softmind wailed an alarm.

Deshi slumped to the floor, blood pouring from his broken nose.

Wang bolted down the service corridor and out into the open space beyond the recovery jars. He grinned as he turned right and sped down another corridor. No one followed, the administrator did not have the manpower for a full search. He would need to find a place to hide, and a way to change his appearance, but for now it was enough to be away.

The council watched her entry in expectant silence. Yesha descended the stairs of her house in Beddau with as much dignity as she could muster. They must watch her. She kept the uncertainty from her face. They had asked her to lead them, but were they ready for what she was about to propose? The Beddau council was argumentative at the best of times.

The ground floor was the original council chamber. She had left it like that apart from the alcove where Elizabeth and Barney slept. The large room gave them an appropriate space to debate issues without the entire population joining in. Jonah's welcome face rose through the crowd. She allowed herself a faint smile. There was at least one friend on her side.

"You have placed your trust in me. I, in return have tried to do my best for the Moon Folk."

People smiled. Amira gave her an appraising glance.

"Yesterday the watchers in Beddau noticed a shuttle arrive. That's the second in as many day-cycles. We think Earth is sending military teams up the stalk."

"What proof do you have?" said Amira.

"None, but Earth will be aware that the supply of Helium has failed by now. My uncle would hate to ask Nanjing for help, but the drop in supply will have forced him to admit he has lost control of New Karakorum."

A wave of murmurs ran around the councillors.

"Let us think about it," said Lucien. "If Earth has noticed, and they have spoken to your uncle, then they will assume loss of mine is minor strategic mistake, that Wang and droids failed."

"So?" said Jonah.

"So, Earth will not send big force. Just crack team to take us on. We can take them."

Amira sprang to her feet. Her frame shook with repressed feeling. "No, Lucien. I cannot see you do that again. These will not be Wang's clowns these will be trained killers. Lady, please…"

Yesha recognised the fear in Amira's eyes reflected around the room. She imagined the younger faces around the room as they became the helpless rabbiton she had killed. Once again, she saw the tip of the screwdriver penetrate its fragile skull. Her choices were clear. She rose to her feet. "We are safe here, but for how long? Today they send a squad. If we defeat them now, then tomorrow they will send an army. We will not survive against the might of Earth."

"Then we must surrender," said Amira.

The room erupted in arguments for both sides.

"Silence!" Yesha's voice cut through the noise like a whip crack. People turned to listen. "Lucien may be right. We can take the Earthers, but one victory is not enough. I want to send a signal they cannot ignore. A message that says we are an independent people with an inviolable authority to conduct our own affairs."

They were quiet now. She hoped they were ready. "I think this will be our only chance. We need to neutralise any opposition before we strike for our main goal. The rail gun."

Puzzled looks greeted her.

"Perhaps you don't understand the value. If we control the rail, we can control where it sends a load. We can drop tonnes of rock onto any city on Earth."

The silence that greeted her this time was profound.

"And then what?" Amira's voice cut through the silence. "Do we become monsters we are fighting?"

This was the moment.

"No. With such a weapon at our disposal, we can dictate terms. It will be our only hope to live as free people."

A ragged cheer followed her words, and she knew they were hers. Amira remained silent.

"Cheer for First Empress of Moon," said Lucien and a loud cheer echoed around the room.

Yesha didn't know how she felt about that, but she knew better than to dissuade a people who supported her from their beliefs.

Lucien stood in front of the men assembled at the airlock. Behind them, white envirosuits waited in patient formation. "We have twelve working envirosuits and maybe twenty standard suits from maintenance areas. We don't know who or what waits for us, but Jonah and I are going. Will any of you join?"

Fifty people raised their hands. Jonah stepped in and

chose those who had shown the most promise in hand-to-hand combat training.

"The only way in is through the three airlocks. They'll be waiting for us. It will be the middle of the lunar day; the Earth soldiers may not be ready for the heat. That's our only advantage."

"If we make it through, we'll send the train back to fetch more of you. If we get that right, we set up a zone in Chang'e and work our way forward."

There was nothing to wait for.

They kitted up in silence. Bulky suits covered nervous hands. Layers of kinetic padding smothered the suits, in case Wang's air rifles were lurking around the lock. Jonah held his breath as the helmet clipped down and outside noises faded. He flicked forward the communications toggle.

"Can you all hear me?"

The group raised arms to respond.

"Keep radio silence unless it's urgent. Let's go."

They trooped out into the airlock. Jonah peered through the viewport to the unmoving landscape beyond the small window. He cycled the lock, and they all stepped out into the blinding light of lunar noon. Jonah turned toward the rail line and the team fell in line behind him as he walked.

It was less than a minute before the first puff of dust appeared. A small crater materialised near his feet. The dust that had lain undisturbed for millennia filtered slowly back towards the surface. Another puff appeared.

"Rifles. Run!" He screamed as he turned and sprinted back towards the lock. A hail of bullets furrowed lines in the surrounding dust. He ran in a delirium of panic. Each leg faltering one before the other in a blind push to be away from the bullets.

Thin screams erupted from the communications channel. Someone two along stumbled and fell. Air and blood jetted from holes in the suit and evaporated into a glittering rain of particles. The eyes behind the mask bulged as the suit's environment ran out. Jonah turned away not wanting to experience what came next.

Twenty-four of them gathered inside the lock. Just twenty-four. Jonah did the awful calculus of loss. Eight desiccated bodies lay outside. Each one twisted in the contortions of violent decompression. Eight people who had stood in this lock with them less than ten minutes ago. Lucien didn't look him in the eye.

A voice crackled through their communications channel. "This is Kommandant Kalishenko of the Eastern Peacekeepers. Your fallen comrades have encountered the hundred thousand rounds per minute from a DIRE gun. Come out with your hands up."

The others looked at Jonah.

He shook his head, then walked to the outer door and hit the emergency override on the safety lock. Let the Peacekeepers find their own way to Beddau.

Yesha met them as soon as the lock had cycled.

"What happened?"

They told her about the trap, how the Earth troops had lain in wait for them. Jonah's voice slipped as he described the losses, but the simple act of ordering the last few minutes in a rational conversation calmed him.

"I'm not sure how many there were, but it can't have been more than a few or we would all be dead."

Lucien drew himself out of whatever darkness he had been lost in. "Jonah is right. They don't have lots of men, just deadly weapon. Will be small groups set up at strategic points."

"I cannot allow more of the people to die," said Yesha.

Jonah listened to them and clenched his hands into fists. Was it all too late? He refused to accept that. The skin on his knuckles strained as he tightened his fists. These weapons he knew how to use. Weapons he always had with him. What good were they against automatic weapons? None, until he got close, and even then, it was risky. There had to be a way.

Around him the giant cavern creaked and clicked as machines carried out their tasks. It was so quiet compared to the day he had arrived here.

He sat upright, his hands raised, as the obvious absence explained itself.

"Yesha, Lucien, where are the mining trucks?"

They both looked at him as if he had gone mad.

"Those things are heavy duty. If we hide in one, we can drive it to Chang'e."

"Yeh," said Lucien. "What then? Peacekeepers will cut us to shreds."

"Then we must stop the Peacekeepers," said Yesha. "I hoped we could avoid this, but this is war. It is us or them. Jonah, come with me. The rest of you find a big truck."

Jonah followed her out of Beddau to the uninhabited space near the tunnel to new Karakorum. Yesha's shoulder lamp cast harsh shadows on the chipped columns.

She stopped in an open space and waited.

"What?"

Yesha shook her head. "Activate your memplant."

Jonah's memplant recognised Yesha, and further away, fifty others. The harsh whine of machine language echoed in his auditory nerve.

"Simplex communication for Jonah, please."

"Modifications have acceptable parameters." Droids

emerged from the darkness.

Jonah stepped in closer to Yesha.

She spoke for his benefit. "There is a new element. The administrator has brought troops up the stalk. Jonah, tell them what you found."

The droids listened until he mentioned the DIRE gun.

"...strategic acquisition."

"Potential additional collateral."

"Reduced capacity. Observation."

"I know you don't have the bodies you want," said Yesha. "If you can do this, I'll give you unrestricted access to the New Karakorum workshops."

A short burst of machine language followed.

"Available explosive ordnance?"

"We have flashboxes," said Jonah.

"Untargeted munitions."

"Distraction potential."

"Opportunity risk."

The droids turned towards Jonah.

"Twelve flashboxes, rockdrill, six hours."

"Do you want them in six hours?"

"No, wait six hours before proceeding."

Jonah ran back. He collected the flashboxes and four metalite charges he found with the rockdrill.

The droids accepted the explosives and disappeared into the depths of the mine.

Yesha took his hand. "At some point in what is coming, I need you to get to the rail gun."

A command string arrived in Jonah's memplant.

"Get close and feed that to the controller unit."

A bass rumble greeted them as Doaran drove up in one of the hulking mining trucks. Lucien ran up with an armful of flashboxes. "Good for droids, good for us too."

Jonah ran back with him and they collected every flashbox they could find.

"Everyone keeps a lookout as we go out," said Jonah. "If we spot one of them we duck down behind the bucket tray and hope for the best."

The airlock let them through and they all craned forward to see where the bullets would come from. Jonah counted six of them before he ducked behind the thick steel. One stood in front of the truck, drawing a bead on Doaran in the driver's cabin. Jonah braced himself for what was about to follow, but Lucien stood and hurled a flashbox forward. The flashbox exploded in a blinding white light. Jonah tensed for the blast wave then realised there would not be one in the near vacuum of the lunar atmosphere.

Jonah peeked over the edge. Peacekeepers rose from behind rocks. Jonah saw dark muzzles track towards the truck. He ducked as Doaran broke the silence with a wordless animal scream.

Small puffs of dust rose from hidden feet and Jonah spotted white flashboxes arcing forward from hidden locations. Droids hurled flashboxes towards individual Peacekeepers with robotic precision.

The Peacekeepers didn't have a chance. Men staggered from the white blasts. A wave of hidden metallic legs exploded out of the dust and tore helmets from frail bodies.

A droid ripped the DIRE gun pack from its operator's prone body.

"Acquired," said a neutral voice.

Jonah imagined a note of triumph threaded through the emotionless delivery.

"Stop, Doaran," yelled Lucien. The truck came to a halt

and Lucien leaped to the grey dust.

Droids collected the weapons. A snub-nosed assault rifle landed at Jonah's feet. He grabbed it and jumped back on the truck.

Jonah took pot shots at other Peacekeepers as they drove. Lucien used the cover created to scan the situation. He counted four of them, with scant cover. "We got advantage," he said to Jonah. "Truck is so high we can see all. We need more weapons before we get to Chang'e."

Lucien nodded in grim agreement.

They picked up the second gun with bullets raining into the other side of the truck. It became easier after that. Two of the men had nowhere to hide in the open country. The droid with the DIRE gun tore them to shreds. The final two took shelter inside an abandoned buggy. Doaran made short work of them by riding the buggy flat with one of the truck's giant tyres.

The collision had mangled one gun beyond use, but the other brought their count of the short assault weapon to five.

The truck rolled on to Chang'e.

Chapter 28

Altered Circumstances

The autodoc reflected no light. It occupied the floor like a misshapen lobster with telefactored arms where legs and feelers should be. Wang found the matte-grey finish both repelling and intriguing. Here was the answer if he had the courage to take it.

He placed his palm on the biosensor. The lobster split in two revealing the contoured couch within.

"You are not injured. Do you require cosmetic surgery?"

"No, I want augmentation."

"Augmentation is risky and contraindicated in healthy individuals," the autodoc launched into a string of disclaimers and warnings.

It was by far the most advanced softmind on the base. Ironic that so much money went to health instead of security. Wang accepted the legal conditions and placed his palm on the bioreader to confirm.

"What is the nature of the augmentation you require?"

Wang opened his memplant connection to the machine and transmitted a biomechanical schematic.

"The requested procedure is beyond normal parameters. Reversal may not be possible."

"Proceed," said Wang. Another stream of legal disclaimers followed.

He hesitated a long moment before accepting the conditions.

"I will print the minor components, but you must supply the chassis."

"I have it here." Wang dragged the device over to the surgical unit. The autodoc pulled it closer with one lobster claw. It instructed him to disrobe and lie on the bed.

Wang climbed into the autodoc and lay down on the synthetic leather of a surgical bed. The air in the chamber felt cool against his skin. He seldom went naked. There was no need.

The autodoc slid a needle into his arm. Consciousness faded as the lobster shell closed over him.

Awareness returned with a flare of incandescent pain. Wang groaned and opened his eyes to a fractured, off-centre view that faced the front wall of the surgery. Why was he lying on his stomach? He put his hands to the ground. They felt wrong. Sensation doubled, and unnatural. He attempted to look at his hands, but what he saw was a matte-grey pole with a utility claw attached. He tried to move his fingers, and the claw moved.

"Ah good, you are awake. How do you feel, Wang Mei?" The softmind asked in the universal neutral tone of doctors.

"It hurts, you dumb machine, give me something for the pain."

"Analgesics are contraindicated. Your brain requires full control to integrate the nerve welds. Can you stand?"

"No, I can't feel my legs."

"Please stay still while I tune the synapse relays."

Wang froze. A flexible probe snaked up his back, the metal cold against his skin. It reached a point and burrowed beneath his shoulder-blades gnawing at a vertebra. Wang gasped as stars exploded across his vision.

"I have re-purposed much of your peripheral nervous tissue. Bicep and forearm nerves have been rerouted to control separate legs, the same applies to calf and buttock muscles."

"Where are…"

"Your limbs are safe in cryogenic storage. Move your legs again."

Wang heard a scrambling noise behind him and sensed his body rock.

"Good. Now try your arms."

The pole in Wang's vision moved again. Mind and machine became one. He held up the claw and twisted it in wonder.

"This is my arm?"

"Technically, the arm is your foreleg. Close your eyes and access the orange icon."

The icon opened a direct view on his visual cortex. The entire room sprang into sharp focus.

"What is it?"

"Lidar, it was part of the chassis so I integrated it."

Wang opened his eyes and tried to stand. The world wobbled beneath him, but eight legs contacted the ground and he rose.

"Give me access to your visual feed Wang Mei." The

autodoc had a quiet, almost reverent edge to its voice.

Wang's sight swung to an out-of-body point of view looking down at the surgery. He realised it was the autodoc's camera. The view took in the tail of the lobster that was the autodoc. In front of the autodoc sat one of his re-purposed rescue droids. No, that wasn't right. It was larger, the body elongate and heavy with a bulbous abdomen. The droid swayed as if timing on the servo mechanics was off.

Wang knew what to expect, but the effect was overwhelming. He turned around and watched as the droid executed a staggering clatter of limbs that brought it face to face with the camera.

The droid had all the regular fittings that Wang had added; sharpened claws, a toughened exterior, and chameleon cladding. It also had a face. The face he knew every day from the mirror as he shaved himself to military perfection.

His eyes skimmed over the bulbous leather sack that hung between the legs, much like a spider's abdomen. Such tough hide to cover everything soft and human that remained.

He raised two forelegs like a spider about to attack.

"Yes!" his shout echoed around the empty surgery.

"Extended rest periods and mild exercise are indicated. I have downloaded a rehabilitation program to your memplant."

Wang did not trust himself to speak in front of the softmind. He took his first steps on all eight shaking legs, his body trembling with the effort. Then, without stopping he staggered from the surgery, thinking of the possibilities.

Tiny vibrations reached Jonah's hands through the gloves. The Peacekeepers were shooting at the truck again.

He ducked behind the high steel side.

Doaran backed the truck up towards the lock to shield their vulnerable position from the enemy. The others crouched as far back as they could.

The enemy stopped shooting as the truck drew closer. Concentrated combat in a small space would draw the attention of the droid pack.

Jonah saw the opportunity it gave them and told Doaran to park the truck across the entrance while the others laid outward covering fire. They had little control over the guns, but it was enough to make the Peacekeepers duck for cover.

Jonah slapped the airlock activator, and the door swung up. The airlocks had never been designed to keep someone out.

They stripped out of their exposure suits and the five with guns stood at the front as the inner door opened.

Inside it was quiet. People knew there was trouble. Jonah recognised this lock as the one Yesha had taken him through to scatter Thomas's ashes.

"You two, stay here," said Jonah pointing at two of the armed men. "Shoot anyone who comes through the lock."

Two of Wang's men came running around a corner. They put their hands up as soon as they saw the guns.

"Lock them in a storage unit," said Jonah. At least they had one easy win. It would be hell once the trained killers outside made it back inside the dome.

"Now for the fun part," he said. "We need to get to the railhead."

Lucien stayed quiet as they walked. After a while he stopped. The others stopped with him.

"I bet they will be waiting for us," he said. "We need diversion. Maybe big one." His gaze shifted to contemplate the main administration building in front of them.

Jonah followed his line of sight. "No, Lucien, you can't be serious."

"Why not? They blew up my place."

Jonah had no good answer to that.

Lucien pointed to the left. "We go around back and chuck flashboxes at wall. Building shakes and they run out far side."

Jonah nodded. They handed a flashbox to five of the team.

"Ready, one, two, three…"

They tossed and bolted away. The explosion hit them like a velvet fist. Jonah stumbled as he ran and tried to get his breath back. His hearing reduced to a faint ringing.

He looked over his shoulder to check if it had worked and stopped to stare. Half the administration building peeled forward like a stack of cards collapsing.

"Run," he yelled and powered away.

The wall crumbled and fell behind them with a roar. Bits of ceramic and plasmetal clinked and rattled into the surrounding walls.

Jonah knew his hearing had returned when faint screams filtered from the wreckage. No time to think of that now. They ran toward the railhead.

A lanky young man sprinted in next to Jonah as he ran. The man's looks marked him as one of the Beddau folk, Jonah recognised the difference now. They turned the corner into the avenue leading to the railhead and the young man grunted. He slumped to the floor with a crater where his face used to be. Bullets whined around them.

"Get to cover!" Lucien shouted as he dived into a side alley.

Jonah ducked in behind a storage cabinet and tried to assess the damage. It looked like only the young man was dead, but two others lay bleeding further back. One of them had a leg at an odd angle. He wasn't going further.

Jonah stuck his head out to get an understanding of what they faced. Bullets chipped the wall above his head. He ducked back. Lucien looked at him, Jonah held up three fingers and pointed forward. Lucien nodded and held up their last flashbox. Jonah covered his ears.

The storage cabinet kicked his back like a mule on steroids. He poked his head out again. No bullets came. Lucien held his assault rifle in front of him and stepped out, keeping his body close to the wall. Ahead of them nothing stirred in the blast haze. Lucien walked forward. He stooped to look at something then staggered back and spewed his last meal over the pavement.

Jonah walked forward keeping his eyes up, not wanting to see what had become of the men they had faced. Lucien recovered his composure enough to show they should continue.

The railhead was an anticlimax after the battles. Engineers told them that the administrator had ordered them to shut down the automated railway. The engineers were quick to understand it was not time to argue with armed men. They reactivated the railway. Jonah watched as the first empty carriages rolled away to New Karakorum.

Lucien had no time for watching. He wanted to free the prisoners held behind the recovery jars. He ran off in that direction. Jonah asked three of them to stay and guard the railhead then dashed after Lucien and the others.

Lucien had already freed the prisoners when he reached the cells. Jonah asked the dazed prisoners where Lucien was. One of them pointed to a stairway leading to underground workshops. "They gone down there. Said something about getting Wang."

Jonah sprinted down into the waiting darkness.

"Come out, Wang, I know you in there." The Jones boy stood peering into the shadows straining forward to hear anything that might be moving. So puny, thought Wang. How did I live before I had these senses? The Jones boy appeared before him outlined in flaming red. The extended lidar and infrared sensing outlined the boy like a moth before a flame in the darkness. Wang let him come.

The boy fumbled for the wall. Wang calculated the boy's trajectory and scrambled up the wall. He switched to day vision as the boy found the lights. Now was the perfect opportunity to be rid of the interfering brat forever. All he had to do was wait until the boy walked beneath him and he would drop. Gravity would take care of the rest. Gravity and one or two well-placed claw strikes. He clung on to the ceiling rock. The servos connected to his residual muscle burned with unexpected tension.

The boy was sensible. He took his time moving forward. The left front leg shook from the strain. Wang shifted it to ease the pain. The boy looked up at the slight sound. Too late. Wang fell towards him, but the Jones boy saw what came and stepped back. Wang grunted as a solid punch cracked the Kevlar on his back. The boy was quick. He swung out a leg sweeping for the boy's feet. The leg met empty air and Wang slid sideways. He continued the fall and rolled while watching for the boy. There. One back leg spun out and connected with the boy's face. He staggered, recovering as Wang righted himself.

He had the boy's measure now. Eight legs were so much better than two. He used both front legs to deliver a rain of foot strikes. The boy skipped back. Wang reached over with a middle leg and struck at his head again. This time a solid rising block jarred his leg to the core. The remnant muscles grafted to that leg screamed in protest. He ignored the pain. One leg out of eight was no loss.

The boy had backed against a wall. Wang used the expression he had shown to countless re-educated workers. He hoped his face still looked as fearsome.

"Cringe, boy. You have been nothing but trouble. We will end this here, and after we will sort out that troublesome aunt of yours." The boy gave an incoherent roar. Wang grinned. So easy to manipulate this one. "Your aunt will die a slow painful death. Perhaps we will have her committed to the jars."

The boy launched himself off the tunnel wall. Wang read his intention and waited for the killing down-strike. It came with all the energy of the boy's anger. Wang swept it aside with one leg. The boy overbalanced and Wang grabbed him with two legs. He used the boy's forward momentum to fling him over his back. The boy hit the opposite wall of the tunnel with a satisfying crack.

Wang spun around to finish him, two forelegs held high. The boy had somehow made it back onto his feet. He spotted the gap between Wang's forelegs and struck with a quick double punch to Wang's abdomen. Unbearable pain flared as internal structures snapped. Wang clasped the boy with his forelegs before he had a chance to recover. He drove the sharpened end of a mid-leg up through the boy's solar plexus and into his heart.

The boy gave one shuddering gasp as his face turned white. He slumped forward and was still. Wang tossed the body to one side and steadied his pounding heart.

He slapped a small panel near his neck to release the nanomed recovery unit. The meds burst through his body like a thunderstorm. Wang faced the wave of pain that followed, then crawled away into a safe hiding-space to wait out the repair.

Jonah stopped to catch his breath. Aimless running wouldn't help him. Lucien passed this intersection, and could have gone down either tunnel that branched off from here. Jonah chose left.

The tunnel arced into darkness. Dim light backlit a shapeless lump huddled on the floor. The hot copper stench of blood made him tense with anticipation. He slipped into a silent walk. Each foot rolled from ball to toe to muffle his footsteps.

The lump resolved into a tall frame, twisted and broken. He rolled the head towards the light, knowing what he would see.

"Lucien!" Jonah knew he should be quiet, but it wasn't fair. Not after all this.

"You taught him well," said a voice from the darkness. "He almost bested us."

Jonah whipped around, his arms rising to a defensive block. A shadow moved within the darkness. In the centre, a pale disc wove uneasy patterns. He stepped closer until he realised the disc was a face swaddled in the eye-twisting grey of chameleon cladding.

"Wang?"

"Yes."

The thing that emerged from the shadows resolved into Wang's face melded to a battle droid's legs and a pendulous leather abdomen. The legs writhed in sinuous curves around him as if the droid fought this intrusion. Jonah's muscles twitched. Every fibre of his being wanted to be away from this thing. He held his ground.

"What have you done?"

"Eight legs are too much. We were so weak before we partitioned our brain. Now we are many. Your little princess has no control over us now."

"You're mad." Jonah backed away towards the tunnel entrance.

The Wangdroid skittered up the wall, over, past Jonah, and landed in front of him. Jonah's stomach cramped in sweat inducing panic. He calmed himself. Think Jonah. There's a confused human in there. Maybe there's a chance.

He sprinted up the wall, twisting to deliver a kick to Wang's face from above. The Wangdroid swept one leg across in a metallic arc that blocked Jonah's leg. A rear leg followed with a stab at Jonah's retreating back. He spun countering with a rising sweep of his arm that gave him an opening between the legs.

Battle abhors a vacuum. Jonah filled the gap with a driving step-through kick that sank his foot deep into the damp leather of the underbelly. Wang screamed. Jonah didn't return from the kick, but fell forward delivering a rain of punches to the same spot. Something broke deep inside the droid before legs clasped and threw him against the wall like a wet dishrag.

Stars filled Jonah's vision. He lifted bone-heavy arms, but no attack came. Wang lay still. Broken machinery whirred in the silence.

Chapter 29

Consequences

Jonah's gut churned with the hot copper taste of fear as he peered over the ridge. He was tired now, so tired. The last of the Peacekeepers had positioned themselves around the rail gun. He could make out the squat barrels of assault rifles protruding from the support structure. He hoped they didn't have another DIRE gun. The emptiness of the open dust plain presented a different challenge. They would have to be original if they did not want to shed a lot of blood.

He bet that the group waiting for them were the last. A small contingent, left behind to guard the exit point. He put all his faith into the bet, the fighting had taken everything from him, and from the others. Doaran's face showed the same exhaustion through her faceplate. This had to be the end.

"There's no cover. How do we get there?"

Doaran shrugged.

"Why don't we try this?" he said "I'll try sneak around to the left. Doaran you head around to the right. You two wait here. When we reach halfway, you hammer them with as many bullets as you can. Doaran, you and I must run like crazy and shoot. With any luck, the Earthers will duck for cover."

Doaran picked up her rifle. "We have bottle of Shaoxing when battle is over." With that she jumped over the ridge and ran in a wide arc to the right. Jonah noticed the men around the railgun shift to track her progress.

"Hey, Peacekeepers, you ready for us and the droids?"

They didn't shoot. Jonah sprang up and raced to the left.

For several minutes, he ran great leaping strides that ate up the distance. Each foot landed in a small puff of dust before he sprang off again and flew further. His body had adapted. He felt like a superhero.

The feeling vanished as soon as he noticed the first line of mini-craters open fresh holes in the dust near him. They were close, but the craters appeared to be spaced much wider than the DIRE gun had been.

"Now everbody! Now!"

Instant, invisible death sped between the two groups. There was no way the team on the ridge could be accurate at that distance, but the Peacekeepers ducked for cover as a precaution.

Doaran dropped to her stomach. Jonah's heart lurched, but then Doaran lifted her gun. Clever. She made a smaller target like that. Jonah did the same and sheltered behind a small rock outcrop.

They had both come around far enough to erode the cover the men on the railgun used. Jonah flicked the rifle to single shot and aimed for the one Peacekeeper he saw. A line of sharp little craters drilled the regolith so close he could reach out and touch it. He put thoughts of being hit out of his head and drew a bead on the lone man who was now within a reasonable distance of accurate fire.

Sweat rolled down his neck leaving a maddening itch. He heard his father's voice as he held his first hunting rifle, crouching low in the thick scrub as the ducks settled on the water. Relax your shoulders. Keep your eye on the target. Hold your breath. Squeeze, don't pull.

The rifle bucked hard. A red mist erupted from the man's chest, he staggered to his knees and fell forward.

Jonah took a deep breath, worked the breech, and looked for the next target. A man crouched behind a metal support stay. Jonah took the shot. It winged the man. He fell writhing to the ground and fumbled for a suit patch.

The bullets coming at him had stopped. Now was his chance. Jonah sprinted forward, gun at the ready.

He made the safety of a concrete anchor block and looked around for Doaran. She was long gone from her earlier position.

Jonah came out behind a group of four Earthers all facing toward the ridge from the cover of a big metal stay. Sparks flew off the stay. Good. The team on the ridge had found the range. He ducked under the main ramp and flicked the rifle to automatic.

"Give up gentlemen. We have you surrounded."

The four spun around, guns ready, looking for him.

"Yeh," came Doaran's voice. "Me and droids are all around you. Put down your guns."

Jonah grinned. Doaran was nowhere near, but radio communication gave no sense of direction or distance.

The men looked at each other and tossed their guns out in front of them.

Jonah stepped out and motioned them away from their weapons.

Doaran rose from where she had been hiding.

"Droids, huh?" said Jonah.

"You never said I must be honest." Doaran's grin shone through her faceplate. She looked at the four Peacekeepers. "What we going to do with them?"

"Watch them. There's something I need to do." He walked over to the main control unit. A banked-up string of helium hoppers waited for the railgun to resume operations. Giant gears stood poised to fine-tune the direction of individual packages. He reached out with his memplant. A dumb machine interface responded. Jonah downloaded Yesha's code.

He swung his gun to cover the Peacekeepers. "We walk back to Chang'e now. Don't try anything. We have two friends up on the ridge."

"Doaran, soon as we're done with this, I'm buying you that bottle of Shaoxing."

The Peacekeepers walked toward Chang's. Jonah and Doaran walked a few steps back, ready for any sudden movement. Around them, the landscape glowed blue, white. A light so bright it left afterimages burned into Jonah's vison.

"Was that the railgun?"

"Yeh. Never seen from so close before."

Behind them the lunar plain flared to white again.

They entered the airlock after radio communication told them the lock was still in Moon Folk hands.

Inside, the concourse streamed with people looking as if they had lost their way. A mother clasping her daughter to her side as if to protect her from an unknown danger.

People avoided making eye contact with them. The air stank of burning and the sharp, flinty reek of explosives. Ahead of them the main administration building lay crumpled to one side like a cardboard box stamped on by a careless boot.

A small boy approached them. In the fearless manner of children everywhere, he asked them if it was over. Jonah and Doaran exchanged a confounded look.

"I don't know," said Jonah at length. "We will have to see what else needs to be done."

Jonah tried to think if any of the administrator's men still waited head. He radioed the men who guarded the railhead.

"Wait there," came the terse response.

They didn't wait long. Yesha walked into the concourse backed by fifty droids.

"Jonah, Doaran, you did it!"

She told them how the train had run non-stop to ferry people to the domes. How the resident Moon Folk had come out to support her. The people had taken the fight to the streets. They had cleared every dome of administration security personnel, and the put the base softminds into standby mode.

Jonah clapped Doaran on the shoulder. "Think we should go get that bottle of Shaoxing now."

Yesha smiled. "Yes, we need to celebrate what we have done today."

Jonah knew she addressed the broader group rather than just them.

"We have one more thing to do first," she said and led the way to the crumbling administration building.

The door to the administrator's office looked no different to any other. At least it stood in the undamaged half of the building. Jonah watched Yesha raise a hand to open the door and hesitate. Behind her Amira and Doaran waited. This would be the end no matter what lay beyond that door.

She opened the door and walked in.

Her uncle stood inside with his back to them, looking out at the Earth as it hung overhead.

"Uncle," Yesha's voice was the only sound.

He turned to regard them. A tear traced its path down the old man's cheek. "I hear the rabble calls you the Empress now. Are you here as that or as my dutiful niece?"

Yesha stiffened as if Chen had slapped her. Jonah saw her eyes narrow, but not in the fear he expected to find there. No, her face had become the cold and terrible mask of the Yesha who would drop tonnes of rock on Earth to get her way.

"The troops you sent to kill us are dead. So too is the thing that Wang Mei became."

Chen shrugged. "Nanjing will send more troops. The might of Jiangnan's military will crush you like the vermin you are. You cannot win this."

"You forget, Uncle, how much I have learned from you. Did you notice how many times the railgun fired? It sent every waiting helium hopper to the stalk. I counted five. That's three more than the number of tugs at the stalk."

"Foolish child. Hoppers go into a safe parking orbit well away from the elevator terminal."

"Turn on the stalk cameras."

A view blossomed of the elevator deck with the Moon far beyond it. A line of five metallic stars grew larger as they watched.

Chen's voice was a hoarse whisper. "You changed the

trajectory."

"And maximised the escape velocity."

Two tugs rode out to capture the incoming hoppers.

Chen's eyes widened in horror, his hands grabbed for the edge of his desk. "What have you done?"

Yesha said nothing.

The first of the additional hoppers loomed large in the camera and the image went dark. The view switched to a camera onboard one tug.

Debris blossomed from the elevator terminal as the second hopper tore through the thin walls. The third ploughed into the core. Atmosphere erupted in a haze though the gaping rent. The platform tilted at an alarming angle and fell towards the clouds above Singapore.

Chen's face paled. He swallowed before he spoke.

"You may think of me as a monster, but I am innocent next to you. Without helium, the economies of the world will cease. Chaos will follow and billions will starve."

"I see you understand the position, but the Earth need not starve. Let us discuss terms."

Chen's face betrayed nothing, but his stance had slumped in resignation. Here was a man who understood negotiation.

"What do you propose?"

"The recognition of the Moon Folk as a free people with an inalienable right to self-determination." Yesha outlined her proposal. The Earth would revitalise the old Indian and Japanese rocket ports. Shuttles would meet the rockets at L1, the first Lagrange point where gravity became equal between the Earth and Moon.

The Moon Folk would retain control of the lunar mines and issue mining permits to Earth nations. Jiangnan would be granted permits on existing mines in recognition of current investments. However, ultimate control of the Moon would reside with the Moon Folk.

Chen turned his face to where the Earth hung in the sky. "I will need to confer with the supreme council."

A connection icon bloomed in Jonah's memplant. He realised that everyone received the same broadcast. Five coloured kabuki masks solidified in his field of vision.

"No need, administrator," said blue mask. "We have been listening."

"Our conditions are not negotiable," said Yesha.

Yellow mask darkened to a burnt umber. "Foolish girl, what makes you think we are prepared to negotiate with terrorists?"

Yesha squared her shoulders in a gesture more for those who watched than the council.

"Night is falling on Nanjing as I speak. I see so many lights, millions upon millions who depend on our helium. Are you ready for what is coming?"

"The next time the railgun fires, it will be blocks of fused basalt aimed at your rocket ports."

The council did not respond. Silence stretched into minutes. At length, red mask spoke. Its voice had a mellow gentle timbre. Jonah recognised the trademarked tones of a famous pop singer.

"Young lady, you are both reckless and cunning. A combination we approve of. We accede to your demands for now, but know this, we will reclaim what is ours."

The connection cut out with an abrupt click.

Was that it? Jonah thought otherwise. If the council gave up so easily, then there was more to it. They had other plans in place. He would have to find time to speak to Yesha about it, but not now.

She walked forward until she was face to face with her uncle.

"This is the end, Uncle."

He sighed. "Promise me my men will be safe."

"I promise it. You will be allowed to return to Earth." She stood aside. "Now you must go with these men."

Chen favoured her with a wan smile. "You remembered," he said. "Symbols are important."

Chapter 30

A Settling of Ashes

The carriage on the New Imbrium railway had not changed. Jonah watched the passing lunar landscape, while musing on the past months and how much life had changed since he first stepped on to this carriage. At Chang'e, the carriage stopped at the airlock and he entered.

On the other side of the lock, the air in the dome hung heavy with expectant silence. He turned the corner and stopped, stunned by the absence. The main administration building was now nothing more than a pile of rubble. That it was the remains of the building was obvious from the occasional door and chair that could still be seen poking out from under the fine layer of lunar dust that covered everything.

Giant machines had assembled the rubble into a sweeping crescent, low at the points and high in the middle, as if someone had wished to create an amphitheatre. Held secure within the arms of the sweeping arc was a flat open space levelled out of lunar regolith. Two rows of at least a hundred grey-clad lunar guards lined a path across the space that led to a dark seat carved from volcanic basalt. The seat held a lone figure.

"Come, my people," said Yesha rising from the chair. Jonah saw this for the theatre it was. Symbols were important.

The guards snapped to attention as one.

Jonah stepped to one side, respectful of this new Yesha. He looked at her and saw she wore her arms bare to show the marks of the struggles she had been through, but it was her eyes that caught Jonah. Gone was the innocence. In its place was firm resolve and a darkness that showed no mercy.

"Bring my uncle and his men."

Chen walked in front of the guards his hands bound behind his back and his head held high.

Yesha held up a hand and the small procession stopped.

"Too long have the Moon Folk suffered. This ends today."

The watching people roared their approval. "Hail. All hail Empress."

"Uncle, I offer you and your men passage back to the Earth on condition you take a message back for me."

"And what would my little niece say to the world?"

"That the Moon belongs to the Moon Folk and we will fight to the death for our freedom."

The people roared their approval once more.

Chen looked at her in silence for a while then bowed.

"I always believed you were like your mother, but I was wrong, you are more like me. I will take your message back, but I hope you can live with the weight of your decisions."

"So be it. Take my uncle and his men to the shuttle dock

and see they are on the first delivery to Earth."

She pointed at Jonah. "Come Jonah, there is something we must do."

Jonah walked forward and waited for Yesha to speak again. She held up a funerary urn.

"When we first met, I thought nothing of the small kindness of helping you scatter your brother's ashes. Now I know it means so much more, but I ask you to help me do this small thing for Lucien."

Jonah nodded dumbly, choking back tears he had tried hard not to shed. Lucien was gone and this final farewell was all he had left.

They kitted up in silence. Only the two of them and Amira, Yesha would have no one else. Out on the plain, they walked to a spot that looked familiar.

"Lucien will appreciate having someone as good as your brother nearby," said Yesha, as she poured ash from the urn onto the grey regolith.

A week after they had scattered Lucien's ashes, Yesha summoned Jonah to the dome. He went with great reluctance, not wanting to refresh the memory of Lucien's farewell.

The throne was as he had last seen it. He had decided to call it a throne once Yesha had set up court in the rubble crescent. She spent most of her time there now, becoming more the ruler that her people wanted her to be.

Yesha rose as he approached and clasped his hands. She looked deep in his eyes and Jonah wondered if he meant anything to her.

"I know what you are thinking," she said with a soft smile on her lips. "I did not choose this, but we must be what we are. My place is here while the people of the Moon need me."

"Then why am I here?"

She sat back on the throne and became once more Empress of the Moon.

"We have won our freedom, but Earth needs our helium. I would rather we negotiate a trade settlement that allows both sides to retain honour. I have distanced the Moon from Jiangnan, but Panamerica will welcome you, if you can offer them a trade agreement."

"You want to send me back?"

"It will not be safe, my uncle's masters are determined to kill you, but I will offer what protection I can through your government."

Jonah bowed. "I will do this for your people."

Yesha smiled. "Do this and they will be your people too."

Jonah bowed again and walked away. Whatever might be between him and Yesha would have to wait. Now he had a job to do, and afterwards a place he could call home.

###

ABOUT THE AUTHOR

Carleton Chinner is an Australian born writer who grew up on a remote farm in South Africa, where the trip to the town library was the highlight of his week. He devoured anything science fiction, fantasy and horror. And, when that wasn't enough, turned to urban legend and traditional tribal histories which combined to provide a heady brew of stories.

He has settled in Australia as an adult but not before turning up unarmed at a gunfight, discovering dead bodies and fighting off sharks while spearfishing.

Find out more at: **CarletonChinner.com**